THE MYSTERY OF RUFFORD ABBEY

Stephen Taylor

SAPERE BOOKS

THE MYSTERY OF RUFFORD ABBEY

Published by Sapere Books.

20 Windermere Drive, Leeds, England, LS17 7UZ,
United Kingdom

saperebooks.com

ISBN: 978-1-80055-847-2

PROLOGUE

Wellow Village, Nottinghamshire 1152

'Tie up the witch!'

The village priest's words to the blacksmith were staccato, laced with odium. Terrified, the young girl felt his rough-skinned, hairy fingers as he tied the hide thongs, pulling them so tight that the leather bit deep into her flesh. He tied her left thumb to the right big toe and her right thumb to the left big toe. All the time the villagers were chanting — 'WITCH, WITCH, WITCH'. They were neighbours, friends of her mother and father, but now — now they saw her as a sorceress; she could see the fear in their eyes — she knew they wanted her dead.

The blacksmith lifted her as if she were no more than a corn dolly, but then she was a starveling, an undernourished fifteen-year-old girl. He carried her to the village pond, following the priest, with the villagers behind shouting their ire. He waded into the water, and it quickly deepened. When it came to his chest, he looked behind, saw the priest nod that it was deep enough, then he tossed her forward as if she were mutton bones thrown on a tip. The icy water splashed and then closed over her, and she went rigid with shock; the November day already had the hand of winter gripping it. She fought the urge to gasp but did not succeed, and the freezing water entered her mouth, stunned her windpipe, and she started to choke. In desperation, she closed her mouth again as quickly as she could.

For some moments her world went silent, her mind filled only with the icy cold on her raw flesh. But, one by one, sounds came back into her consciousness — bubbles popped in her ear as they rose to the surface; she heard the muted chanting of the villagers above the water. *Sweet Jesus will protect me, though*, she thought. *I am a good Christian girl. I go to church every Sunday and say my prayers every night.* She knew she would sink to the bottom, and her innocence would be proven — *I am no witch.* She prayed they would fish her out before she drowned.

But soon she felt herself rising to the top. She had never learned to swim, yet, somehow, she was rising as if she were being pushed by an invisible hand. The way they had tied her meant she was curled into a ball. She broke the surface and started to bob there, like a summer apple in a water pail. She gasped for air, coughing and spluttering as she did so, but she was the right way up, her head out of the water.

Her wet hair clung to her face, but through the streaming strands she could see the villagers, see the look of satisfaction on their faces.

'WITCH, WITCH, WITCH!' they chanted as she bobbed.

Sweet Jesus, why have you done this to me? she thought. *Jesus save me, please Jesus save me. You know I am not a witch.* She started to sink again; she took a deep breath, closing her mouth as her head went under. She held her breath as bubbles escaped from her hair. But in filling her lungs she had sealed her own fate, the village priest knew — and she rose back up to the surface.

Jesus had not listened to her pleas. *I must have done something evil for him to condemn me like this — perhaps I am a scurvy because I have sinned with my bad thoughts.* She continued to bob on the surface of the muddy brown water for some moments. The villagers' chanting was now directed at the village priest. Then she heard his words.

'The witch's guilt is proven,' he said as he kissed his bible. 'She floats, the water has rejected her, spurned the sacrament of baptism.'

Briefly, she saw her mother and father: her mother's hands held over her mouth in disbelief; her father's arm around her shoulder, his face a befuddled mask.

The priest turned and nodded at the blacksmith. He waded back in and took her up in his powerful arms. She was thrown down on the bank, her whole body shivering and trembling, as much with fear as with cold. The thongs were cut off, and she was dragged away.

'WITCH, WITCH, WITCH!' the villagers chanted.

PART 1: THE GIRL WHO TOLD THE TRUTH

CHAPTER 1

February 2019

Opening the door, I stepped out of the swirling February wind into the warmth of the Nag's Head.

I looked around and down the bar and saw a hand go up, holding a pint of Bombardier as my enticement. Underneath was the serious face of James Postlethwaite, head of the history department.

I manoeuvred my way to the bar. 'Ah, good man, James,' I said. I grasped the glass he held out and took a long swig. It tasted perfect; I needed it.

He had sent me an email to arrange a meeting in his office. I told him we should meet in the pub after work. He finally accepted after he realised I wouldn't take no for an answer. I knew that if I got him out of the university, I could get at the real James — he was good company, and my oldest friend.

'So, what have I done wrong? Have I overspent the paperclip budget?'

'Have you?' he asked with a critical look — but soon it cracked, and a smile erupted.

'Nah,' I sniggered, 'I spent all my budget on beer and fags months ago.' He laughed — it was good to hear him laugh again.

'Well, I've had a tip-off,' he said. 'You're a medievalist, and I thought you might be interested.'

I straightened up; source documentation was always gold-dust to a historian. 'What — what have you heard?'

'What do you know of Rufford Abbey?'

'Cistercian monastery — The White Monks, Nottinghamshire, founded in the twelfth century, if I remember correctly — dissolved in the sixteenth century as part of the dissolution of the monasteries by Henry VIII. One of the relics that *Enery knocked abaht a bit*, to quote the old song,' I replied.

'Cromwell,' he said, and I looked at him, confused. 'The song, it's by Marie Lloyd,' he continued. 'It's called — "One of the Ruins that *Cromwell* Knocked About a Bit".'

'Pedant!' I said. 'It was still Henry VIII that dissolved the monasteries; Thomas Cromwell was just his henchman, despite what Marie Lloyd sang.'

He grinned. 'Does the name Brother Roger of Hathern mean anything to you?' I shook my head. 'Well, what about Philip de Kyme?'

I shook my head again. 'Should I know them?'

'Probably not, they're both obscure — Philip de Kyme was the first abbot of Rufford Abbey from 1147, known as Abbot Stephen.'

'And Brother Roger of Hathern?'

'He was a monk there and the abbot's chaplain — and he seems to have acted as the abbot's chronicler.'

'Don't tell me these chronicles have turned up?' I was getting excited now.

'Okay, I won't,' he said, as he took a long swig of his pint.

'Come on, James,' I said, 'out with it — what have you heard?'

He turned to me, lowering his voice. 'Well, the abbey and lands were granted to the Earl of Shrewsbury after the dissolution and converted into a country house, and so it remained for centuries, but by 1952 it was in a bad state and was acquired by Nottinghamshire County Council. It's now run by English Heritage.'

'And?'

'And — they have been doing some cataloguing and have come up with these chronicles, and they asked me if the university is interested. So I thought of you.'

'Well, that's worth another pint,' I said, raising my hand at the barman.

When the courier arrived, I signed for the package enthusiastically, made room on my desk, took some scissors and snipped the plastic envelope at one end and gingerly slid out the bubble-wrapped contents. It was addressed to me — Toby Fielding, History Department. I cut away the tape and unfolded the bubble-wrap to reveal its contents — two leather-bound volumes which I could see had once been engraved, but the letters were now obscured as the leather had darkened over the centuries to a deep, rich black. This must be why they had been overlooked for so long, as there was no indication as to their contents.

I opened the first volume to reveal the Latin script; the ink had faded so that there was no contrast with the discoloured parchment. I knew there was several months' work of exacting translation ahead of me; it would be arduous, but I also knew from past experience that the task would not be boring. I would be the first person to read the words for centuries. Occasionally we got a genuine glimpse into real people's lives, how they lived, how they thought and the emotions that drove them; ordinary people speaking in their own words from across time. It would be a privilege to study them — this was why I had become a historian.

CHAPTER 2

I was sat at my desk when my phone started ringing. I recognised the ringtone. It was an internal call, so I ignored it. I didn't want to be disturbed. It was a quarter past six, and I gazed about at my department — I was the only one here — and wondered who else would be ringing at this time. I looked at the last entry I had made, but before I continued, the caller, I realised, was probably James Postlethwaite. He was always the last to leave.

It was May, and I'd been so busy over the past few weeks; the third semester was examination time, and with that came hours of marking. I was also the mentor for my students, and I needed to give them guidance on their dissertations. I had little time for my own work, squeezing it in when I could. I had now come to an unusual and exciting discovery and I didn't want to put it on hold.

The door burst open and James came in. I threw my pen down in frustration, mumbling under my breath. He looked at the chaotic desk and opened his mouth to speak, but I beat him to it: 'I take it that was you on the phone?'

'Yep,' he said, 'so why didn't you answer?'

'Why d'ya think?' I said, gesturing at the textbooks on my desk. 'I'm trying to work.'

'What's this? The Rufford Abbey chronicles — haven't you finished the translations yet?' I knew he was being playful, but it was still irritating. 'Is the medieval monk-Latin particularly tough?'

I sighed. 'You know what medieval Latin is like, James — there's no single form of it. It was always spoken as a second language. This guy will have been influenced by his mother tongue, his native dialect, the depth of his studies. It's adulterated, but this Brother Roger of Hathern fella's monk-Latin is not bad.'

'So you are getting in sync with him?'

'Yep, he has a relatively easy style.'

'So why haven't you finished?'

'Look, what is it you want, James?' There was exasperation in my tone. 'Haven't you got the great paperclip shortage to deal with?'

'You know your trouble, Toby,' he said, 'you can dish it out, but you can't take it.'

'Take what, for Christ's sake?'

'You tease me mercilessly, but when I do it back, you go all *dedicated* on me.'

A smile cracked my face. He was right, of course. I did tease him for his devotion to duty. 'Yeah, okay, touché,' I said, putting my pen down. 'So what is it you want?'

'A pint of Bombardier at the Nag's Head.'

That sounded good — I looked at my watch. 'Can you give me half an hour to get these notes down while they're fresh in my mind? Have a read of this while I finish. It's a bit of a mystery — an 800-year-old mystery, in fact.' I lifted the lid of my laptop, clicked to open the document with my translation of the chronicle on it, and scrolled down to the relevant part.

James pulled up a chair and started to read Brother Roger's words.

AD 1152 — The sixteenth year of the reign of King Stephen. 8th Day of November.

It is three years since Abbot Stephen was appointed a justice. He takes these duties as seriously as he does his abbatial tasks in the monastery. He is skilled in the liberal arts and in the Holy Scriptures, being a learned man, brought up in scholarship, but he has since studied in civil law to add to his knowledge of ecclesiastical statute.

He is now regarded as a wise judge, because of the books he has read and the cases he has tried. He has established a reputation for impartiality, and it is known that his courts will not accept gold nor silver to sway his judgements. His cases are tried according to the form of law, much to the displeasure of the noble families in the county.

But he has been troubled in the last week by a case referred to him by Guy FitzHugh the Under-Sheriff of Nottingham. The case concerns a young girl by the name of Margaret of Wellow. The under-sheriff's letter said the case was more suited to his capacities as an abbot, being one of witchcraft. Wellow itself is a manor endowed to the abbacy and is only two miles away. Abbot Stephen had the girl brought to the monastery from the village.

She is a fifteen-year-old girl, but looked no more than a child of twelve, having none of the feminine curves of womenfolk. He questioned her first for an hour, and her story is certainly one of incredulity. Abbot Stephen would not give judgement hastily but proceeded in a judicial manner, knowing that the merits of the case were unclear. She claimed to be a good Christian girl who attended church each Sunday and said her prayers every day. I think he considered her story was more to do with the fanciful imagination of a young girl than the dark forces of witchcraft.

He questioned her two more times, but the girl was convinced her words were sooth, unaware that every protestation to that effect brought a terrible judgement closer, for her claim was thus — that by some unexplained happening, she did find herself in some future time, the year she claimed was the Year of our Lord 2020.

'What?' James exclaimed. 'The Year of our Lord 2020!'

'Exactly,' I answered, looking up from my notes. 'How about that? A document written in 1152 with a connection to 2020.

That's why I want to get on with the translation — working late and all that.'

'I see a book deal in this for you as well, Toby.'

'Let's not get ahead of ourselves — it might not come to anything.'

'You're right to be cautious, but let's hope Brother Roger has more to say on this. Will you keep me in the loop? I want to know what comes out of this.'

CHAPTER 3

I emailed James later that week, with an update on my progress:

James, I have translated the next entry that is relevant to Margaret of Wellow. See what you think.

P.S. I got it in the neck from Carol for getting back late the other night. I was supposed to take my daughter to guides. I am in her bad books now because of you.

AD 1152 — 11th Day of November.

At the behest of Abbot Stephen, I went to see the young Margaret of Wellow in the cell she has been given that acts as her prison while under the jurisdiction of the monastery. He was concerned that the naive child would continue to incriminate herself if she persisted in this make-believe story of hers. I was charged with questioning her to see who had put such fanciful thoughts into her confused mind. I knew she could not read or write, and so she has not read something that her childlike mind has interpreted wrongly.

She has the face of innocence and bewilderment on her in equal measure, but I know that evil can sometimes hide behind a comely mask.

I started by asking her the furthest she had travelled, and she said that she had been to the market at Newark once with her father when she was ten. Her father is a cottier and works on the abbey's land and has only a cottage, no land in his possession to work as a villein would have, so in the evenings, he works as a weaver for extra coin. He takes his wares to market to try and sell them.

The town is about eleven miles from her village and about a three and half hour walk. I asked her who she had spoken to, but she replied she did not talk to anybody — her father had warned her not to or even to leave his side. As a dutiful girl, she had obeyed him.

I then asked her if she had listened to any street preachers when they went thither, but she did not at first understand what I meant by a street preacher. I explained that there were certain men who were not learned priests or monks, who sometimes expressed their heretical views to crowds at the marketplace.

She did not understand the word heretical, and it is hard to interrogate her as her knowledge of words was so limited. I asked if she saw jugglers, stilt-walkers, tumblers or storytellers, but the only thing she remembered was setting off at dawn on a summer's day, the throng of people, and being exhausted by walking 22 miles in a day.

She had been to Ollerton, a larger village approximately one and one-half miles from Wellow on some occasions, but each time with one or other of her parents. Again she said she had not listened to any preacher.

I next asked her if she had ever listened to a fortune-teller. I am aware that most fortune-tellers are common rogues and tricksters who use a variety of devious illusions to create dramatic effects and fool gullible country people. Some more educated fortune-tellers, however, do use lunar and celestial patterns to predict probable outcomes — I wondered if this was the source of her fantasies.

She replied that the village priest warned them regularly from the pulpit not to listen to fortune-tellers as they were profane. Only God knew what would happen in the future, she said, her eyes full of purity. On the face of it, she seems the most goodly child.

I still think that somebody has put these ideas into her fanciful head. I will visit the village to see if any fortune-teller or storyteller has been there recently.

An email pinged back from James a few hours later:

Toby — I'm hooked on this — thanks for keeping me in the loop.

P.S. Don't blame me for taking you to the pub. You were working late anyway.

I continued to send him passages of my translations as I finished them.

AD 1152 — 15th Day of November.

The priest at Wellow is a zealous fellow, I found. His piousness is to be admired, but after talking to him, I found his devotion laced with bigotry. He sees the devil all around him, regarding it as his Christian duty to root it out with belligerent vehemence. I cannot help but think that if he had considered the possibility that the child was a confused innocent rather than a disciple of Satan, Abbot Stephen would not have been so troubled by this accusation. He confirmed, however, what the girl had said — he had no truck with fortune-tellers; he sent them on their way so that they would not poison his congregation.

His indignation also extended to storytellers, and he was proud that he also sent such people on their way. I, myself, like nothing more than to listen to a storyteller; they are great entertainment. The common folk have no reading and writing, and storytellers are a source of information passing around the country and even from generation to generation.

I say this even after admitting they often embellish the facts to make their stories more exciting. Travelling storytellers earn a few coins for their stories, but there are usually some, within each village, who have good memories that also beguile their neighbours with stories.

I asked Margaret's parents who were the storytellers within Wellow Village, but they claimed there were none. I also asked their neighbours and was given the same answer. I am unsure whether this is truth or whether they are afraid of their village priest and his fervour.

I travelled to Ollerton and talked to the priest there. He said fortune-tellers were more likely to go to Newark on market day, rarely coming to

Ollerton. The odd storyteller did come, and he liked to listen to them himself. He was unaware of any story, however, that had a tale about events in the future — it was not the sort of thing storytellers told. They were usually about great heroes or pious saints. He had no knowledge of Margaret or her family and could not recognise such a family at a storytelling.

He gave me the names of the storytellers in Ollerton village, and I also spoke to them. None of them knew of the girl or her family, nor of a story about the future. I will have to report back to Abbot Stephen that I have been unable to trace where these fanciful stories have come from.

AD 1152 — 21st Day of November.

Abbot Stephen gave his judgement with a heavy heart. I think he felt he had let the maid down. I certainly had a feeling hanging over me that I had failed to find the culprit — the manipulative rogue who had planted this story, this uncommon tale in the girl's controllable mind. It is a burden that also troubles me greatly.

The village priest was examined again, and Abbot Stephen's incisive questions highlighted his bigotry, but the man was so entrenched in his prejudice he could not even see the points the abbot was making. He was convinced the maid was a disciple of the devil and that her guilt had been proved in trial by ordeal.

He railed about Exodus 22:18: 'Thou shalt not suffer a witch to live' and Leviticus 20:27: 'A man also or a woman that hath a familiar spirit, or that is a wizard, shall surely be put to death: they shall stone them with stones.'

The girl continued to damn herself by insisting she had not been listening to stories and that the events she described were sooth.

Abbot Stephen could find no counterargument and reluctantly passed judgment that the charge of witchcraft was proven. However, he gave the maid the chance to repent and admit the story was untrue and submit to the authority of the Church.

At this, the child became frenzied and through her tearful sobs reiterated that Jesus knew her fanciful tale was true. There was a smug look on the priest's face. He could see Abbot Stephen was trying to spare the maid, but she had been too naive to understand that.

The priest demanded the girl be burnt at the stake, but Abbot Stephen would have none of that. She will be hanged next week — a small comfort to the abbot and me.

CHAPTER 4

I reached over and filled everybody's wine glass. We had a dinner date with James Postlethwaite and his partner Grace once a month, and it was our turn to host. The atmosphere was frosty, though; Carol and I had had a blazing row before they'd come. It was the same festering sore — about me not doing my fair share around the house and with the kids and always being at work. But this time, things had got out of hand. She had suggested a trial separation might be the answer, so I could 'get my shit together'. I was stunned. I had thought we were basically stable, despite the constant friction — I filled my wine glass to the top, intent on getting drunk.

The kids had left the table and gone to their rooms. Tom was fourteen and happy to spend time in his room on his computer games. Emma was eleven and liked nothing better than to spend hours texting her friends.

'You two had a row?' asked Grace, but her words were playful, her eyes sparkling.

'Is it that obvious?' said Carol, giving me a sideways hostile stare.

'A bit,' said Grace, still trying to keep things light. 'Is it the usual thing?'

Carol sighed, but soon a torrent of words cascaded out of her, and I could only sit there, sucking my lip. 'I could bloody well understand it if I had married a chuffing policeman. I could understand him never coming home, but he's a chuffing historian. It's a chuffing nine to five job, isn't it? No, I had to marry the only historian that is always working late. I work full time as a solicitor — it should be me that works late, but I have to be at home for the kids. And when he's supposed to be home picking them up, or whatever, I get a phone call saying he hasn't turned up — again!'

Grace looked at me sympathetically, suppressing a smile. 'No, he's not the only one,' she said, nodding in James's direction. 'He gets carried away with it all too.'

'But you're a historian as well,' said Carol to Grace. 'Surely you understand what they're up to. You understand this — this shit that gets hold of them.'

'You would think so, wouldn't you?' said Grace. 'But did you know we split up a couple of years ago?' Carol looked at her, stunned, and Grace knew she had to tell the full story. 'He got his head in some sort of a bubble; he was obsessed by a woman he was researching. He started to judge *me* by everything *she* did 200 years ago. Well, I wasn't having any of that, so I left him.'

'How long?' asked Carol.

'A couple of months, until he came to his senses. But I did think it was all over between us.'

'Perhaps that is what Toby needs. A good kick up the arse to bring him to his senses.' There was still anger in Carol's voice. She exchanged a sort of *all girls together* look with Grace.

We all laughed, but my laughter was uncomfortable. I knew she was basically right yet, I thought, being dedicated was not the greatest sin in the world, was it? James looked at me, knowing he had to come to my aid.

'The third semester is examination time, you know, and that comes with hours of marking. He also has to mentor his students and give them guidance on their dissertations.'

'He can do his marking from home,' said Carol, dismissing James's argument.

There was an uncomfortable silence until James spoke again. 'Carol,' he said tentatively, 'have you ever had to deal with a case at work that might define your career? Something that you are immensely proud of?'

Carol thought. 'No, not really. I don't do criminal work. It's mainly family matters. But I see what you're getting at. I've worked with colleagues who have spent years taking cases through the courts to get justice for clients. If you're suggesting Toby is working on something comparable, I am going to take some convincing, I assure you.'

'I'm suggesting just that. What Toby is doing now will define his career. He is translating one of the most remarkable chronicles I have ever seen. I think it will make him famous.'

Carol looked at him, dumbfounded, and he told her of the newly found chronicles and their translation into modern English and their connection to 2020. 'Toby might not be the best husband and father at the moment,' said James, 'but I promise you what he is doing is special — very special indeed.' He turned and looked at me. 'Why haven't you told Carol?'

I twitched a smile, shrugged my shoulders. *Damn it — I don't know why I keep it all to myself*, I thought.

'Have you translated any more since the last bits you sent me?'

'Yes, I have the deathbed confession.'

'How about letting us all see it?' said Grace. 'Do you have your laptop with you?'

I could only nod. I collected my portfolio case from the hall, opened my laptop, and scrolled down to the last entry — the deathbed confession. The three of them moved their chairs closer as I started to read.

AD 1152 — 30th Day of November.

Guy FitzHugh, the Under-Sheriff of Nottingham, sent his men-at-arms to escort the maid Margaret to Nottingham — they took her away two days ago. I asked Abbot Stephen for permission to go to Nottingham to give the maid the last rites before her execution on the morrow. I was fearful her village priest would not give her these rites, knowing his fervour against witchcraft.

The abbot readily agreed, and I now find myself in the blind house attached to the Church of St. Mary The Virgin, with the condemned child. She sits, with her knees drawn up, shivering in soiled straw, trying to keep warm in this bitter cell. There is a small pool of light from my candle safely engulfing us, as if keeping out the horrors of the morrow.

After I administered the sacraments, I did not feel like leaving her alone, and I hoped I could comfort her. Of course, the uneducated child was unaware of the principle of 'novissima verba' — a dying man's last words should be respected, but I prompted that she ought to make a full confession of her sins, and she agreed readily to do so.

She rolled over and sat on her knees, shivering, and I took off my thick woollen winter cape and put it around her shoulders.

'Forgive me, father, for I have sinned,' she quoth, but the trespasses to which she confessed were so trivial. She confessed to not always paying attention at Mass and not always doing straight away what her father and mother bade her do. Yet she was adamant that she said her prayers every day, was not mean to people, was not lazy, did her chores, and did not blame other people for the thing she did.

This dying confession revealed her as a goodly and dutiful daughter and a credit to her parents. As she looked up at me, her rosy pink complexion was gone, now dirtied and pallid. Nevertheless, I saw again that face of innocence and bewilderment I had seen when I first met her.

I was more puzzled than ever as to the source of the tale she told. I reminded her she was making a deathbed confession and asked her to tell her story from the very beginning while trying to remember every detail as she did so. I will relate the wondrous tale that she said to me thus.

Her story began in June of last year, the Year of our Lord AD 1151. She had been sent by her mother to gather wild brambleberries. This was not a chore she liked because the thorns can tear through clothes with ease. But she knew a place at the skirt of a copse a few yards from the Newark Road.

The long stems amongst the brambles had some fruit on them; it was yet early in the summer, but she could see that the ripest fruit was in the centre of the hedgerow. She stretched in, trying to avoid the thorns, but overreached and fell into a ditch. She yelled out in pain as she felt the thorns piercing not only her clothes but her arms and legs as well.

She found herself in a gloomy hollow, the wooden bowl with her harvest now scattered on the dark ground around her. The bramble was so thick that it was closed over her head like a canopy and at first, she was fearful, there being so little light. She was also angry, as she would have to start picking all over again; it was too gloomy to regather the scattered fruit.

'I knew I had to climb out,' she quoth, 'and I used the long stems of the old growth as a sort of a ladder and climbed up carefully, still trying to avoid the thorns. I was heading for a small hole of light, and when I reached it, I threw the bowl out in front of me and put my arm through, followed by my head, and squeezed through as cautiously as I could.

'When I was clear, I lifted up my woollen dress to look at the scratches on my legs, some of which were weeping and were starting to sting. And that is when I heard it — a great sound the likes of which I had never heard before. It was like a —' She was at first unable to find a description, but then she added, 'It was like a dragon. I looked about me, and it was as if I were in the same place but not the same place. The copse was still there, but somehow it looked different, smaller, not as rambling.

'I walked towards the Newark Road that was nigh to see what had made the noise. I was afeared, but I went anyway. But the road was not the same. It was still hard like it was when the summer sun dried up the

mud, but there were no furrows in it from the cartwheels — and it was black — and it was wider than the last time I had seen it, and it was not lined with trees.

'But I heard that sound again; it was quieter than before. I looked down the road and saw this runaway covered wagon, and the sound it was making, I thought, must have been its wooden wheels on the hard black mud. The sound got louder and louder as it came hither, but then I saw it was being pulled by a demon horse I could not see. I jumped back behind a bush until the demon carriage passed me by, my heart thumping in my chest, I was so afeared.

'I sat trembling there for some minutes, before running back to the bramble bush by the copse. I climbed back down the blackcurrant stems into that dark hollow, hoping I would be safe there. In the darkness, I said my prayers over and over again and asked Jesus to save me.

'I was there for at least an hour until I could not hear any demon wagons anymore. I wanted to run home, so I carefully climbed out of the hollow again, but this time I walked as far as I could down the hollow so that the slope was not as steep. When I emerged, I seemed to recognise where I was. I tiptoed back to the road, but now it was hard, baked mud again with the wheel furrows in it, lined with trees. I ran home.

'I was scolded for not bringing the fruit, and for losing the bowl. I tried to tell them my story, but Father thought I was making excuses for not doing my chores, despite my scratched legs that showed I had been to the bramble bushes and my story was sooth. I was sent back the next day.

'When I got to the copse, I walked past it to the Newark Road. Everything was as it should be: baked mud, no demon carriages, so I went back to my chores. I found my lost bowl and filled it with berries. I had started to return home when something made me stop, and I walked back the few steps to the bramble. I cannot explain why, but something drew me there as if it was the ditch below the hedgerow that was the magical place.

'I wondered if I had had a vision from Jesus and he was testing me — though I now fear it was a vision from the devil. I climbed down into the

ditch, leaving my bowl of berries at the top. It was colder down there, the hot June sun not warming it, but there was something else. I shivered as an icy chill touched me from my head to my feet, and I knew something had changed.

'I climbed out again carefully, even though I had now made the hole larger. I knew at once I was back in the vision. It was again the same place, yet not the same place. I heard that sound again of the demon carriages travelling faster than a galloping horse. I went to the strange road in time to see it flash past me. It was as shiny as the polished chalice the priest uses for communion. I watched for a time from behind a bush and saw several of these dragon carriages gallop along as if they were part of a hue and cry, but they were going both ways so they could not have been.

'I was less afeared than the day before but knew I had to go back home, as I did not want another scolding from Father. I climbed back down into the bramble hollow and out again, but I was still engulfed in the vision. My fear came flooding back to me, and I tried this several more times, but each time I emerged still in this strange place. I sat at the bottom of the hollow, panicking, and started to cry in my terrifying fear.

'I was befuddled, and I prayed to Jesus, asking him to explain this confusing vision to me, and he came to me and put a thought in my head. There was a way into the vision and a way out. The day before I had left by the far end of the ditch, where it was less steep. I went that way and climbed out. I saw my bowl of berries and knew straightaway that I was no longer in the vision.

'I ran home, thinking of what I would say to Father for taking so long, but when I got there, I was not late at all; the sun was still not high in the sky, but I knew I had been away long enough to take it past sext. Our priest had regularly told us from the pulpit that time belonged to God, and it was not ours to waste. I thought these visions must have come from Jesus because only he had control of time. I also knew I would return to the vision, as it was the will of Jesus — he had a task for me.

'I went thither again to the vision several more times, each time getting bolder. Sometimes I saw people, but they were dressed strangely so I avoided them, always hiding. I walked further and further down the road each time towards Ollerton, and one day I got to where Ollerton should be, but I found a wondrous city of God — or was it the devil? — as far as the eye could see.

'There were demon carriages galloping all around it. The noise was deafening, and I feared Jesus's task for me was to bring his word to this evil place. I was a mere girl, and such a task was beyond me, I knew.

'I did not go back again for some weeks after that, but at one Sunday service, the priest told the parable of not hiding your light under a bushel, the one that Jesus spoke in his Sermon on the Mount. The priest said it meant that we believers should not hide our faith. Was I doing that by not going back to the vision that had been sent to me?

'So I started to go back again, trying each time to understand what Jesus had in mind for me. Why had he chosen me? Was it my purity that had made him pick me out? Yet I had kept these visions to myself. I had not lied to my parents about where I was going. I told them I had found a really good place for brambleberries — which I had.

'It was in September that I first saw the devil's work. The brambleberries were now ripe and bountiful, and the summer was coming to an end. I thought this would be my last visit to the vision until the coming of spring next year. I had walked some miles beside the road of demons, trying all the time to keep out of sight, when one of the shiny horseless carriages slowed to a canter and turned off the road. The dragon within it stopped growling, and the doors opened. Two angels got out.

'They were giants; they must have been as tall as a knight on his steed. The lady angel, though beautiful as a princess, was dressed as a man in white breeches, and she walked on the toes of her beautiful white slippers. Her hair was white and curled, hanging long down her back, her fingernails long and red.

'The man angel came around to her side of the dragon wagon, and he was dressed all in black, and he had a mask of dark glass over his eyes.

'At first, they spoke quietly, and he called her by the name of Catherine, and I wondered if she was Saint Catherine herself appearing to me to explain God's purpose for me. But I saw that the lady angel seemed to be pleading with the man angel. His voice became louder. I could not understand his words, but they seemed to me to be wicked as the lady recoiled from him. I think he was baiting her, as I could see fear in her face.

'His hand came up and he tried to strike her down. She brought her hand up to defend herself, and with her other hand she scratched his face with her long, red nails and blood started to weep straightaway.

'His wrath was clear to me, and I crouched down further so that I would not be seen. I heard the lady angel start to make noises, and I looked back again — he was choking her. His hand was gripped around her neck, and he was trying to force her back into the dragon wagon, and that's when I saw it — the mark of the devil on the back of one of his hands — the Eye of Lucifer.

'I saw him squeeze with his left hand while his right held her other hand to stop her scratching him further. He turned her round, put his arm across her throat and she went limp. The carl dropped her body and she fell to the ground.

'I first thought she was dead, but then I saw her writhe on the floor, making a moaning sound, trying to crawl away. He looked about him to see if there was anyone abroad that would be witness to his deed. Seeing no one, he went back to his dragon carriage and commanded a door at the back to open, and it did so obey him. But he went back to the writhing lady angel and lifted her body and put it into the back of the carriage.

'His snarling carriage soon roared to his command, and it galloped away as if he were pursuing a stag in the hunt.

'When I was sure he was not coming back, I went thither and looked at where the beautiful lady angel had lain. There were two of her bright red

fingernails in the dirt, and one of her white slippers had fallen from her foot into a bush and was partially hidden. I picked them all up and held them to my bosom. Terror took me, and I ran back to the ditch as fast as my legs could carry me, and I hid the white slipper down there in the darkness, the fingernails tucked inside. When I emerged from the vision, I ran home so afeared.

'I did not even go abroad for many weeks after that, always staying close to father's cottage. My fears subsided over the following months, but I still did not go back to the vision. It was at Mass on Good Friday the next spring that Jesus came to me again. The priest told us all of his sufferings for our salvation, and he made me think of my own cowardliness. He had called me, but I had run away from his word.

'It was on Easter Sunday that I returned again to the copse. I climbed in and out again and was once more in the vision, but this time, I looked abroad, trying to understand what task Jesus had for me. But I was still unsure.

'I went to the road that was nigh, and again I saw the dragon carriages but could not understand what they had to do with Jesus and what he wanted of me.

'And then I saw a man; I was again afeared, but this time, I did not hide. He came to me and knew my name. He spoke in a strange way, but I understood something of what he said.

"Are you Margaret?" he quoth. I nodded and knew he was an angel from God. He said he was the man to be — and that his name was Ristorian. He had come from the year of our Lord 2020 to speak to me. He showed me his hand, which lit up with a picture of the Virgin Mary — then he asked me to show him from where the lady angel was taken.'

CHAPTER 5

'Phew!' said James when I had shared the translation. 'It gets better and better, doesn't it?'

Carol looked at me over the top of her wine glass. She swirled the red liquid languidly, her face reflecting interest and irritation at the same time. I think she saw the value of what I was working on, but at the same time was exasperated as it negated the strength of her anger towards me.

Grace gave Carol a sideways look, as if wanting permission to break the female code, the women's union. There must have been some gesture of confirmation, but I didn't discern it.

'It's remarkable stuff isn't it?' Grace said. 'What does everyone think?'

'Is it real?' asked Carol, looking at me. 'Is it a fake, a hoax?'

'Oh, it's real, all right,' I said, relieved Carol was showing some interest in what I was doing. 'The manuscript is original — well, I need to get the boffins to verify the writing material and the ink, but I am sure it's genuine. The source is impeccable.'

'So what are we saying here?' my wife said, her investigative lawyer's mind at work. 'Surely we have to start from the premise that she is not a time traveller, because there's no such thing as a time portal, is there? They only exist in novels, in the movies.' She looked at us in turn, and one by one, we agreed, although Grace with less conviction. 'So where does that leave us? Either she has indeed had some sort of vision, or she is making the whole thing up.'

'You had better take this one, Toby. You're the medievalist,' said James, urging me to expand.

'You have to understand the medieval mind,' I said. 'Take Margaret's trial by ordeal, for example. They believed witches were all about them. Witches had spurned the sacrament of baptism, so if they floated, the water was rejecting them and proved their guilt.'

'But it was probably more to do with the fat content in their body,' interrupted James, 'or the fact they were often tied up in the foetal position, enabling them to fill their lungs with air.'

'Exactly,' I said. 'The medieval mind was different — to them, the trial was real. They were in constant fear of their immortal souls. This was immensely important to them. A medieval deathbed confession was made to wipe out all past sin. It was always accepted that people did not lie if they gave a deathbed confession.'

'*Nemo moriturus praesumitur mentire*,' said Carol, 'if I remember my law training correctly.'

We all looked at her — she smiled as she explained further. 'It's an ancient principle of English law — going back to medieval times, I think. No-one on the point of death should be presumed to be lying. Dying declarations were admitted as evidence as far back as English law itself goes.'

'So,' I said, 'that leaves us with one possible explanation, however ludicrous it seems.'

'No, it doesn't,' said Carol. 'Hold on a minute. You don't actually believe she did have a religious vision?'

'Is that so ridiculous?' interrupted Grace. 'She's saying things that are clearer than Nostradamus ever said. His predictions are vague and tenuous, and it's wishful thinking that links them with subsequent events. But this girl refers to —' she pointed her finger at the laptop, running it down the lines — 'shiny demon carriages, either pulled by invisible horses or having dragons roaring inside them. It's not such a leap to say she saw motor cars, is it?'

'And the man angel has a mask of dark glass over his eyes — that could be sunglasses, could it not?' added James.

'Yeah, okay,' said Carol, 'but what about —' she ran her finger down the screen as Grace had done — '*he said he was the man to be — and that his name was Ristorian.* That's pretty vague stuff, isn't it? And what about — *his hand lit up with a picture of the Virgin Mary*?'

'It may be vague to us,' I said, 'but this girl has no education, very little vocabulary. It could be that she couldn't articulate what she saw and heard. She has no points of reference to rationalise what she sees. Remember — a young, uneducated medieval girl. Even Brother Roger of Hathern who *has* education has no points of reference to explain her vision. We are able to interpret some of what she said but not everything. I don't think it devalues the other parts.'

'It's a hoax!' Carol screeched, her eyes widening as she looked at us each in turn. 'I know it's three historians to one lawyer, but come on, guys — that's the most likely answer, isn't it? A hoax?'

We looked at each other. It was clear *we* thought the chronicle was genuine.

'I don't believe it is,' I said, 'but you are right — we have to eliminate the possibility. I'll scan the chronicle into my computer; I can finish the translation from there. I'll get it to the university boffins in palaeography to do their tests as soon as possible. They can verify the writing materials used as well as the form of Latin to see if it's compatible with the twelfth century.'

The evening became more amiable from that point on. I had James and Grace to thank for that. They had involved Carol in my passion. Why I had not thought to do that myself, I didn't know, but they may have saved my marriage. I wouldn't continue the translation, I decided, until the end of term. It would also give the boffins time to validate the document — I was wasting my time if this *was* a hoax.

It was a Sunday afternoon in July, and the university summer graduations had been completed. I was reading the Sunday paper, enjoying a cup of coffee, and Carol was busy packing for our family holiday in Cyprus. She suddenly asked if I had done any more translations of the Latin in the chronicle. I was surprised — she was casually folding some of Tom's clothes, but she raised an inquisitive eyebrow as if she was genuinely interested.

'You said a couple of weeks ago that palaeography had verified the paper and ink, pronounced it genuine — I was just wondering.'

'I was going to start translating again when I got back from holiday.'

'Mmm, pity,' she said, laying the clothes in the suitcase, having, I thought, seen the look of surprise on my face.

'Are you interested?' I said warily.

'A bit,' she said, her face buried in the suitcase.

She had opened a door, I thought, but seemed anxious about crossing the threshold. 'Oh,' was all I could say, and I went back to the article I was reading.

'When do you finish at work?' she added.

'Wednesday, why?'

She came over and took a drink from my coffee cup. 'I was wondering what became of the girl.'

'Margaret of Wellow, you mean?' I said, lowering my paper.

'Yep, that's her.'

'I suppose they hung her the next morning.'

I saw her face crease into a grimace. 'Aw, poor little thing.'

'It was 900 years ago, you know.'

'I know, but … she has been on my mind these past few days — well, since you ruled out a hoax. I don't know why.'

'That's how *I* get,' I said. 'I understand — they are real people to me as well, even if they are long dead.'

'Could you translate the bit about her, you know, this week?'

I looked at her, dumbfounded. 'Well, yes, I could. The chronicle is not indexed or anything but it is in date order, so it should be the next day — the next entry.'

'It would be interesting to know,' she said, again going back to her packing.

'I need to go and get the foreign currency and stuff,' I said.

'I'll do that, shall I?'

'Okay,' I said, 'I'll translate the entry in the next couple of days.'

CHAPTER 6

I lost no time in translating the next section of the chronicle. I then emailed it to James, Grace and Carol:

Thought you might be interested in the translation of the day covering the execution.

AD 1152 — 1st Day of December.

The morning dawned cold, overcast, a light drizzle falling from a cloudy, grey sky. The sheriff's men-at-arms came for poor Margaret after first light, well before nine of the clock. I walked with her, shivering myself; I had not the heart to take my heavy winter cape from her.

They took her to the hangman's cart, which made the short journey to Gallows Hill at the northern entrance to the town on the Mansfield Road, where a scaffold with three ropes stood ominously in the gloom, the nooses swinging in the gusts of drizzling rain.

She was calm, but I had had a hand in that. I had brought with me a vial containing a draught of dwale that I had obtained from Brother Augustine, the abbey apothecary. He said it contained various herbs including extract of poppy seeds, henbane, bryony, mandrake root, hemlock, and vinegar.

'Some of these are poisonous,' he said, 'but given in small quantities the dwale will induce calmness and sleep.' However, if the dose is exceeded, it could easily kill. I had given her a few drops when I had heard the boots of the men-at-arms coming along the cobbled streets. As she walked, I saw that her eyelids were hooded, half open. I was relieved the draught was doing its work.

When the cart reached Gallows Hill, there was little delay in the execution. The sergeant-at-arms read out the names of the prisoners, who were brought forward. Each had a noose placed around their neck and was then manoeuvred to stand on a bench.

The other two were outlaws convicted of robbery on the Nottingham Road through Sherwood forest. They were visibly shaking.

I saw Margaret's legs buckle slightly as she climbed up, but nobody thought anything of it. A priest from Lenton Priory spoke words in Latin, but I fear I was the only one present who understood, and the prisoners must have gained little comfort from them.

There were a few bedraggled onlookers, but the inclement day had kept most of them in their homes. If it had been summer, and the prisoners more notorious, there would have been jugglers and stilt-walkers to entertain the crowds, and ale to drink.

The hangman came and pulled on a lever, the bench fell away, and all three prisoners fell, the nooses tightening around their necks. Little Margaret hung there, but the other two on the outside swung violently on the end of their ropes, eyes bulging, lips turning blue as they writhed. After a time their tongues engorged, black, protruding from their lips as the strangling nooses tightened ever more firmly around their necks. Urine stained their breeches and dripped from their feet.

It took some time for them to die, but eventually, the thrashing stopped as the life left them. God rest their souls, *I prayed to myself.*

They were cut down at twelve of the clock. I was pleased they were not left there as they sometimes are for days as a warning to others, but another hanging was scheduled for the morrow. I retrieved my heavy cape and went back to the inn where I had stabled my mule. I took a meal from the landlord, but despite my impending journey, sustenance was not what I wanted. I ate little of the rabbit stew.

I was tucking some bread into the pannier, about to mount the animal, when an errand boy came shouting after me. 'Are you Brother Roger?' he quoth, so that I would not leave. 'I am Brother Roger,' I answered, and the lad said that he had been sent by Guy FitzHugh, the under-sheriff. I went with him to the sheriff's hall at the runner's insistence, where I met Guy FitzHugh himself.

'This is a rum do,' he said, nodding his head at the three bodies. I was confused, and I asked him what he meant. Go and put your fingers to the girl's neck, he demanded. I did so, and at first, I felt nothing, but then, unmistakably, I sensed a faint but regular pulse. 'Do you agree?' quoth Guy, and I nodded my confirmation.

'The maid is not dead,' I said.

'I fear she did not have enough weight to pull the noose tight,' he said. 'She is a waif, and the rope has not throttled her.' I could see the truth in his observation, but I also suspected the dwale I had given her had contributed. If she had thrashed, the noose would surely have tightened.

'Her village priest has already been to check that the maid is dead,' said Guy. 'He was the one who found the pulse. He is demanding she be burnt at the stake, as witchcraft is involved in her survival.'

'What did you say to that?' I asked, and he said that he could not stand the fellow and was not going to let him have a say on what is not within his jurisdiction. The problem, he went on, was that he did not know either, what the law was in these circumstances. The girl has previously failed a trial by ordeal, but it seemed to him that the failure to die on the scaffold could itself be said to be a trial by ordeal. One that has now proved her innocence.

'So,' he said, 'I am assigning the whole matter back to the Abbot of Rufford for him to consider what the correct law is in these circumstances. When the maid is fit to travel, I want you to take her back to Rufford.'

I received three replies soon after.

Amazing stuff, Toby, wrote James. *Have a great holiday. Work to do when you get back.*

Girl power, wrote Grace.

Yippee! wrote Carol. *She's alive.*

PART 2: THE PEACOCK SYNDROME

CHAPTER 7

Day 1: Tuesday, 10th September 2019

Susan Devlin looked up at the clock on the far wall of the control room. 8.40 p.m. She sighed; her shift finished at 10.00 p.m. — more than an hour to go. Her job as a radio officer was to answer 999 calls and non-emergency calls alike for the Nottinghamshire Police, Central Division.

It had been a sunny late summer's day, and the city had been relatively calm. It was Tuesday, so it was not a peak time for calls, but the control room had a target of handling all emergency calls within ten seconds. She knew it would not be long before her next call came in.

On cue, her computer screen alerted her, and she answered: 'Nottinghamshire Police.'

'My wife is missing.' The caller's voice was quivering, and she recognised his anxiety. She had heard it many times before.

'How long has she been missing, sir?'

'She didn't show up for her meeting at her office.'

'What time would that be, sir?'

'Two-thirty this afternoon.'

Only six hours or so, Susan thought. 72 hours was the trigger for reference to the Missing Persons Bureau, but she also knew that if the circumstances warranted it, she could authorise an immediate response.

'She's not answering her phone.' The caller's voice was little more than a murmur.

'Phones get lost or run out of battery, sir.'

'I've been telling myself that for hours,' he said, 'but she would have found some way to call me by now. She's an intelligent woman.'

'Your name, sir?'

'My name is Gerald Talbot.'

'And your wife's name?'

'Katarina … but everybody knows her as Karrie.'

'How old is she, sir?'

'Thirty-two.'

'Her occupation?'

'She's an architect, works from her office on High Pavement, in the city. She's a partner there — Turner Talbot Associates.'

'Does she sometimes work late?'

'Sometimes, but it's all logged in her diary when she does. I've spoken to her business partner. He rang this afternoon when she didn't turn up for their weekly briefing. That's the last thing scheduled for today, according to her log. She should have been working in the office for the rest of the day and therefore home at the usual time.'

Susan Devlin made her judgement call. She would authorise the deployment of frontline staff.

'I'll get an officer to come and see you, sir,' she said.

CHAPTER 8

Day 2
Nottinghamshire CID Central Division

Coffee cups and empty croissant wrappers littered the tabletops, purchased on the way into work. The morning briefing was a good time to fuel up for the day — the chief inspector in charge had no objection, and some took advantage, but they knew enough not to get on the wrong side of him. There was the buzz of gossip humming around the room; there had been a promotions board. Speculation was rife.

The chatter stopped immediately, however, when Detective Chief Inspector Donald McMillan entered. He perched his lean, muscular frame on the edge of the desk at the front of the room, his leg swinging — he never sat behind it. He looked around the briefing room at this syndicate, some experienced, some inexperienced, some fast-track graduates with law degrees. He was a fifty-two-year-old who had come up through the ranks and was suspicious of the latter, but he was a fair man — at least, he tried to be — judging people on their merits.

Most DCIs liked their senior investigative officers to brief them in private, but he preferred to touch base every day. He was old school; budget control came with his grade, but he was a detective to his fingertips. He controlled several syndicates of detectives, but he wanted to see how they performed close up, day to day. He didn't like surprises, and the best way to avoid them was to head them off. He was aided by his intellectual capacity — the ability to assimilate information without writing it down. He was a walking database of information. A difficult man to get to know, but everyone respected him. He was known as 'Big Mac,' but not to his face, although it was a nickname he was comfortable with.

He turned to Detective Inspector Jilly French, who stood to the side of him, waiting to take the meeting. She had the team's caseload list — the running investigations. He hated that name, *Jilly* — why couldn't she be a *Jill*? *She* was one of the law graduates, thirty-one and fast-tracked. She dressed appropriately: a navy blue business suit and white blouse, the collar over the collar of her jacket. Her blonde hair was swept back severely into a ponytail. A hint of eyeshadow highlighted her green eyes, but otherwise she wore no make-up. *Plain clothes*, he mused, *yet they all wear the same uniform — look at me, I'm the sharpest pencil in the box. I sharpened it at university. I got a 2:1 for having the most pointy nib*, he thought. He caught himself; he was being unjust.

'Jill, if you please?' he said, his voice low and guttural.

Each of the running cases was reviewed by her in turn, and those officers working the cases gave their updates. Jilly questioned them, giving advice where necessary. McMillan said little, but all the time his brain registered what was being said. He knew about every case his syndicates were working and the state of play.

'Anything new overnight?' McMillan asked when the reviews had been concluded. He never raised his voice. It made people strain to hear him and ensured they were paying attention.

'Yes, Mac,' said Jilly French, shuffling the papers in front her to find the thin file she wanted, 'a missing persons.'

'A child?' Mac's eyes darted to her. He knew missing kiddie cases were traumatic for all concerned, but they also burned his team's resources. Everything else stopped until the child was found — dead or alive.

'No, Mac,' said Jilly, 'a city architect.' She took a photo from the thin folder, stepped to the whiteboard, and put it up. There was wolf whistling from the back, but it stopped abruptly as Mac stared at the culprit.

'Sorry, Mac,' said DC Reader sheepishly, looking down at his desk, 'but she's some looker, isn't she?' His voice had fallen away as he spoke.

Mac looked back at DI French, nodded, and she continued.

'Nottingham architect — Katarina Talbot, known as Karrie. German mother, English father. Yes, she *is* stunning, if her photo is anything to go by: long platinum-blonde hair, blue eyes. Last seen wearing a white, tailored trouser-suit late yesterday morning after visiting a client in Rainworth. Did not return to her office for a meeting at two-thirty p.m. Reported as missing by husband at eight-forty p.m.'

'What do we have so far?' asked Mac.

'DC Anderson did the preliminary interview with the husband last night, ten-twenty p.m. According to him there are no marital problems or financial problems. The husband is a surgeon and, by all accounts, Ms Talbot is something of a star architect — a big earner.'

'That doesn't mean the business isn't overstretched,' interrupted Mac. Years of detective work had made him cynical; he knew appearances could be deceptive. Things were rarely as they seemed.

Jilly French nodded, reinforcing her chief inspector's observation. She lacked his years of experience, but she had an incisive brain.

'Any thoughts?' whispered Mac, looking around his team.

'A looker like that will have every randy dog in town chasing her,' said DC Eric Boone. 'She'll be shacked up somewhere and will turn up all shamefaced this morning. You mark my words.'

There was another short silence as everybody looked back to Mac. He'd expected that of Boone — *he* was the randy dog in this police station, and it was typical he should think that way. Mac continued to nod, though, seeming to agree with his DC, but his mind was making connections — then he sat up. His team waited in anticipation. 'No,' he said, pausing for a second before continuing, 'people who are playing away cover their tracks. Well, anyone with intelligence will, and we must assume this lady is a smart cookie. If she were "playing away", she would have fabricated a story for her husband.'

DC Boone put his papers down — he was not going to get away yet.

There was something at the back of Mac's mind: other missing women being investigated by other area commands. 'I smell foul play,' he said, looking round at DI French. She nodded her agreement. 'Right — we elevate this case from a missing persons to top priority. I want a timeline established from eight a.m. yesterday morning, or whatever time she left for work. I want a check on her mobile and credit cards, and we need to find her car — what was she driving?'

'Aston Martin DB9,' said DI French.

Mac looked round at her, raising an eyebrow.

'Brilliant yellow custom paint job as well,' she added, raising an eyebrow to match his.

'Well, even the greenest new PC should be able to spot that bugger,' said Mac.

'Should I get the techies in to set up the husband's phone to record and trace any ransom demand?'

'Yeah — do that,' he said as he stood to leave, 'and record all incoming and outgoing messages, too.'

In a clearing close to the A616 Nottingham Road, a man dressed in an expensively tailored black suit searched frantically in the undergrowth. There had been a heavy dew, but he still rummaged in the wet shrubbery until his stylish black brogues were scuffed and muddied. He cursed under his breath — his plan had been thought through to the end; his plans always were. How could he have been stupid enough to leave something behind? He did not make mistakes — mistakes were for others.

He went to the boot of his car, took out a shovel and used it to sweep away as much of the foliage as he could, slashing it from side to side as though he were a swordsman. There should have been no loose ends to tidy up, he cursed to himself. His face stung from the scratches he had received — he had tried to reason with the woman, use the strength of his personality to mould her to his will as he had done previously, but she wouldn't have it. They had been face to face; she had managed to scratch him before he could subdue her. He wouldn't make *that* mistake again.

He got down on his hands and knees, the cut of his stylish suit now irrelevant in the face of his dilemma. He reached through the undergrowth, grasping at anything that might be a shoe or a false nail. But he found nothing.

He went back to the roadside and looked up and down the road. After a few moments, he confirmed to himself that he had the correct clearing, the one that he had pre-selected as the scene of the abduction. He reached up and scratched his head, the movement of his cuff revealing the tattoo of an eye. He looked down at it and pondered its significance to him — perhaps he was not worthy of it.

He turned, went back into the clearing and started his search all over again. He was not to find what he was looking for.

CHAPTER 9

Day 3

'Katarina Talbot,' said DI French, standing at the presentation board, 'left the family home at seven-forty-five a.m. on Tuesday morning, arrived at work at eight-forty, logged on to her computer eight-forty-three. She logged off again at ten-twenty, when she left to visit a client to review the work on a rebuild at Rainworth that she had designed. She met the client and the contractor at approximately eleven a.m., which agrees with her computer diary for the day. She left to return to the office shortly after twelve, but we know she never arrived back.

'What about her mobile?' As usual, Mac's words were kept to a minimum, his voice matter-of-fact. He chewed his cheek, staring at the floor.

'It was turned off at two-twenty-one p.m. — the last location we have for it is the old market square in the centre of the city,' said Jilly.

Mac looked up. He swept his fingers through his dark hair, greying at the temples, spreading them as if a comb. He knew the significance of this and saw that his team understood too. *Phones run out of battery; it could be as simple as that*, he thought, but the fact that she was missing suggested it had been switched off or, more likely, destroyed.

'So she *wasn't* "shacked up" somewhere, DC Boone,' he said.

'No, Mac,' said the young detective constable contritely.

'Any ransom demands yet?' Mac's words were directed at the floor.

'No, nothing yet, Mac.'

'Credit cards?' He looked at DI French.

'Her credit card was last used at one-ten p.m. at the Travellers Rest pub on Mapperley Top. It would be on her way back to the office. It seems she stopped for a bite of lunch. According to the manager, she had a tuna baguette and a small glass of Chenin Blanc.'

'Do we have CCTV?'

'Yes, Mac. We have it inside the pub and the main car park.'

'And?'

'We have her arriving in the car park, and she is seen inside — you can't miss her in that white trouser-suit, but she dined alone. Doesn't appear to have spoken to anybody.'

'So what about CCTV on the road outside? Have you tracked her movements from that point on?'

'That's the problem, Mac,' said DI French, biting her lip. 'We don't have any CCTV showing her leaving the pub.'

'You must have,' said DCI McMillan. 'If you have her entering the car park, you must have her leaving.'

'The Aston Martin is still there, Mac — DC Reader noticed it on his way into the pub.'

Mac ground his teeth as he thought, the muscles in his cheek twitching. 'So let me get this straight: we have her entering, we have her eating inside, she gets up to leave, then nothing?'

'Yep, that's about the size of it — the problem is the CCTV doesn't have full coverage. Inside, the camera looks down into the central room, but there is no coverage of the main entrance. Likewise, there are a few parking spaces at the front of the pub that are not caught by the CCTV which covers the main car park.'

'So we must assume she met somebody in the entrance and then went off in another vehicle, leaving hers behind.'

Jilly nodded, adding, 'But we must then ask ourselves why she would do that. And the answer must be that this person was known to her.'

'And this man, or whoever, was either very smart or very lucky not be caught on camera.'

She nodded again. 'And there's no point in us reviewing the CCTV cameras on the road, because we don't know the car she left in.'

'We've hit the buffers,' said Mac. 'Better start interviewing all her associates.'

CHAPTER 10

Day 4

'Sit down, Jill,' said Mac. He was by his office window, staring out as he spoke. Jilly knew he didn't like to sit behind a desk — what she didn't know was that he had taken a bullet in his hip as a DC twenty-five years ago, and prolonged sitting made him stiff.

She sat and took the opportunity to study her boss from behind. He was immaculately dressed as usual in a tailored, lightweight, pale grey suit that looked stylish and fitted his lithe frame like a glove, but then everything he wore suited him. As older men went, he looked good, Jilly thought — he even smelled good. But she couldn't work him out. He treated her respectfully, listened when she spoke, appeared to respect her opinion, but then deliberately called her Jill. Was it a put-down?

'We're not covering ourselves with glory on this one, are we?' Mac said over his shoulder, his steel-grey eyes seeking her out.

'The Katarina Talbot case? No, we bloody well aren't,' Jilly responded, launching her mind into work mode. 'The critical first seventy-two hours are up, and we've got zilch.'

'No suspect, no motive, and our timeline is broken at one-ten p.m. when she last used her credit card at the pub. I suppose at least we can say that soon after this is the time of her abduction.'

'You think she was abducted, then?'

'Don't you?'

'I do — it doesn't look good for the poor woman, does it? If there'd been a ransom demand, we could speculate that she's still alive — but nothing.'

'Yep, if it were a ransom case we would have heard from them by now — but we proceed on the basis she's still alive, until we know for certain that she isn't. What about her associates?'

'We have her computer diary, and we have a list of all her clients and anybody she has met in the last three months,' said Jilly. 'We are interviewing everybody on that list, but so far, nothing, and everyone has an alibi for the time of the disappearance. It was during a working day, after all.'

'What about the pub staff?'

'Well, it was peak time, the lunch rush. Everybody was busy.'

'True, but come on, she's extremely noticeable, isn't she?'

'She is, Mac, and she *was* noticed, but the staff lose her the moment the CCTV does when she leaves. The exit isn't visible from the bar either.'

'Send somebody back at lunchtime to see if there are any regulars in there who remember her, especially her leaving.'

'Will do, guv.' Jilly paused. 'Have you seen the morning papers, Mac?'

'Yep, and so has the chief constable. The bastards are not painting us in a good light, are they?'

'Time for a press briefing?' Jilly raised an eyebrow.

'Unfortunately, it is. The chief constable has approved it — we need the help of the public. Three o'clock this afternoon — you'll be with me as the senior investigative officer.'

'It's going to be a bit uncomfortable, Mac. We've virtually nothing to tell them. We'll be admitting that on camera.'

'I know, but you can leave Johnny Journalist to me. I know how to handle him. But be prepared for information overload, and the usual set of nutters burning your resources checking their stories.'

CHAPTER 11

Day 4
Press briefing

'Katarina Talbot,' said DCI McMillan as he pointed to the picture of the stunning woman, 'was last seen at one-ten p.m. on Tuesday afternoon.' His voice was silky yet matter-of-fact. Camera flashes went off as he started to talk, but he knew to expect that. 'She was last seen at the Travellers Rest Pub on Mapperley Top. She was wearing a distinctive white tailored trouser-suit, and she parked her bright yellow Aston Martin DB9 in the car park. The car is still there, but we have no sightings of her since. We are appealing to the general public for any sightings after this time or anyone who has any information as to her whereabouts.'

He was sitting in the middle of three, with DI French to his right and Gerald Talbot to his left. Talbot looked gaunt, his skin pallid as though he had not slept for days, but then he probably hadn't, thought McMillan. He turned to him and nodded imperceptibly. It was Gerald Talbot's opportunity to speak.

'Karrie, if you see this…' His voice caught in his throat, and he had to stop and swallow down his emotions, but he was a surgeon and used to giving bad news. He steeled himself and regained his composure. 'If you are seeing this, Karrie, and you can get to a phone, just ring me or the police — please!' Gerald Talbot heard the words come out of his mouth, and realised how inadequate they were — he had been advised to say them, to show hope, but they did not even convince himself.

McMillan was about to speak again, but Talbot decided he had to explain further; he did not believe his wife had gone off on her own, so why should the general public? He cleared his throat. 'Look, I believe my wife has been abducted, and I appeal to the public at large. Somebody must have seen her or have information about her. Please get in touch with the police.'

McMillan took a deep breath as flashes went off, this time aimed at Talbot. He waited for the assembly to quiet down. Jason Aston stood and raised his hand, his pen twiddling between his fingers.

Mac looked at him with contempt. The crime correspondent for the local newspaper, Aston was in his late twenties with a shaven head despite not being bald, and the designer stubble on his face made it look as if he had his head on upside down. A round, fleshy countenance and small, beady eyes spoiled the cool look he was obviously going for. He had the characteristics of a pit bull, and his target, as always, was the police — he knew that painting them in a bad light sold papers. They exchanged a look. *Go on, then*, thought McMillan. *Do your worst.* He prepared to take the question, and nodded at him to proceed.

'How many days did it take you to find the bright yellow Aston Martin?' There was irony in his delivery; the question provoked laughter around the room.

'The first morning of the investigation,' said McMillan unemotionally, looking around for another question, but Aston remained standing — he was not going to yield his platform.

'And how many sightings of this striking woman have you established so far?' The laughter erupted again.

'We have a timeline to one-ten p.m. on the day of the disappearance.'

'Are you treating this as an abduction, then?' continued Aston.

'We are keeping an open mind,' said McMillan, batting back the question.

'Do you see any connection with the disappearances of Emily Jackson and Caitlin Morgan?'

McMillan *had* seen a link — the fabled policeman's hunch. It had jumped into his mind at the first morning briefing. Emily Jackson, a barrister, had disappeared in November 2018 near Peterborough; Caitlin Morgan, a marketing director from Leeds, had vanished in April 2019. Neither had been seen since. Both top professional women, and now Karrie Talbot — and all last seen no more than a few miles from the A1. Sexual abductions, Mac knew, were usually local affairs; sad opportunists who acted on their perverted instincts, but the access to the motorway network and major roads gave some of the more devious ones the opportunity to put distance between them and their victims — and with distance came anonymity. The perpetrator could be hundreds of miles away before the crimes were discovered. They were the hard ones to find.

'We are keeping an open mind,' McMillan repeated dismissively, his voice little more than a murmur.

He continued with this stock answer for several more minutes. He knew that being open with Aston would only lead to his words being misrepresented, and anyway, he could see Aston getting more and more frustrated — he liked that.

When the barbed questions dried up, he looked around the room and made his closing remarks. 'We will be setting up a Major Incident Room later today to pursue this case. Thank you all for attending.' He stood to emphasise that the briefing was over.

CHAPTER 12

Day 5

McMillan sat on the corner of the desk at the front of the major incident room, swinging his leg as usual. There was the pleasant aroma of coffee and croissants in his nostrils, a smell he found comforting. That feeling, however, began to dissolve when he looked at the whiteboard; there was a picture of Karrie Talbot, and pictures of Emily Jackson and Caitlin Morgan had now been added, but the board was still sparse, lacking anything concrete.

He looked around at his assembled major incident team. DI Jill French was the senior investigating officer, with DS Satinder Kaur as deputy. Both graduates and fast-tracked and did things by the book. Mac smiled to himself — when he was a DS and then a DI, he'd had no time for those who did things by the book; it got in the way of good policing. Coppers, he'd thought, should use their instincts — but now, as a DCI, his view had changed. As the manager, he now not only had to consider results, but know how they were obtained. He knew he could rely on these two: no surprises, no messes to clean up.

But he too was a graduate, though he had earned his degree as a mature student in archaeology at the age of forty-three. That didn't count, in his mind; he was not the fast-tracked privileged type — he had paid his dues, pounded the beat, done the legwork as a young DC, learned the job from the bottom up. He had taken a career break at the age of forty after his first marriage had failed. It had shaken him up, made him re-evaluate his life. It was the usual coppers' problem, though — never at home, leaving a policeman's widow there to fear for his safety. He had met his second wife at university. She'd been one of his lecturers — as a mature student, he'd had more in common with the faculty than the younger students.

As to the rest, DS Jimmy Jackson was a gnarled fifty-something who had seen it all, from homicide to vice; white hair with a white goatee beard. Nicknamed *Whacko* because of his surname, but that was not an insightful jibe — he was ultra-reliable; no problem there. DC Peter Reader, a scruffy, forthright, opinionated slob who had something to say about everything. You could dress him in an Armani suit, and he would still look like a layabout. Bright, though — he would have been promoted years ago if he had been able to keep his mouth shut and had stayed out of the pub. McMillan smiled inwardly — in times gone by, being first into the pub was a positive — but not now. Finally, DC Eric Boone, known to all as *Dan'll* — he was the joker, a scallywag who hadn't grown up. He was also a womaniser, and had been transferred so often after leaving a trail of broken hearts that his personnel file was as thick as a serial killer's dossier.

Not bad, McMillan mused to himself, nodding imperceptibly. And he could bring in resources from other syndicates if necessary, or call on uniformed officers to do some of the legwork if the information started to pile up.

'What do we have from the appeal last night, Jill?' he asked, his voice discreet and silky. He looked up to catch her eye for the first time that morning. *Another blue business suit*, he thought, *another white blouse, but she has lipstick on*. He raised an eyebrow to acknowledge it. He saw she had registered his reaction, and he immediately looked down again at the floor.

Bugger — why did I put lipstick on? Jilly thought. *He'll think it's for his benefit. Damn, I* have *put it on for him*, she admitted to herself. *What am I doing?* She admonished herself inwardly, then got on with her job. 'We have a couple of dozen sightings, Mac, all over the city. Probably anybody wearing white on Tuesday.'

'To be expected, I suppose. Have them followed up anyway.'

'Already on it, Mac.'

'Anything else?'

'Three loonies offering their services to lead us to the body. One claims to be a clairvoyant, one has a Native American spirit guide, and, get this, one is a guy who says the murder was foretold in a twelfth-century chronicle.'

'Usual stuff, then?'

'Yep.'

McMillan scanned his team. 'Anybody got anything else?' he asked, raising an inquisitive eyebrow. But there was nothing; no leads, no evidence.

'What about HOLMES 2, Mac?' asked DI French, her voice rising in anticipation. HOLMES 2 was the police's information technology system, a database set up to provide consistency across UK police forces. She knew that serial murders were one of the categories it was designed for.

'Aren't we getting ahead of ourselves?' DS Jackson cut across her. 'We have no body, no ransom demand. Isn't this technically still a missing persons case?'

His DI shot him a look, but there was no admonishment in it. She welcomed his input, but she didn't agree with him. 'You don't suspect foul play then, DS Jackson? I do.'

He paused and thought, then started to nod. 'Yes, I do, boss. I believe she has been abducted, and probably murdered.'

'I agree,' said Mac. 'We've already crossed that bridge. This case has already been elevated from a missing persons. Yeah, go ahead — input our case on the system, but the damn thing is supposed to help SIOs with the management of complex investigations. You know how it works, it processes a mass of information so that vital clues do not get lost. But we have *no* mass of information. No forensics, no blood, no hair, no skin samples, no body, no suspects. Chuffing hell! We don't even have a bloody crime scene.'

'So we carry on with the legwork?' asked DI French, sucking at her lower lip.

'Yeah, carry on with the legwork,' Mac said. He stopped at the door and looked back. 'Her diary shows she's been to a couple of architectural conferences, doesn't it? Get a list of the attendees — see if any of them live near the A1.' It was the best suggestion he could come up with.

When Gerald Talbot answered the ring at his front door, he went rigid at the sight of DI French and DS Kaur. 'You've found her body, haven't you?'

'No, sir,' said Jilly, trying to make her voice as calm and reassuring as she could, 'but we need to ask you a few more questions, if you are up to it.'

She scanned the man's face: it was unshaven and he had red-rimmed eyes, every inch of his countenance etched with anxiety. He stepped back, gesturing for them to enter.

They sat in his living room; it felt cold to her, as though love and affection had been sucked from it and all that was left was despair. Gerald sat up in his armchair, and she could see he was bracing himself, adopting his professional persona.

'Did you get any leads from her diary?' he asked.

'No, sir, I'm afraid not. So we are going back a further three months and starting interviewing again today. It's a slog, and it's about eliminating people, but that is where leads come from.'

'So what do you want to ask me?' he asked.

'You kindly gave us a list of her friends and associates outside work, and we asked you to keep thinking of people she has met recently. Have you been able to come up with any more names?'

'I've racked my brains, but I can't come up with anybody else.' Gerald's voice rose, as if he was afraid he was letting his wife down.

'Is she a member of any societies, any fundraising organisations — anything like that?'

He sighed and looked away as he thought, shaking his head. 'She's so busy professionally,' he said, 'she hasn't time, really, for that sort of thing. Have you checked the stables where she rides her horse?'

'Yes, sir, we've interviewed everybody who knows her there. There've been no disputes, and everybody has nothing but kind words for your wife.'

'She is so very personable; everybody loves her. Who would wish her evil?' He looked away. 'She *was* asked by the city council to sit on a focus group considering a new development,' he added suddenly, as if the thought had just sprung into his mind.

It wasn't much, but Jilly could see it gave him some relief. It was something positive that he had done for his wife. She jotted down the details. *No, it isn't very much*, she thought.

CHAPTER 13

Day 7

Big Mac inclined his head. It was enough for DI French to take the briefing — she was the SIO, and he wasn't going to tread on her toes. She stood at the whiteboard, but it had little further information added from yesterday.

'None of the sightings from the general public have given us a positive lead. They are unlikely to be Karrie Talbot. As we thought, no more than an assortment of ladies in white — the ages, hair colours, and locations are wrong. We'll log them anyway, in case anything else arises later that suggests a connection — but to be honest, it's unlikely.'

DC Reader made a *tsk* sound. 'So we still have no bloody leads?'

'There is one possible lead — Karrie Talbot sat on a council focus group as a technical expert. A London developer wants to build an entertainment complex on the edge of the city centre. You know … cinema, bowling, restaurants, pubs, that sort of thing, but that would mean pulling down more of the inner-city housing. There isn't much of it left.'

''Bout time they pulled that dump down,' said DC Reader. He was sitting back with his legs out in front of him, crossed at the ankle.

He sat up when DCI McMillan looked at him. 'A closed mouth gathers no feet, DC Reader.'

Jilly went on. 'Well, it seems our Ms. Talbot had the same reservations as some of the councillors and suggested that the developer should build some affordable housing as part of the redevelopment. Now, the MD of the property company didn't like that at all, and a row broke out.'

'Have you scheduled a meeting with this MD?' asked McMillan.

'Yes, Mac, later today.'

McMillan waited to see if anything else was on the agenda, then he stood. They all looked at him — he never did that at a briefing, he was usually only an observer, keeping his finger on the pulse. He walked to the whiteboard and tapped the photos of the two other women. 'Do we have a serial killer on the loose here?' he asked, looking around the room.

'We have no M.O., Mac,' said DS Kaur. 'No scene of crime means nothing for SOCO to explore.' DS Kaur was twenty-eight, another law graduate with her eyes on a DI position.

Mac looked at her intently. She was a tall, in-your-face, sturdily built woman, and a good interrogator. She wore the same uniform as the other fast-tracked women officers — a dark business suit over a white blouse, her hair swept back in a ponytail.

'I've been on to the area commands for Leeds and Peterborough and asked for a copy of all they have — it came through this morning.' Mac turned and looked at DI French. 'Something for you to look at, Jill. Both investigations have been run down, if not actually closed. They are not operational runners anymore. Both hit the same brick wall as we have — a disappearance … then nothing. No sightings, no crime scene, no forensics — and —' he stopped then, emphasising his next comment — 'no ransom — so we are possibly looking at "sexual gratification" as a motive.' He paused to let it sink in. 'But there are similarities, even if we have no M.O. So what do we have?'

'If it's a serial killer, does he have a *type*?' asked DS Kaur.

'All three are blonde and blue-eyed,' said Jilly. 'Is that enough to establish a *type*?'

'Not necessarily,' said DS Kaur. 'They were all taller than average as well, so their physical appearance suggests a link, but I think it's more complicated — I think his type could be *powerful* women. He might get off on degrading strong women — bringing them down, so to speak.'

Mac nodded. 'Yep, I agree. My instinct tells me these cases are connected, and the common factor is powerful women. What does *your* instinct tell you, DS Kaur?'

'Same as yours, Mac,' she said. He had never sought her view so publicly before. She smiled, pleased with herself — and him. 'But what on earth can we do to follow it up?'

McMillan looked around the room. 'Anybody?'

'I don't think this is an opportunistic abduction, guv,' said DC Reader. 'He must have been stalking her.'

'And?'

'Well, we can't look at the CCTV on the roads outside the pub where she disappeared 'cos we don't know which car she left in, but we can tell from her diary when she was out and about and where she was going. So if we can find that yellow Aston Martin on CCTV on those days, let's see what cars are following her — does one of them keep turning up?'

Mac turned to DI French, with a gesture that implied it was her call.

'Will you take that, Pete?' she said, looking at Reader.

He sighed. Hours of sitting in front of a computer was not how he wanted to spend his day. 'Sure, guv,' he said, trying to display some enthusiasm. 'Me and my big mouth,' he mumbled under his breath.

DI French and DS Kaur stood before the glass-fronted office development that towered above them. Jilly put her hand over her eyes to shield them from the sunlight that was reflected back from the glass windows. 'Not much money in this property development game,' she said sarcastically. Satinder Kaur tried to hide a smile.

They took the lift to the twelfth floor, flashed their warrant cards to the receptionist, said they had an appointment with the CEO, Piers Barford-Black, and found themselves seats. After twenty minutes, Jilly French had had enough and went back to the receptionist.

'Does Mr. Barford-Black have somebody with him?' she said, her tone impatient.

The receptionist studied his computer diary. 'No,' she said, 'but he may be on the phone. I'm sure he will be with you shortly.'

DI French was not going to accept that. 'Will you go and see him, please,' she said, 'and find out what is causing the delay?'

'Oh, I couldn't do that,' the receptionist said. It was clear she never had been asked to question her boss before.

'Okay, I'll do it. Which room is his office?'

'No, don't do that.' Alarmed, the receptionist picked up her phone and hit some buttons. 'Sorry to interrupt you, Mr. Barford-Black, but the police are asking what is causing the delay.'

'Oh … tell them that I will be with them as soon as I can.'

Jilly heard the words over the phone and snatched it from the receptionist. 'DI French, Mr. Barford-Black,' she said. 'We had an appointment scheduled for twenty-five minutes ago. If you have somebody else with you, can we reschedule the meeting at the police station in Nottingham? Will you consult your diary, please?'

There was a pause, then he said, 'No — that won't be necessary. I'll break off and see you now. Will you put the receptionist back on, please?'

Jilly handed the receiver back. 'He'll see us now,' she said, her words reinforced by a stare.

The CEO's office was huge, with views across London. They both took seats but were still some distance from him, his desk was so large.

'I didn't see anybody leave, Mr. Barford-Black,' Jilly said. 'What was keeping you from seeing us?'

He was visibly taken aback by her directness, but then he smiled and adopted an open pose. 'The phone,' he said, gesturing towards it. 'How can I help you? Can I get you some coffee?'

'No, that won't be necessary — we are investigating the disappearance of Katarina Talbot.'

'Disappearance?'

'Yes — you must have seen it on the TV, read it in the newspapers?'

'I've been out of the country. I flew back last night.'

'When did you leave, sir?' interrupted DS Kaur.

'I flew to Frankfurt on Wednesday morning.'

'So you didn't know that Katarina Talbot was missing?'

'No, I didn't,' he answered, showing little concern.

'Karrie disappeared on Tuesday. She hasn't been seen since *Tuesday* lunchtime.'

'What has that got to do with me?' said Barford-Black.

'Can you please tell me your whereabouts on Tuesday, sir?'

'I was here in London at my desk, all day.'

'We understand that you knew Ms. Talbot, sir.' Jilly French's words were polite but probing.

'Depends what you mean by *know*.'

'How would *you* describe your relationship?'

'Well, there was no *relationship*. I met her a few times when she was acting as a consultant for the council. I didn't know her personally.'

'And would you describe your meetings as cordial?'

'Oh, I see,' he said, as a realisation dawned. 'No, I bloody well wouldn't. I guess you've been told we had a blazing row? She wanted the company to build some social housing next to a prestige development, and then wanted us to cough up for it.'

'So there was some friction between you.' Jilly leant forward to reinforce the question.

'You could say that, but if I killed business rivals, the bodies would be piled up three deep by now, wouldn't they?'

Barford-Black was arrogant, but Jilly knew what he was saying was probably true — she needed more than a row to make him a suspect. 'How many times did you meet her?'

He sat back. 'Two — no, three times.'

'And where did those meetings take place?'

'At the council offices in Nottingham.'

'Did you ever meet her outside the council offices?'

'How do you mean?' He set his jaw hard and gave both officers an uneasy stare.

'Well, Karrie is a striking-looking woman, isn't she?'

Jilly saw his fist clench. She searched his face and saw comprehension cross his features. He could see what she was suggesting.

He gave a hollow laugh, but he was clearly shaken. 'Yes, she is a striking-looking woman, as you say — but I repeat: I had no personal relationship.' He had emphasised every word.

DI French gave him a hard stare, searching for an indication that he was being evasive, but she saw nothing. He was an egotistical sod, but he was not slippery, she thought. Nothing he had said implicated him in the disappearance. *Another dead end*, she thought, but there was something there — something to file away in her analytical brain.

She turned to DS Kaur, giving her the merest of gestures. Kaur responded equally as subtly, confirming that she had no further questions either.

Outside, Jilly was more forthright. 'What do you think of him, Satinder?'

'Condescending shit!' she said. 'But I don't see him in the frame for this. Another dead end.'

'My thoughts exactly — his alibi is not watertight, though. He flew out on Wednesday, the day after the disappearance — will you check anyway? If he *was* elsewhere, we can eliminate him.'

CHAPTER 14

Day 8

The team were back in the major incident room.

'Did the CCTV reveal anything, DC Reader?' asked DI French. He had already reported his findings to her, but her question was for the benefit of the team.

'Yep,' he said, 'some cars can be seen following her on more than one occasion, but I think we can split the sightings into two categories. Firstly, most sightings fall into the rush hour. She went to work, it seems, at about the same time each morning. A little less regular coming home, but still a routine. I think it's reasonable to deduce that other commuters do the same thing, and it would be expected to find some of the same cars showing up on CCTV each morning.'

He looked around the room and saw heads nodding.

'We won't waste our resources interviewing the owners of these cars,' said DI French, 'but we'll check the names against the Peterborough and Leeds investigations to make sure none of the names have cropped up before.'

DC Reader continued. 'But when we checked the CCTV against daytime journeys as indicated by her diary entries, you would *not* expect to find the same car following her more than once, but we have identified two vehicles doing just that.' Mac looked up, his leg no longer swinging. This was the first lead they'd had. 'A black Range Rover Sport SVR tinted windows, shows up three times. And two sightings of a BMW X5, also black.'

'And who are they registered to?' asked DI French.

'That's the problem, ma'am. Both are registered to the same car hire company.'

'What don't we like?' asked Mac, still looking at the floor.

'Coincidence, Mac,' most answered in unison.

'So we find out who hired the cars on those days,' interrupted Jilly, looking at DC Reader, 'and?'

'Been onto the hire company first thing this morning, ma'am. Both cars were hired to the same person. James Smith, with an address in Bottesford, a village about eighteen miles from the city.'

'Bring him in,' said Mac, his voice quiet but laced with authority.

There was a brief silence, and DC Reader and DI French shared uneasy sideways looks.

'We can't, Mac,' said Jilly.

He looked at her, his mouth gaping — then the lines in his face creased as realisation dawned. 'Both the name and address are false, aren't they?'

'Yep, Mac, they don't exist,' she said. 'James Smith is not quite John Smith, but we get the picture.'

'And I take it he paid cash on each occasion, so no credit card trail?'

'You got it, Mac.'

DCI McMillan's leg started swinging again. *We haven't got him*, he thought, *but we now have a partial M.O. — he stalked her, alright.* He knew that psychology analysts said that serial rapists usually had a history of violence going back to their childhood, but he was not convinced rape was the primary reason for the abduction. He exhaled heavily. 'What do you think, Jill? Is this our man?'

'Absolutely, Mac. This guy is covering his tracks. He's our man, I'm sure of it.'

'Do we have a description from the hire company?'

'They remember him — he was so distinctive. Late thirties, tall, dark blond, piercing blue eyes, well built, expensively dressed, black suit, dark tie each time, expensive haircut and grooming.'

'So he's as conspicuous as the victim's yellow sports car, then?'

'It gets better, Mac. He has a tattoo on the back of his hand.'

He looked at her. A tattoo was inconsistent with a well-groomed man.

'It's an eye — some sort of religious symbol, maybe.'

Shit, the last thing we want is some religious nut, thought McMillan. 'So we see if HOLMES 2 tells us if anyone with a tattoo of an eye was identified in the Peterborough and Leeds enquiries — yes?'

Jilly nodded. 'Already on it, Mac.'

McMillan chewed on the inside of his cheek as he considered the lead. This man was something of an enigma. He was bright, was covering his tracks, had left no clues in the Peterborough and Leeds enquiries — yet he was conspicuous. He'd made no attempt at disguise, his appearance even suggesting something of a peacock syndrome. The psychological profilers identified serial murderers as loners, insignificant people who blended in and were easily overlooked — unless the flash clothes and grooming *were* the disguise. And why not cover up the tattoo? That suggested carelessness, though everything else about him pointed to meticulous planning. *Ego — his ego is getting in the way*, Mac thought. *If so, then it will be his downfall.* He looked up at Jilly French and shrugged his shoulders. 'See if anyone on the sex offenders list has this tattoo.' But he knew that was a long shot.

CHAPTER 15

Day 9

It was another day, with little progress to look back on. DI French was aware she had to remotivate her team.

'HOLMES 2 doesn't give us a hit on a suspect with an eye tattooed on his hand,' she said, 'so it's unlikely this guy was questioned in Peterborough or Leeds.'

'Another bloody dead end, then,' interrupted DC Reader.

'It was never going to be easy, Pete. What about the delegates at the conference? Do any of them live near the A1?' she asked, looking round at DS Satinder Kaur.

'It depends on how you define *near*, ma'am,' she said, 'how wide we cast the net — but I have identified five possibilities — men who live within ten miles of the A1.'

'Anything interesting?'

'I interviewed four of them yesterday, and I'll see the last one this morning. All played down any connection with the missing woman, saying they had little to do with her. I doubt if any of them was being absolutely truthful given that this woman was such a looker, but they have alibis for the day she went missing. And I've checked them out.'

'Well, I suppose it *was* a long shot,' said Jilly.

'Something is interesting, though,' continued DS Kaur. 'One of the men was there with his wife, who's also an architect. Now she had a different take on the events at the conference — I got the impression she looked at Karrie Talbot with, shall we say, *jealous* eyes. *She* told me that, in the bar at night, the men were around her like bees to honey. She handled them with consummate ease, though — striking as she was, she must have had years of practice at fending off unwanted attention. But there was one guy who was hitting on her, big time. To the point that he was making himself a nuisance, and our informant says she thought she saw some distress in Karrie's features.'

'So he was making a pest of himself?' asked DC Boone.

'Well, you'd know all about that,' quipped DC Reader and everybody laughed.

'Pest is putting it mildly,' continued DS Kaur. 'He stuck to her at breakfast, during the seminars, in the dining hall at lunch time and the bar at night. She even thinks that Karrie left the conference a day early to get away from him.'

'Was she able to give you a name?'

'Oh, yes. Dougie Jardine, an architect from Manchester, divorced, remarried, three children, one child by his first marriage, two by his second. No criminal record, but a lot of speeding tickets — been banned twice.' It was dangerous to make assumptions, Satinder knew that, but she thought she knew this guy's type — arrogant alpha male, fast car, womaniser, went after what he wanted despite the consequences. He was a possible suspect, she thought. Others thought that too.

Mac's leg stopped swinging. 'Will *you* take Don Juan, Jill,' he said in his quiet voice, his face fixed on the floor. Looking up, he added, 'And take DC Boone with you as a sort of expert consultant.' He had a kind of deadpan humour which escaped every now and then. Everybody laughed — except DS Kaur; she had wanted to get her teeth into this guy.

Mac stood, and everybody started to gather their papers. 'Anything else?' asked DI French, but she too stood as she spoke.

'Yep,' said DC Reader. 'There's another connection in this case, guv.'

McMillan was at the door, but he looked back at Reader's comment.

'Go on,' said Jilly.

'Expensive cars, guv. Aston Martin, BMW and a Range Rover Sport SVR'

Jilly paused and thought about this observation. It was obvious, yet everybody had missed it — except DC Reader. 'I get that,' she said, then bit her lip uneasily, 'but I'm not sure where we go with it.'

'Well, I've been on to the car hire company again, for a list of all the cars this James Smith has hired over the last two years, and particularly if he hired a car on the day Karrie disappeared.'

McMillan came back into the room, fixing his eyes on Reader.

'Go on,' said Jilly again.

'Sorry I haven't briefed you on this, guv,' he said to his DI, 'but I only got off the phone before the meeting started. James Smith did hire more cars, expensive top-of-the-range ones, in the couple of months before the abduction. I'll check these against Karrie's diary to see whether she was out and about on those days, and I expect we will find him on CCTV.'

Jilly nodded her approval.

'But there was nothing hired to him on the day of the abduction, and nothing for the time of the Peterborough and Leeds abductions.'

There was a groan around the room.

'So another bloody dead end,' said DC Boone.

But McMillan and DI French had both understood the significance of Reader's words.

'Our man covers his tracks,' said Jilly. 'He will have used different car hire companies.'

'Yep, guv,' said Reader. 'So we check them out but narrow it down to cash rentals of expensive cars, particularly from a smart dude with a crazy eye tattoo on the back of his hand.'

'And if that draws a blank,' interrupted Mac, 'you start ringing round car hire companies in Peterborough and Leeds. Good work, DC Reader.'

DC Boone stopped the pool car when the sat-nav said they had reached their destination. They were in a smart, leafy residential area of Manchester, but it was not what they had expected. They were looking for the architectural practice office of Dougie Jardine, thinking it would be a commercial office building.

'It's there, boss,' said Boone, pointing at a bungalow.

Jilly spotted the business plaque on a small boundary wall — *Douglas Jardine and Associates: Architects.* The front garden had been converted into a car park for visitors, and Boone pulled their pool car into one of the four available spaces. There was one other car: a Porsche 997. *Small-time practice*, Jilly thought. The guy probably did designs for middle-class clients looking to build an extension. Certainly not in the same league as Karrie Talbot, with her city centre practice.

'That's the turbo version,' said Dan'll Boone, nodding at the Porsche.

There it is again, Jilly thought, *the upmarket connection. At every turn, there seem to be bloody flash cars.*

'This architecture lark must pay well,' added Boone as he looked in the side window of the Porsche. Jilly wondered if it was all show.

Inside the house, the illusion of affluence was repeated. The reception room was eerie in its silence and smelled of air freshener, but it was a picture of professional interior design down to expensive artworks on the walls.

The receptionist's desk was empty, and Jilly looked around for a bell to ring, but there wasn't one. She was about to shout *shop* when a door opened and a woman exited, pulling a large handbag over her shoulders.

'Oh!' she said. 'I was about to go to lunch.'

Jilly flashed her warrant card as she spoke. 'DI French, and this is DC Boone — can we talk to Mr. Jardine, please?'

Her eyebrows furrowed and she made a *humph* sound. 'Has my husband been speeding again?' she asked in an apologetic tone.

'No, not today, Mrs. Jardine, but we'd like to ask him some questions.'

She paused as if confused, then went back through the door without saying anything. They could hear some muffled words — indistinct, but the tone of the female voice suggested she was giving her husband a hard time.

The door opened, and they were shown through into Jardine's office. There was an easel to one side of the desk, but the primary focus of the office was the desk and an elaborate PC installation. The modern architect did most of their work with a computer, it seemed, not a pencil. Jardine was sitting behind his desk, his eyes fixed upon his wife, and they followed her to the door. As soon as she left, his body language changed. He stood, came around the desk and thrust out his hand.

'Dougie Jardine,' he said forcefully. 'How can I help you?'

Jilly took in the man. He was all things masculine: broad shoulders, deep chest, full mouth, long jaw. Expensive shirt, open at the neck, a smart suit jacket draped over a dumb-valet standing beside his desk. He wore his blond hair unfashionably long, collar-length — it put her in mind of one of the three musketeers.

She took his hand, and his cologne entered her nostrils. 'DI French, and this is DC Boone,' she repeated, but then she looked down at her hand, surprised. He was still holding on to it. In all the time she had been a police officer, this had never happened. She looked at him, making no attempt to hide her displeasure; she considered his behaviour inappropriate. What she saw in return amazed her; there was a twinkle in his eye.

'Mr. Jardine!' she exclaimed, nodding at her hand, her tone unmistakably reprimanding, but he still did not let go. She pulled her hand away and looked back at Jardine; there was no contrition in his features. His look was openly sexual. He gestured to the chairs with his hand, and she sat in front of his desk. Boone followed her, and Jardine went to his side, all the time keeping eye contact with Jilly.

'Mr. Jardine, we are investigating the disappearance of Katarina Talbot,' she said. 'I understand you know her?'

'Do I?' he answered.

'Are you saying you don't know her, Mr. Jardine? Because if you are, I must advise you that lying to the police is a serious matter. Section 89(2) of the Police Act 1996 makes it an offence to obstruct a police officer acting in the execution of their duty.'

He took time to register what she had said, but then his eyes widened. She saw the expression on his face change as he snapped back to reality.

'No, no. I know her,' he said. 'Well, slightly.'

'And can I remind you that a woman's life is at stake here.' She gave him a hostile stare.

'Of course, of course,' he grunted. 'How can I help you?'

'Can you tell me where you met, Mr. Jardine?'

'Purely professionally.' He sucked at his lips all the time, his eyes taunting her. 'We met at a couple of architectural conferences.'

'And how would you describe her?'

'Oh, an accomplished woman.'

'Accomplished?'

'Oh, yes, very capable. A real high-flyer — she's definitely going places, Karrie.'

'You called her Karrie. Does that mean you knew her socially, Mr. Jardine?'

For the first time, that leer on his face dissolved. He sat upright as he mulled over his faux pas. 'No — no, we never met socially.'

'But you would have liked to, wouldn't you, Mr. Jardine? Good-looking woman, wasn't she?'

'Well — yes, she was, but that doesn't mean … you know.'

'Know what, Mr. Jardine?'

'It doesn't mean that something was going on — some sort of a relationship.'

'And was there — some sort of relationship?'

'Certainly not.' He had regained his equilibrium; even a hint of that leer had returned.

'We have a witness who says you spent a lot of time with her at her last conference — a *lot* of time, Mr. Jardine.'

'That's what happens at conferences.'

'So you admit you spent a lot of time with her?'

'Look, Inspector, I am a bit of a ladies' man — I admit it, but there's no crime in that, is there? As they say — what goes on at a conference stays at a conference.'

'Do they indeed, Mr. Jardine?' Jilly tried to read the man. There was something of the sociopath in him — a disregard for others, superficial charm, inflated sense of his own importance. A lack of remorse for the chaos he left behind. Her eyes searched out his hands — there was no tattoo on the back of them, but she sensed he could be capable of abduction. 'You'll have no objection to me looking at your diary, then, Mr. Jardine. Does your wife keep it for you?'

The arrogance vanished, his eyes widened and his face coloured at the mention of his wife. 'My wife? Can we keep my wife out of this?' His eyes darted from Jilly to Dan'll Boone and back.

'Why, is there a problem?' Jilly said with feigned surprise.

'It's — well, my wife is a very suspicious woman.'

'Well, you had better open up your computer diary and print it off for me now, before she comes back from lunch, hadn't you?'

He froze for a second, then he reached for his mouse. After numerous clicks and a short delay, his printer burst into life.

'And you will have another diary for your non-business *liaisons*, won't you?' Jilly said pointedly.

Jardine tried to adopt a stance of righteous denial, but then it seemed to drain from him. He slipped his hand into his jacket pocket and took out a notebook diary.

'I'll keep this for the time being,' Jilly said. 'I'll let you have it back later — unless you want to photocopy it for me now?'

Dan'll Boone pulled out onto the main road and hit the gas.

'Whoa!' said his DI. 'You're not driving Jardine's bloody Porsche. The last thing we want is to try and explain ourselves to the boys in blue from Manchester.'

'Sorry, boss,' he said, easing off. He settled back into his seat. 'You see Dougie as a viable suspect, don't you, guv?'

'I do, Dan'll — why? Don't you?'

'No, not really. He wouldn't have come on to you so strong if he was hiding something. He would have been slippery, not lecherous.'

'Unless it was a tactic. I've seen them all in the last few years. It's about deception, what magicians call misdirection. You're directed to look at the right hand, so you don't see what the left hand is doing. Some use anger — *how dare you accuse me?* Some use the — *don't you know who I am?* Sometimes: *I know the chief constable, you know.* It doesn't work with me — he was trying to put me off my game.'

'I'm not so sure, guv.'

'Look, we know he is predatory. He openly pestered Karrie at the convention. You saw him — you couldn't get a better example of the peacock syndrome. Peacocks fan their tails to catch a mate's eye. I can see through that — the flash car, the smart clothes. He's looking for sexual conquests all the time.'

'I get that, guv, but…'

Jilly cut across him. 'Look, what if his game plan was to get a job at her prestigious city practice? To use his good looks to…'

'Get into her knickers?'

'Yes, get into her knickers, as you so indelicately put it. Now, what if he couldn't take that rejection at the conference? He pursued her, his arrogance making him believe every woman was his to be had. But after abducting her, and finding she was having none of it, he panicked.'

'And killed her?'

'Worst-case scenario, but — well, yes.'

'Well — maybe, guv, but…'

'But what?'

'Strictly between you and me, boss?'

'Okay — go on then.'

'It's the one-in-ten principle. It's what I use, guv,' Boone said reluctantly. 'Dougie is more upmarket than me, goes after high-flyers. He's a good-looking dude as well, and flash, but it's still basically the one-in-ten principle he uses.' He took a quick sideways look at his DI. 'I try it on with every new woman I meet, and I get lucky about once in ten. Now, out of those I get lucky with, one in ten of those will be a corker.'

Jilly looked at him with disbelief. 'I always wondered what women saw in you, Dan'll — you're no oil painting, are you? But I never put it down to mathematics. But okay — so he uses the one-in-ten principle. Your point?'

'The point is — rejection, boss. You have to develop a thick skin, because the one-in-ten principle comes with constant *rejection* — nine times out of ten. Our Dougie would not be incensed by a rebuff. He would have simply moved on to the next one.'

DI French turned and gave him a long look, grinding her teeth. 'It's a theory, I suppose.'

They drove in silence for some minutes — then Jilly turned to Dan'll, her forehead furrowed in confusion. 'You mean you try it on with every woman you meet?' She paused. 'Then how come you didn't try it on with me?'

He bit his lip, trying to pick his words carefully. 'Wouldn't have dared, boss,' he said. 'You're too scary. And anyway, you've got the hots for Mac — everybody knows that.'

Jilly stared, a thunderous look on her face. 'And what's that supposed to mean?' she screeched.

Dan'll Boone swallowed. He had nearly got away with it. But he knew enough not to say any more.

'That's cobblers!' she exclaimed. 'He's old enough to be my dad.'

They sat in silence all the way back to Nottingham.

CHAPTER 16

Day 10

DI French stood alone in front of the whiteboard — DCI McMillan was away at a senior officer's seminar. She felt relaxed — she knew Mac was good, very good, but other DCIs didn't sit in on every damn morning meeting. She resented it, felt it undermined her — and the bugger still kept calling her Jill.

She also now knew what other people were calling her — she'd overheard them sniggering. She was Big Mac's French fries on the side. There were variations on the joke: *Do you want French fries with that, Mac? Fancy a French fries sandwich, Mac?* They were getting cruder by the day: *Relish on your fries, Mac? Does French like a gherkin with her Big Mac?*

Jilly pointed to the board. Dougie Jardine's name was now prominent, with an arrow connecting it to Karrie Talbot. 'Suspect,' she began as she tapped her knuckles against his name. 'He's been pestering her at conferences. Dan'll and I interviewed him yesterday — lecherous sociopath, superficial charm, thinks he's God's gift, as they say, inflated sense of his own importance. Private life in chaos — good-looking guy, though,' she added. She paused as something came into her mind — it was there again: the peacock syndrome. Eye-tattoo man had it as well. He had the flash cars too. It was all wrong, all counterintuitive — serial killers were misfits, loners, not peacocks.

'Do you want me to check the CCTV we have of Karrie driving, guv?' said DC Reader. 'See if I can spot Dougie stalking her?'

'Absolutely, Pete. He drives a red Porsche 997 Turbo.' She saw Reader's eyebrows arch and knew what he was thinking: another flash car.

'We have his diaries so we can tell where he was, or at least where he was supposed to be. Satinder has them.' She turned to look at DS Kaur. 'Anything yet?'

'It'll take me a few more hours to go through them in detail, but his business diary shows he had client meetings on the day Karrie was abducted, and also on the dates Emily Jackson and Caitlin Morgan disappeared.'

Damn, Jilly thought. 'We need to check them out — see if he was where his diaries said he was.'

Satinder nodded. 'His personal journal uses only initials, and there is no "KT", so unless it is a code, he doesn't appear to have had any rendezvous with Karrie.'

Jilly sighed inwardly. Day ten, and still virtually nothing. No sightings since the day she went missing, her credit cards unused, no crime scene, no forensics. It was standard practice to establish the victim's final moments, but they were nowhere near doing that. *Final moments*, she mused to herself — it was still officially a missing person case, but deep down she believed it to be a murder case. No one was saying that, but she knew the whole team thought it. The only two suspects they had both looked less likely by the day. But there was something about Jardine — she felt it in her water.

CHAPTER 17

Day 11

DCI McMillan was back, sitting on the desk, swinging his leg. Jilly had already briefed him about the interview with Dougie Jardine. He was up to speed.

She looked across at Pete Reader. 'The CCTV of Karrie when she was out and about in the city. Did you find anything of the red Porsche 997 Turbo?'

He shrugged his shoulders. 'No, guv, not a trace. A flash motor like that wouldn't have slipped by me. I think we can say he wasn't stalking her — well, not in that Porsche anyway.'

Jilly bit her top lip; this case was like swimming through treacle. 'Anybody got anything else?'

'Yes, ma'am,' said DS Jimmy Jackson. 'You know I've been overseeing uniform systematically ringing the car hire companies in Peterborough and Leeds?' Jilly nodded. 'Well, a firm in Peterborough remember a guy with a tattoo of an eye on the back of his hand.'

'Did you get back to them?' she asked, her words eager. 'Description?'

'Oh yes, ma'am. It was a long time ago, but they remember him all right. Tall, well built, expensively dressed, black suit, well groomed. It's our man.'

Mac looked up at DI French and gave the merest nod. They had their link between Karrie and one of the other abductees. Eye-tattoo guy was their man.

'Same M.O., though, guv. He paid cash, gave his name as Alan Jones, but no such person lives at the address provided.'

'Yep, he's covering his tracks, we expect that. But now we know for certain — we have a serial abductor. Let's get on with it. Let's find him.'

But DS Kaur raised a hand. 'Do you think that eye-tattoo guy has any connection with Dougie Jardine, guv?'

'In cahoots? Why would you think that?'

'Well, according to Jardine's private diary, about four weeks ago he had an appointment with TT. Karrie's architectural practice is Turner Talbot. Well, there's nothing in *her* diary for that date, but I have spoken to her secretary, and somebody turned up without an appointment. She doesn't remember the name, but she remembers this good-looking guy because he came on to her — I'd bet it's Dougie Jardine.'

DI French darted a look at Mac and then back to Satinder. 'Bring him in,' she said.

DS Kaur twitched a smile — she wanted a crack at this guy.

DI French and DS Kaur sat in the interview room made available to them by Manchester police. They recognised the familiarity of it: grey table, grey chairs, grey walls, no windows — they could have been back in Nottingham. It was 5.30 p.m., and Dougie Jardine sat opposite next to his solicitor.

DS Kaur studied him. The conceit was still there — he was sitting back in his seat, one arm resting on the back. On the surface he seemed unphased by the prospect of questioning, unphased by the trip to the police station. That was not normal, whether the suspect was innocent or not. Serial offenders got used to it, she knew — they had learned the ropes, but he was not one of them.

She turned on the tape, and announced the date and time and those present. She took a sidelong look at Jilly, who gestured for her to continue.

'Mr. Jardine, thank you for coming today…'

'Did I have any choice?' he interrupted. 'Am I under arrest?'

Satinder smiled inwardly. *Today's tactics are arrogance and aggression, are they?* she thought, looking forward to stripping the self-importance from him. 'No Mr. Jardine, you are not under arrest, but we'd like to speak to you about some inconsistencies in the information you gave us the day before yesterday.'

'What inconsistencies?'

'Is your business solvent, Mr. Jardine?'

'What's that got to do with anything?' he said. He turned to look at his solicitor.

'Where are you going with this, Inspector?' the solicitor asked Jilly, ignoring DS Kaur as if he was trying make her look insignificant.

'Mr. Jardine's financial status is relevant to our enquiries,' she said. 'Will he answer the question, please?'

The lawyer nodded to his client.

Jardine sat upright in his chair. 'I turned over a little north of £300K last year.'

'And what was your net profit, for tax purposes?' Satinder knew that turnover meant nothing in isolation.

'£55K, or thereabouts.'

'That's a good income, Mr. Jardine,' she said, feigning envy, then added, 'and how much did your Porsche cost you?'

'I got a deal on it.'

'And how much was that deal?'

He made a *humph* sound. '£120K, if you must know.'

'A lot more than your profit, Mr. Jardine.'

'It's a business asset — it impresses the clients.'

'So it's an asset on the business balance sheet?'

He nodded as if the answer was obvious.

'If I asked you to produce the balance sheet from your last accounts, would it show that your assets exceeded your liabilities?' He gave her a fiery glance but initially did not reply. 'Is the question too difficult for you, Mr. Jardine?'

His face screwed up into a scowl. 'Well, no, actually. So what?'

'By how much do your liabilities exceed your assets, Mr. Jardine?'

'I can't remember. I'd need to look at the accounts.'

'A ball-park figure, then, Mr. Jardine — ten, twenty thousand?'

He could see she was not going to let this go. He ground his teeth, dropped his eyes to the table, and wrung his hands. 'About £280K,' he said.

'Let's go back to the original question, then. Is your business solvent, Mr. Jardine?'

'It could be healthier. I have a lot of business loans, but with one good contract I could pay them off.'

Satinder could see his swagger was beginning to evaporate. *Easier than I thought*, she mused. 'So you are looking for a nice, big, juicy contract, are you?'

'I'm a self-employed architect — I'm always looking for business.'

'Is that easy from a converted bungalow in the suburbs?'

'My work is my shop window — people see it and come to me.'

'But not enough work to pay your bills, meet your lifestyle, it seems? Particularly since you take out far more than you earn.'

'Look … what is this?' Jardine blustered. 'So my business is up against it, but what has this to do with Karrie Talbot?'

'Yes, Karrie Talbot, Mr. Jardine — let's talk about her. You have previously stated you did not meet her outside the conferences you both attended. Is that correct?'

He swallowed, his Adam's apple rising, but then he set his mouth hard. 'Yes, that's correct.'

Not very bright, Dougie, Satinder thought to herself. *You can't even see the next question coming.* 'So you didn't ask her for work?'

'No,' he said, but his voice faltered.

'This *is* your diary, Mr. Jardine?' she said, taking it from the file and handing it to him.

'You know it is.'

'Can you turn to the 1st of August? What do the initials TT stand for?'

She saw the realisation in his eyes. His fists clenched, then his whole body seemed to collapse before her. 'It's Turner Talbot — yes, I went to see her, looking for work or even a job.' His shoulders fell. 'I'm a good architect,' he added, as if to justify himself.

'So why did you lie, Mr. Jardine?'

He paled at the question. Satinder caught his eye, but he could not hold her stare. 'I didn't want to get involved,' was all he could say, stuttering.

'You didn't want to get involved?'

'I hardly know her,' he pleaded.

'You hardly knew Karrie Talbot — so that's your explanation, is it? So let's review the situation. We have a missing person, and in the few weeks before her disappearance, you were seen harassing her at a conference, and then you turn up without an appointment at her office. You *are* involved, aren't you, Mr. Jardine? Was she pleased to see you?'

He hesitated, then his shoulders fell. 'I can usually get women to do what I want,' he said. 'I complimented her on her looks, her success, put my charm into overdrive — but she was having none of it. I was even reduced to begging, but she couldn't get rid of me fast enough. Said she had a client coming, but I knew she didn't — I got that out of her secretary before I talked her into calling Karrie on the intercom.'

'Did that make you angry, Dougie?'

He looked down at his hands. 'No, of course not.'

'Oh, come on, Dougie. I bet you found her rejection emasculating, didn't you?'

'No — look, I'm a chancer, I know that, have been all my life. I like it, it gives me a buzz. But I can handle rejection — you have to get used to that. I took a chance by turning up at Karrie's office, but that's all I did.'

Dan'll's one-in-ten principle popped into Jilly's mind. She had rejected it at the time, but now she reconsidered. Dougie seemed to fit the bill. She gestured to DS Kaur that she would take the next question.

'Do you know a man with an eye tattoo on the back of his hand?' she asked, watching his face, but she saw only puzzlement.

'A what?' was all he could say.

Jilly held out her hand to demonstrate. 'An eye — here, on the back of his hand, by his thumb and forefinger.'

Jardine shook his head.

'For the purposes of the tape, Mr. Jardine has answered no,' she said.

DS Satinder Kaur had revealed his arrogance but had not exposed any guilt. She sighed, resigned — there was nothing to support the theory that he was involved with eye-tattoo man.

CHAPTER 18

Day 12

DI French tapped the picture of Dougie Jardine on the whiteboard and updated the team on his interrogation. 'Looks as if we have established that Jardine is an arrogant tosser, but we've not found any connection with the abductions. Let's cross the t's and dot the i's, though — Dan'll, will you take his picture to the two firms that hired cars to tattoo-hand man to see if they recognise him as well?'

'Okay, guv.'

'We need to concentrate on eye-tattoo man,' she said, looking at her team, her expression inviting input. 'What do we know about him?'

'Sod all.' Peter Reader was his usual gobby self.

'A little more than that,' Jilly argued, her irritation evident. 'We know he is flash, likes expensive cars, and we have a good description of him.'

'But we don't know *how* he is connected to his victims,' added DC Reader. 'The inference is that he is *not* — they are random, based on a type — blonde, blue-eyed, and successful. Yet Karrie left the Travellers Rest with him — so he must have found a way in. He makes contact with them before he abducts them. We need to know how it works — something to get us launched, but we haven't found it yet.'

He was a mouthy bugger, but Jilly French knew he was right. 'I agree,' she said.

'We have assumed he has been following her and took his opportunity at the Travellers Rest,' continued Peter Reader, 'but I've been looking again at the CCTV. If you look at her body language while she is eating, she keeps looking up — she's waiting for him, but tattoo man won't come into the main room because he has checked it beforehand. He knows where the CCTV cameras are. I think he had arranged to meet her there.'

'Do you mind if I come in here?' said Mac, looking up from the floor and turning to Jilly, his voice low. She nodded to defer to him. 'What do we believe the tattoo is all about?' He looked around the room.

'It's only decoration, surely,' said DS Jackson. 'He's another flash bugger, isn't he? That's the recurring theme in this case.'

'Maybe, yeah — but has anybody considered if this tattoo of an eye might have some special significance?'

'Like what?' said Pete Reader.

'Well, could it be some form of symbolism — does it refer to an organisation he may belong to?'

'You mean like the National Front using the Union Jack?' DS Jackson's brows furrowed in confusion.

'Perhaps, but I was thinking of something more subtle. Something to symbolise a secret organisation, maybe?'

'But everything we know about our man suggests he is a peacock, not secretive at all,' added Jackson.

'I disagree, DS Jackson. I think what we have here is a man full of contradictions. We are having trouble finding him because he is so good at covering his tracks — yet he leaves us this big clue: the tattoo.' He saw Jackson purse his lips. He continued, 'I've been doing some research on t'interweb. There's something called the All-Seeing Eye, or sometimes the Eye of Lucifer or the Eye of Providence. It's an eye surrounded by rays of light. It's fundamentally a Christian symbol, representing the all-seeing eye of God. It's also a historical symbol going back hundreds of years — it was depicted on the Great Seal of the United States and is on their dollar bills. But over the years, it has also been connected with various secret societies — the Masons use it.'

'You think he could be a Mason, Mac?' interrupted Jilly.

'Possibly.' He screwed up his face and moved his head from side to side. 'Or some other organisation. If he is a serial killer, then it is more likely to be some form of crazy cult. But we don't know if it *is* the Eye of Lucifer. There are others. There is an ancient Egyptian symbol, "The Eye of Horus". It's a symbol of health and protection. Horus was the sky god depicted as a falcon.'

'What are we talking about here?' interrupted DS Kaur. 'Are we going into conspiracy theories, shadowy figures pulling the strings of the government, the media, pursuing its own agenda?'

'Probably not.' Mac's expression was open. 'But DC Reader is right. We have to widen our thought processes if we are to get this investigation to the lift-off pad. But cults and obsessions are on a spectrum: at one end we could be looking at a member of some powerful underground organisation, and at the other some lone individual with whacky ideas. And remember, whacky beliefs can still be firmly held. DC Boone,' he said, looking up at him, 'when you take the picture of Dougie Jardine to the car hire companies, take pictures of the Eye of Lucifer and the Eye of Horus with you as well — you can get them off t'interweb. See if they fit the tattoo on eye-tattoo man's hand — but don't show them the pictures straight away, or you'll put thoughts into their minds. Ask them to draw it from memory first.'

Jilly bit her lip, unsure of her next request. 'Any money in the budget, Mac, for...'

'For a profiler,' Mac cut across her. 'I've been unsure up to now how much a standard profiler would help in this case. I don't think our man is your typical misogynist — you know, the indicators rooted in his childhood and all that psychobabble. He's not an invisible social inadequate, either. But I've changed my mind — I've done some figure juggling, and I'm arranging for a clinical psychologist to come in to see if he can give us an offender profile.'

Jilly tipped her head in thanks.

'And I've also found money for specialist computer support. If I'm right about the tattoo being a symbol, then we are going to need it.'

CHAPTER 19

Day 14

There were two new people at the daily briefing. At the front sat DC Tim Book. He was the computer whizz kid. And he looked like a kid: jeans, T-shirt, and a baseball cap on backwards. He looked nineteen, but he was actually twenty-eight, with a first in computer science from Manchester University. A career in the police force seemed an odd choice. Jilly introduced him.

'Yo, dudes!' he said, waving his hand around the room.

Mac looked up from his favourite spot on the floor. He disliked the man immediately. But he had to swallow that particular pill; Tim was *his* choice. The guy was a misfit wherever he served. But he had a reputation for finding investigative connections, and Mac needed somebody to think outside the box.

Jilly French then introduced Dr. Leo Adams, the clinical psychologist. He sat at the back and nodded when his name was mentioned, but he'd said he was only observing at this point.

Jilly had met him an hour before the meeting and was stunned by his appearance. Even from his sitting position, she observed, it was evident he was tall, significantly taller even than Mac, with his long legs stretched out before him and crossed at the ankle. His face was angular, his skin tanned, his eyes dark and hooded. His black hair grew past his collar. He had a neatly manicured beard that diminished a prominent chin. But it was those eyes — large, deep-set; she could have sworn they'd seemed to sparkle when she'd been introduced. When she had taken his hand to shake it, she'd become tongue-tied, like a naive teenager, and had rebuked herself for her reaction.

She went to the whiteboard. 'According to Dan'll, nobody at the car hire firms recognised the picture of Dougie Jardine, so we can cautiously eliminate him from our enquiries — unless something else comes to light.' She then tapped a surprisingly accomplished drawing of an eye. 'Dan'll has managed to get this, though.' She looked up at him.

'I did as Mac suggested and asked anyone who remembered eye-tattoo man to draw a picture of the tattoo. Most were pathetic, and you couldn't tell if it was some sort of symbol or decorative image — or if it was anything at all. But this one girl was real good with a pencil — she could draw,' he said, pointing at the picture on the whiteboard, 'and I think we *are* looking at a symbol.'

'I agree,' said Jilly. 'I think Mac was right. The eye tattoo drawing is similar to the All-Seeing Eye — the Eye of Providence. Look, the artist has remembered the sun's rays. This is where you come in, Tim.'

'You want me to search the internet for any organisations that use this as a symbol? Lists of members, etcetera?'

'Exactly, Tim. We already know the Masons use it, and it is on the Great Seal of the United States.'

'Is it now?' he replied, as though that tweaked his thought processes. He paused. 'What about Hell's Angel chapters?' The connection was obscure to Jilly French's non-geek mind.

'We hadn't thought about that — but yes, see what you can find.'

'And what about Karrie Talbot's computer?'

'We've already been through her computer diary, Tim.'

‘Let me have another go. I’ll go through her email history, see what webpages she has visited. Extend that to the home computer, and any tablets she’s been using.’

Jilly clapped her hands to gesture for them all to get on with it. She felt better than she had for days; the enquiry had been stalling, and they now seemed to have the impetus she had been looking for.

CHAPTER 20

Day 15

Printouts littered the desk at the front of the incident room. Tim Book had been busy.

'I'll split these up between you,' said DI French. 'These are organisations that have used the Eye of Lucifer as a sort of symbol — or similar symbols that Tim has identified.'

'Look, guys,' Tim put in, 'they range from organisations that are probably innocent, to some way-out whacky ones.'

'Well, you would know about whacky,' mumbled DC Reader. Most heard him, and there was some snorting. It stopped when Mac looked up. He gave Reader his own evil eye, and he shut up.

Tim Book went on, 'I have also, in most cases, obtained for you a list of their members.'

'Are you on any of them?' mumbled Dan'll Boone, taking up the baton from his mate. This time, the snorts were suppressed. Mac's leg had stopped swinging.

'How did you get these lists?' asked DI French.

'You don't want to know, guv,' Tim replied.

Jilly knew what he meant. He was taking a coach and horses through data protection legislation. She did things by the book — always had. It now put her on the horns of a dilemma — anything established by this line of enquiry would be tainted; they might be unable to take it before a court. But she was desperate to get this investigation moving. She looked up to search out Mac's eyes, but they were where they always were — fixed on some random spot on the floor. After some moments, however, he seemed to feel her pleading gaze. He looked up and fixed her with a stare that said it was her call — but it also said that this was vital, something not to be missed. She nodded imperceptibly towards Tim.

'I have split them into three categories,' Tim continued. 'The first list are cases that look like the innocent ones — give them low priority. The second list is…'

'Will that be Tim Book Two?' Pete Reader sneered. He knew he was bringing down Mac's wrath on himself, but he couldn't resist it. Even Tim heard it this time — there was laughter, and the meeting stalled. But Tim laughed as well.

'Not original, Pete,' he said. 'There's been a wag in every team I've worked with, and each one of them has come up with the Tim-Book-Two line.'

He had handled himself well — Jilly realised that and was pleased. But she wouldn't let it go. 'DC Reader — my office, after the meeting,' she said.

Tim Book carried on. 'The second list is of more clandestine organisations using the Eye of Lucifer as a symbol — high priority. The third list is — well, covert groups using similar symbols. Something to fall back on if you draw a blank — but they look iffy to me.'

As bollockings went, Peter Reader had had worse. DI French used the guilt trip technique — *there's a woman's life at stake*; *you have let me down and let yourself down*; *disrupting a meeting was juvenile*; *no wonder you are still a DC*. That last one stung, but he still felt he had got off lightly — a bollocking from Mac was much more intimidating.

'Now, clear off,' Jilly said, pointing at her door.

Pete Reader had, for once, enough nous to bow his head and take his reprimand. He shuffled off, a rueful smile on his face, then looked back as if unsure this was the right time. 'Guv?'

'What is it now?' she snapped.

'I've been thinking, boss.'

'Well, it was bound to happen sooner or later.'

'We'd assumed tattoo man followed her from her meeting and intercepted her at the pub — the Travellers Rest.'

'Yeah, that seems a fair supposition.'

'But at yesterday's meeting, remember, I flagged up the possibility he had *arranged* to meet her there. The pub's on the way back to her office, I can see that — but what if it *was* a rendezvous?'

'Possibly.' Jilly considered it again. 'Because of her behaviour on the CCTV footage. She kept looking up at the doorway. You believe she was expecting someone.'

'Yeah, I think he'd checked the pub beforehand, knew where the CCTV was and kept to the entrance to avoid it — and then he waylaid her on her way out, maybe pretending to be late.'

'So he was following her in the weeks before to establish her routine, then he set up the Travellers Rest as his interception point. Yeah, that works,' Jilly said, sucking on her teeth, 'but it doesn't explain why she left with him.'

'Agreed, boss, but he has found his *way in*, and I think we all know that's the key to finding him. If it *were* a rendezvous, he would have sent her a message or contacted her to arrange that meeting, probably in the forty-eight hours before the abduction.'

DI French stiffened in her chair. 'So his number will be…'

'Will be on her phone, guv.'

She steeled herself, trying not to get carried away. 'But we've already been through her phone records — we've identified everyone, haven't we?'

'We think we have, but we need to cross-check all those numbers against the phone records for Emily Jackson and Caitlin Morgan.'

Jilly jumped to her feet, opened the door, and looked down the central office. 'Tim!' she yelled, waving him over. He wasn't even through the door when she spat the words out: 'Can you check the phone records of different people against each other, looking to see if they have been called by the same person?'

'Easy-peasy, boss. I have my own algorithm for that.'

'Right, I'll get Leeds and Peterborough to scan Emily Jackson and Caitlin Morgan's phone records and get them sent over. Drop what you're doing as soon as they arrive.'

'But I've found something interesting, guv,' he said. 'Karrie Talbot's search history, boss — she's been checking out car dealers. I think she was after a new car.'

'I knew it!' interrupted Pete. 'I knew flash cars had something to do with this…' Then his eyes widened. 'You don't think tattoo man is a car dealer, do you?'

'Boss,' said Tim, 'get me Emily Jackson's and Caitlin Morgan's computers so I can check their search histories. We might find the same dealer.'

'And, boss, I'll go back to the CCTV for the Travellers Rest in the previous month — see if I can spot tattoo man casing the joint,' said Pete.

CHAPTER 21

Day 16

Dr. Leo Adams's long legs searched for a comfortable place to settle. He had taken a seat on the visitor side of Mac's desk alongside DI French, and their legs kept accidentally touching.

'Have you a preliminary profile for us, Dr. Adams?' Mac said, cutting through their embarrassment.

Leo leaned forward and slid his report across the desk, handing one to DI French. Mac picked up the document. He turned it over disdainfully to see if there was anything on the back — there wasn't; it was barely half a page long.

'This it?' His eyebrows arched in confusion.

Leo ran his hands through his long, dark hair. ''Fraid so.'

'My team was expecting a lot more, Leo,' Jilly said. 'Isn't the whole point of offender profiling to identify likely suspects?'

'Yes, it is,' he answered, 'and I would love to give your team something to get their teeth into, to take the investigation forward — but I can't.'

There was silence as Mac and Jilly looked at each other, then at him. He knew he had to explain further.

'Look,' he said, 'profiling is only one tool to be used in the investigation — it will never identify a particular person who has committed a crime. What it attempts is to determine the *type* of person who committed it. There are several techniques I can use — the geographical approach, the investigative psychology approach, the clinical approach, but they all require information to evaluate.'

'I'm not sure I follow,' said Jilly. But Mac did — that was why he had been reluctant to call in a clinical psychologist in the first place. He knew Leo would have the same problems as they did — too little information to analyse.

'I need to establish patterns,' Leo said. 'I need to do a detailed appraisal of the crime scene — but we don't have a crime scene, do we? So I can't evaluate what he did there and what he left behind. I want to establish the abductor's personality, and I would do this by looking at his behaviour before and after the crime — but we have so little information about what he did before the crime and nothing about what he did after it. Then we come to homology…'

'That's the theory that similar crimes are committed by similar offenders possessing similar characteristics, isn't it?'

'It's exactly that, Jilly. But this guy doesn't fit the standard profile of a sexual abductor. It would be easy to say to you, he is misogynistic, a woman-hater. But — and this is simplistic — they are usually sad loners with mother issues. I don't think our guy is that. If it is tattoo man, there is something of the peacock about him, as you have identified yourselves. But therein lies a danger — I must not assume that tattoo man is the culprit.'

'I follow that, but surely you can make a stab at a profile you can update as the investigation uncovers more information,' said Jilly.

'Profiling doesn't work that way, I'm afraid. If I give you a *steer*,' he said, 'then that will determine the course of your enquiry, and you may find a suspect that fits my *steer*. Alternatively, that guess may lead you to ignore the real guilty person. I mustn't point your enquiry in the wrong direction and send you off at a tangent.'

'So you're not prepared to do it?'

'No, I'm not. But I will, I hope, be able to be more specific when you can get me his "offender signature." Random disappearances are not enough — I need a more detailed M.O.'

Mac interrupted, reading down the page. 'You agree he is most likely a sexual predator, but you don't know his motivation. You say he is male, but you can't say if he is a man of physical strength, because we don't know the M.O. of the abduction. You won't make a stab at his psychological profile, other than to say he is a sociopath. You think he is sane, but you don't know if he is subject to sexual mania or whether he is calculating in the abductions.'

'That's about the size of it, Mac.'

I'm wasting my bloody budget money, Mac thought to himself.

CHAPTER 22

'Thanks a lot, Leo,' said Pete Reader. He made no attempt to hide his contempt after reading the offender profile. He screwed up the sheet of paper and threw it over his shoulder.

'It goes that way sometimes, Pete,' said the clinical psychologist, 'but I think I'll get you something to get your teeth into before long. I'll read through the case files at length, and also start on a profile of the victims.'

'The odds are these women were dead within twenty-fours of their abductions, anyway,' said Pete Reader. 'We know that. The stats tell us so.'

'Unfortunately, that's true,' Leo said, scratching his beard. 'They are probably dead, but we have to do right by them and find this man. You should know I'm committed to that.'

Jilly interrupted to defuse the situation. 'We know this guy will likely abduct again, and we have a duty to find him before he does. Pete, you had a hunch the CCTV for the Travellers Rest in the days before the abduction might show our man casing the joint.'

'Yes, boss. Unlike Leo, I've been busy. I am going backwards from the day of the abduction, but I haven't found anything yet. I'm seeking a man looking directly at the CCTV, so I have to do it in real time, I can't fast-forward. Can you get me some help, boss? Otherwise it will take me forever.'

'Yeah, I'll see if I can get uniform to assist.' She turned to Tim. 'Anything?'

'Yeah, boss, I think I've found something. Karrie's computer search history shows she had been looking at car dealers. I've looked at Emily Jackson's and Caitlin Morgan's computers as well — and bingo! They were doing the same. Pete's hunch that our man may be a car dealer could be spot on. I've cross-referenced those dealers' phone numbers with the numbers in the women's mobile phone histories, and some come up in both. But the same dealers don't turn up for the three women. They live in different cities, and different main dealers act in those places.'

'So we can link each of the three women to car dealers, but not connect any specific car dealer to all three,' said Jilly.

'Spot on, boss.'

'Not to worry, Tim. It's time for some legwork. We go to each of these dealers. See if anyone working there has this tattoo on their hand. And I suspect car dealing is a small community. If our man is in the business, someone should recognise him, may have worked with him previously.'

Jilly shuffled her papers to wrap up, anxious to get her teams sorted out, but Tim raised his hand again. She stopped and nodded to him.

'I've used my algorithm to check the phone records of the three women against each other, looking to see if they have been called by the same person. We have a phone number for all three.'

Mac looked up; others sat up or shuffled in their seats.

DC Book put his hand up to stay their enthusiasm, and gave a sheepish look. 'I have no doubt this is our man, but…' He held his breath and bit his bottom lip. 'He's still covering his tracks. It's a pay-as-you-go phone, I'm afraid.'

There was a visible anti-climax in the room.

Jilly shot a look at Mac, but he just stared down at that elusive spot on the floor. 'So it's not registered to any phone company,' she said, 'and I bet he bought it cash and also tops up using cash, so the phone company won't have any subsequent records either.'

'What about GPS, boss?' asked DS Kaur, but without enthusiasm. 'Can we put a trace on it now? Find out roughly where he lives?'

Jilly French's shoulders fell. 'We can try, but I suspect he has thought of that as well. My bet is it's an old bog-standard cheapo phone with no GPS.' She paused. 'Okay, guys, back to the legwork.'

DI Jilly French was sitting in her office. Her mood had soured during the meeting. The rays of the late summer sun were intensifying as it rose in the sky. Without thinking, she took off her blue suit jacket; the heat in her office was beginning to cling to her. She had been upbeat for the last two days, but that enthusiasm had drained from her, and she didn't know why.

A knock on her door disturbed her reverie and she saw Leo through the glass. She gestured for him to come in.

'Are you busy?'

'Always,' she replied, her expression severe.

'Not to worry, I'll come back later.' He started to leave.

'No — no,' she said, calling him back. 'I'm not in the middle of anything. I'm trying to put my thoughts into order. What can I do for you?'

'I've come to apologise.'

'For what?'

'For demoralising your team.'

'They didn't like your profile, that's for sure, but you hardly discouraged them. They know the score. It's about the long slog until you get that breakthrough.'

'But Peterborough and Leeds didn't get that breakthrough, did they? And you thought you had that lead with the linked phone numbers.'

'Yeah, it's disappointing, but we'll get him, I'm sure. Pity you have no ideas yet about our man.'

'Oh, my mind is bursting with ideas, with scenarios, with possibilities.'

'But you said you could come up with only the obvious traits of this man? Ones my team had already deduced for themselves?'

'I know I did, because there's no point at this juncture in sharing my ideas. They are numerous and speculative — if you based your enquiries on them, it would burn all your resources.'

'So you are keeping them to yourself?'

'For the time being — they stand in my head, and I will eliminate them one by one as you gather information. All the time I'm narrowing down the possibilities. Homing in on the type of man we are looking for.'

Jilly sighed deeply. 'Yeah, I'm sure we'll get him before he kills again.'

Leo recognised some whistling in the dark. For a reason he couldn't have explained, he wanted to lift her mood. It was probably simple: he liked her — she was an attractive, capable woman. She was his type. 'Your staff really respect you, you know? That's something for you to take pride in.'

'It doesn't stop them talking about me behind my back, though, does it?'

'Oh — that you have a crush on DCI McMillan, you mean?'

Jilly gave him a hard stare, her mouth gaping. 'You have been here less than two days, and you have heard the stupid gossip already. It's ludicrous — and what's more, it affects my authority.'

'No, it doesn't. It's office banter, that's all.'

'I'm not so sure about that.'

'You're wrong, you know. Look — why is DC Boone called Dan'll? It's because it's a play on words — and not a particularly clever one at that; probably been with him since school. His surname is Boone, so they call him Dan'll 'cause there was an American frontiersman named that. Why was Tim Book's profiling mocked as Tim-Book-Two? It's just office humour. People have a need for it — it's part of bonding. And all teams tease their bosses — it's gentle when they like them and can be brutal when they don't.'

'So you think it's gentle, then?'

'Absolutely — DCI McMillan has been called Big Mac for years, and then you come along and are called French. So it's obvious you're going to be his French Fries on the side.'

She started to see it in a better light, but then what came next undid it all.

'Your problem is that, although your team doesn't know it, there is some truth in what they have been saying?'

'Bollocks!' She spat the word at him. 'I haven't got a crush on him.'

'How long has he been your line manager?'

'About fifteen months — but what's that got to do with anything?'

'Have you had a relationship with another man in that time?'

Jilly hesitated and bit deeply into her bottom lip. 'Well, no, but that's a coincidence. I moved down from Manchester on promotion. My personal life had been disrupted.'

'Is it a coincidence?' Leo fixed her with a challenging stare.

'Of course it is — I don't fantasise about DCI McMillan, for goodness' sake. He's old enough to be my dad. You're as bad as that lot out there.'

'I never assumed you did fantasise about him — but your eyes seek him out when you head up the meetings. Could it be you are looking for his approval?'

'He's my boss — it's natural I should want him to consider me good at my job.'

'Absolutely. But it's the extent of that *wanting*. How old were you when your father died?'

Her face coloured at the question. 'How do you know my father is dead?'

'I didn't. Let me guess — you were a daddy's girl. Got on better with him than your mum?'

'So what? That's not unusual. And Dad died when I was fifteen, if you must know.' Her level of exasperation was growing with every sentence.

'So he never saw you pass your A-Levels, get your degree, become a detective inspector?'

'Come on, then, let's have your psychoanalysis of me.'

'The theory goes something like this — most women who lose their father don't look for relationships with older men. But some do — they are drawn to an older man to replace him. These men are usually successful with power, status, and influence. Remind you of anyone?'

'So you put me in that particular psychobabble box, do you?'

Leo steepled his hands before his face. Then a rogue smile took the corner of his mouth.

Jilly noticed it. 'Are you teasing me?' She gave him a hard stare.

'A little,' he said.

'So what do you really think, then?'

'I believe you are just on the spectrum. Mac is a father figure to you — but no, I don't think you are looking for a relationship with him.'

Jilly hmphed and looked out of the window to avoid Leo's eyes.

'There's a cause and effect thing going on here, though — I can see it. Mac sits in on your briefings, which I understand is not normal, and subconsciously you interpret that as a lack of trust. So your eyes keep searching him out for approval, to reinforce your sense of self. But Mac has this habit of staring at the floor — so you never get it. And that makes you look to him even more. And then you catch yourself doing it and overcompensate by launching into your alpha rank mode, throwing out orders to show your team you are the boss, the one in charge.'

'So I'm really screwed up, am I?'

The lines by his eyes deepened as he gave a warm smile. 'No, far from that — but you need to fine-tune your relationship with DCI McMillan. He looks at the floor, I think, so as not to undermine you. You should accept it as that and not a slight on your ability.'

'Boss,' said DS Kaur over her mobile later that day, 'I'm in Leeds.'

'Hope you have good news, Satinder.' DI French sat up in anticipation.

'Sorry, boss — no. We've done half a dozen dealers, and none of them has tattoo-hand man working for them, or recognises such a person as working in the trade. It gets worse. Our victims are not on their computer systems, so the implication is they never contacted them about the new cars available. Never got past browsing the internet.'

'Bugger! That's a downer — so why are you calling?'

'It's something the last guy I spoke to said. That if our victims are busy, successful women, then time is not something they have a great deal of.'

'Yeah, makes sense — but I'm not sure I follow where this takes us.'

'He suggested they may have used a broker instead, to do the legwork. I didn't know such a thing existed.'

'Neither did I.'

'Well, this guy said they operate by finding cars for their clients, doing the deal, then introducing their customer to the dealership. They earn their money by way of a referral charge from the dealerships on every car they sell. They claim to get a customer a better price than they could get themselves because they know where the best discounts can be found, which dealerships are prepared to shave their margins to move excess stock — that sort of thing.'

'And the customer doesn't have to traipse round showrooms and forecourts?'

'Exactly. So I thought I'd give you the heads-up as soon as possible. Tim Book identified activity on their search histories that they were looking at car dealers. Can he narrow it down now to car brokers?'

'I can ask him to narrow it down further — Karrie Talbot drove an Aston Martin DB9. We must be looking for a car broker specialising in prestige vehicles.'

CHAPTER 23

Day 17

'Settle down, now.' DI French clapped her hands. 'You know we got precious little yesterday from the car dealers in Nottingham, Peterborough or Leeds, but it wasn't a total waste of time. Satinder has identified that our man could be a car *broker* rather than a dealer, and I've asked Tim to examine the computer search history of the missing women to see if there was any activity with such brokers. Tim?' She looked round.

Despite being up until after midnight on the task, Tim was beaming; he was dying to share his news with the team. 'Yes, all three women showed activity with brokers. The footprint was minor compared to the traffic with dealers, but then there are so few brokers compared with the number of dealerships. There is another similarity in that this broker traffic comes in towards the end of the activity.'

'That makes sense,' interrupted Jilly. 'They probably admitted to themselves they couldn't afford the time to go looking around showrooms.'

Tim continued, 'I have put together a list of these brokers, but the important thing is that we have a match across the victims. All three had looked at one particular broker. A company called Valkyrie Classic Cars Ltd. This guy specialises in finding high-end classic cars.'

'What sort of a name is that?' interrupted Dan'll.

Mac's eyes ascended from his favourite spot on the floor. 'It's Norse mythology told in the Volsunga Saga,' he said. 'The Valkyrie were women who decided which soldiers died in battle and which lived. There's also an opera by Wagner, and the best known bit of it is *The Ride of the Valkyries*. I suppose it's a play on words — *riding* in classic cars.'

'Can I come in here?' Leo sat up in his chair. 'I have been profiling the three victims. One of the linking features is, as you know, that they are powerful, successful women. There may be a connection here — the Valkyrie were certainly that. His using that name for his company may suggest that he *admires* powerful women.

'But if you know the story of the Volsunga Saga, it's about the men taking revenge for acts of treachery, but it is the women who *goad* their men to take that revenge. It could still be part of his sociopathy to want to degrade women.'

'Leo,' Jilly continued, 'do classic cars fit with your profile of the victims?'

'Absolutely. We know all three drove expensive cars.'

'What's the guy's name, and where are his offices, Tim?' Jilly asked.

'Franz Fischer, but he doesn't have office premises — he works from home, an isolated pad between two villages, according to Google Maps — about fifteen miles north of Nottingham.'

Jilly nodded. 'We interview him as soon as possible then, but I want to know everything we can find out about him before we do. Jimmy?' She turned to DS Jackson. 'Will you get onto the Financial Investigations Unit — see what the FIU can do for us. I want background checks — bank accounts, credit cards, etcetera. I want to know about his wealth, his lifestyle, his spending patterns, whether he has any financial problems, where he went on holiday, his hobbies, his interests.'

'Will do, boss,' said DS Jackson, shuffling in his chair. 'What about his company's accounts? Do you want to get them from Companies House as well?'

'Absolutely, Jimmy — and tell them it's urgent.' She turned to DS Kaur. 'Satinder? I want a full criminal record check. Will you get onto that?'

CHAPTER 24

Day 18

DI Jilly French stood by the whiteboard. The name Franz Fischer was emblazoned in bold letters at the top under the heading: "Suspects". The names of Dougie Jardine and Piers Barford-Black had been relegated to the bottom. There was no photograph of Fischer, however.

'Satinder, what have you got for us?'

'We had problems, boss. Well, that is until we established that Franz Fischer isn't his real name. He's plain Frank Fisher. Age thirty-eight, born in Lincoln. His father and mother were both university lecturers; his father in German, his mother in Classics. Frank has a BA in Viking and Old Norse Studies from UCL. His father is Oliver Fisher; he came to the UK in 1955 as an eight-year-old with Frank's grandfather, Helmut Fischer. The family changed their name to Fisher shortly after — anti-German feelings after the war, I suppose, but Frank has now changed his name back.'

'So another connection with Karrie, then,' said Jilly. 'Both have a German and an English parent.' She nodded for Satinder to continue.

'Frank Fisher has virtually no criminal record. A caution for cannabis while at university, then some speeding offences in his early twenties. Significantly, nothing as a juvenile either.'

Leo bit his bottom lip as he contemplated that fact. Serial killers usually had juvenile offences suggesting cruelty, which escalated into killings in later life.

Satinder continued: 'He was married when he was twenty-six, but it doesn't appear to have lasted long — divorced two years later.'

'Jimmy, what have FIU come up with?'

DS Jackson had already pre-briefed Jilly, but now he turned and looked at his DCI. 'You won't believe this, Mac. According to FIU, this guy seems to be some sort of business guru. They say they have never seen such a successful business model. He has virtually no business overheads and no premises, trades from his private residence, which he owns outright. He runs the business without any employees, does everything himself. His turnover has risen steadily, and last year it was just under £750K — but get this: that 750K brings him a profit of over 700K. The company balance sheet shows it has £2.65 million in cash at the bank, and his private bank account stands at over £2 million. But that's not all — he also runs an investment company, Valkyrie Investments Ltd. This has been funded by the classic car brokership over the years, and he seems able to increase its portfolio whether the market's rising or falling. According to his last balance sheet, the company assets stand at over £10 million. This guy is worth about £15 million in total. The only employees he has are a cleaning lady and a cook, neither of whom, we believe, live in.'

'What about his outgoings? What do they tell us about his interests, his hobbies, his lifestyle?'

'Cars obviously, but other than that he doesn't seem to have any expensive vices. No indication of betting, so he's not a gambler. He takes his holidays in Germany and Scandinavia. He appears to be a sightseer rather than a sun worshipper. He does eat at expensive restaurants, though, and his personal wine merchant must like him. He pays out a fortune. No standing orders to any organisations, so it's hard to see what his interests are.'

'Have we got anything from DVLA, Jimmy?'

'Yep, according to Swansea, he has five cars registered. Three are classics, a 1993 Aston Martin Virage Volante, a 1948 Bentley Mk VI Pininfarina Cresta and a 1969 Ferrari 246GT Dino.'

There was a whistle from Dan'll Boone at the back.

Jimmy Jackson smiled. 'They mean nothing to me, but I'm told these are unique collectables indeed, worth north of a million. Then he has a Bentley Continental Flying Spur Saloon and a Mercedes GLS Coupé SUV.'

Jilly turned to Leo. 'Does any of this fit your profile?'

'It doesn't take us much further, I'm afraid. I've said this guy doesn't fit the standard profile of a sexual abductor. What you have established now reinforces that. There are even more contradictions — he is certainly a peacock, in the way he dresses, the cars he drives, but then he lives in an isolated location and trusts nobody with his business activities. It would be interesting to know if those expensive restaurant meals are for two, but then the credit card receipts won't tell us that, will they?'

'Pete,' said Jilly, 'can you look at his favourite restaurant, give them a ring and see if he dines alone?'

'Yes, guv.'

She turned back to Leo and raised her eyebrows again. 'Anything else?'

'If this man is a sexual predator, I need to establish his motivation and, to be honest, I am no nearer to that.'

'So the next step is to interview our man. We'll do it today. I'll lead.' She turned to DS Kaur. 'Satinder, you're with me, please — and Dr. Adams, will you come along too? I'd appreciate your psychological opinion of him.'

'Turn round and go back,' said DI French to DS Kaur. She pulled the pool car off the country lane into the muddy entrance to a farmer's field and engineered a three-point turn.

'The sat-nav says we have reached our destination,' said Satinder, 'but I can't see a house.' They went back about a mile, but there was still no sign of the property. 'I'll turn and go back again.'

Travelling back, she slowed her speed to about ten miles per hour, cautiously looking in her rear-view mirror in case another car came up behind.

'Why would a man running a business from his residence make it so inaccessible?' said Leo.

'He can do his business over the phone or online in this day and age,' mumbled Jilly, concentrating on scanning the road. 'There!' she grunted. There was an opening, and a small gravel track snaked away.

Satinder turned off the road, then pulled up, looking about her for a house sign, but there wasn't one — nothing even to help the postman. The trail continued for about a hundred yards, then disappeared over a hill. She turned to Jilly sitting next to her, who shrugged as if to suggest it was the best option they had. She put the car into gear and followed the path slowly to the brow of the hill. From there they looked down towards a house another half-mile distant. It looked stunning: a wonderfully presented stone-built, period-character building, Jilly thought. There were two substantial annexes and a paddock at the side, where a Bay Morgan horse trotted around like he owned the world. She heard Leo whistle his admiration from the back seat.

They pulled the car up on the gravel at the front. Leo noticed a double garage, but it was evident that one of the annexe buildings was also used as a garage. The use of the second annexe was less apparent.

There was no bell on the solid wooden front door, so Jilly rapped the door knocker forcibly. She heard activity and then bolts being shot to unlock the door. She looked at her watch and noted the time: 11.50 a.m. *The house is still bolted,* she thought. *This man is either very nervous of intruders, or is hiding something.*

The door opened to reveal an impressive figure: about six-one, dark blond hair, black shirt, black trousers, both expensively cut. His forehead was expansive above a handsome, square-jawed face, his hair thick and handsomely groomed — short, formal, and straight with a side parting and the beginnings of grey at the temple. The only concession to casualness was the absence of a tie. His eyes were piercing, the irises the palest flint-blue. His expression was open and inviting.

'Yes, can I help you?' he said. His tone was as welcoming as his features.

'I am DI French, and this is DS Kaur and Dr. Leo Adams,' she said. The two police officers brandished their warrant cards. 'I wonder if we could come in and talk to you?'

At the mention of the police, his eyes darkened and his whole visage changed. He turned cold and intimidating as he stepped forward a pace, folded his arms over his chest, and stood with his legs apart. Partially defensive, partly aggressive, Leo noticed.

Jilly looked for a tattoo — there was nothing on the right hand, though. She thought back to the description the witnesses had given; it was the left hand, she remembered — but that was tucked under his right arm. She had no view of it.

'Yes,' was all he said. His voice was low and menacing.

'Mr. Fischer?' asked DI French.

'Yes,' he answered, again tersely.

He unfolded his arms, and his left hand went into his trouser pocket. Jilly dropped her eyes, but not in time to see if he had a tattoo.

'Sorry, but I'm working. Make an appointment and come back.' He stepped back to close the door.

'Mr. Fischer, sir,' Jilly said with authority, 'we can certainly rearrange this meeting for the police station, if that is what you prefer.'

Fischer stalled and fixed her with a hard stare. 'What is your authority for that?'

'Police and Criminal Evidence Act 1984, sir,' she shot back.

'And that would be an interview under caution, would it not?'

'If that is how you want it, sir — then so be it.'

'To do that, you must have grounds to suspect me of an offence. What crime do you suspect me of?'

DCI French paused; this was new territory for her. Such arguments were usually with defence solicitors, where each side knew the rules. She had not expected him to be so savvy. She softened her tone. 'At this point, sir, we are investigating the disappearance of three women. We are looking for you to help the police voluntarily, as any good citizen would.'

'Is it usual to send an inspector and a sergeant to make routine enquiries, and you, Dr. Adams?' He paused. 'What are you here for? What sort of doctor are you?'

DI French was now caught on the horns of a dilemma. She knew that to question a suspect with a view to getting evidence that could be presented in court, that questioning had to be under caution. She would need to take him back to the police station for that. However, she had made the judgement call to question him informally first. She wanted an impression of the man, wanted a look around his house, to see his lifestyle. Leo could make an initial psychological assessment of Fischer, and they could find out if he had that tattoo. That tactic had now been challenged. She didn't want to lie to this man, conscious of his shrewdness, mindful that a prosecution could fail if she didn't follow procedure. She decided to tell the truth, if not the whole truth.

'No, sir, it's not normal, but when we are dealing with a large investigation, then it burns my manpower. It's all hands to the pumps, so to speak. Dr. Adams here is a psychologist — he is helping with this complicated investigation. As I say, it would be a great help if you would voluntarily answer some questions.'

Fischer's eyes broke away, and he looked over her shoulder into the distance. He was contemplating something, but his face remained a mask.

'Very well.' His voice was monotone, but his stare was still hostile. He stood to one side so that they could enter. 'Will you go to my office … to the left, please.'

He followed them in, walked behind a large vintage oak desk, leaned back into his leather swivel chair and fixed them with his hard stare. He didn't invite them to sit in one of the two seats on the visitor side of the desk. Leo looked around at the beautiful design. It was a mixture of a home office and a country house library. It had modern office paraphernalia — computers, printers, and so on — but on sliders, ready to be concealed by oak furniture. The walls were covered in bookcases, and the room had the feel of a gentleman's club. It even smelled of furniture polish. Leo edged to his side, away from the other two. He saw Franz Fischer's eyes follow him, irritation crossing his features. Then his eyes shot back to Jilly and Satinder. *Good*, Leo thought, *I am out of his direct eyeline; I can observe without being seen.*

'Mr. Fischer,' DI French started, 'a beautiful house you have here.'

He didn't respond, but fixed her with a stare. She ditched that strategy at once.

'Mr. Fischer, we are investigating the disappearances of Karrie Talbot, Emily Jackson, and Caitlin Morgan. I understand they were customers of yours?'

'No, that is incorrect. They have never been clients of mine.'

'Are you certain, Mr. Fischer? Would you like to check your client list?'

'I don't need to. I have an eidetic memory.'

'That must be very useful in business, Mr. Fischer.' She held his stare, but he did not respond. 'Would you like to check anyway?'

He turned to his keyboard and tapped rapidly, then moved his hand to his mouse as he scrolled down a page. He looked back at Jilly. 'No, as I said, they are not on my client list.'

'Could I have a copy, please?'

'No,' he said tersely, his expression bland.

'Why not, sir?' Jilly probed.

'Because my clients expect confidentiality from me.'

'Can I remind you this is a possible murder enquiry?' Jilly said.

'Then come back with a warrant.' He sat forward, adding, 'If you think you have grounds for that.'

DI French sighed. 'Did you hire a car from Newton Ridge Road Car Hire on the thirtieth of August 2019?'

'So you *do* suspect me of involvement in a crime. If you want to ask me that question, you will have to caution me. But if you do, my answer will be "no comment".'

'So you are not prepared to cooperate, to help find these missing women?'

'On the contrary, if I can give you any information that would help find them, I will be happy to do so. But as I have told you, I do not know any of these women. I have never met them.'

'We know from their computer search history that all three visited your website, Mr. Fischer.'

'Ah, so they were browsers. Browsing doesn't always lead to custom. I would be elated if that were true. I would have a lot more business.'

DI French paused and exchanged a sideways glance with DS Kaur. She saw the impotence that she felt reflected back in her eyes. It was time to regroup. 'Okay, Mr. Fischer, thanks for your help,' she said. She stood, and DS Kaur followed. He, too, rose — she expected a satisfied, smug expression from Franz Fischer, but his face remained a mask.

At the door, she looked back over her shoulder. 'Oh, one last thing, Mr. Fischer.' She gestured to his left hand, still hidden in his pocket. 'That's an unusual tattoo — what does it represent?'

He looked at her and his jaw set. *He's wondering if I have seen the tattoo, or if I'm bluffing,* she thought.

Then, slowly, he brought out his hand. There was that tattoo — the Eye of Lucifer. He looked down at it. 'It represents nothing,' he said, 'just a youthful indiscretion.'

A small victory for DI French, perhaps, but it gave her immense satisfaction.

DS Kaur pulled the car off the side road back onto the country lane.

'Nice one, guv,' she said as she manoeuvred, 'getting him to show his hand that way — no pun intended.'

'Yeah, but come on, it didn't go very well, did it?' Jilly said. 'He had me for bloody breakfast.' She was angry with herself. 'I made the wrong judgement call. I should have arrested him, brought him back to the station and interviewed the bugger under caution.'

'Oh, I don't know,' said Leo from the back seat, his tone appeasing, 'I think we have learned a lot about Mr. Fischer.'

'Like what, for instance?' Jilly snapped.

'Well, that he's a control freak, for starters. He didn't tell you anything because he had pre-planned that interview. He had his strategy in place, ready to go. As soon as you showed him your warrant cards, he put his plan into action. He'll have read up about your powers, and he has used their limitations to his advantage. I suspect, if you had interviewed him under caution, he would have said, "no comment" to every question.'

'And, "no comment" means we can't catch him out in a lie,' agreed Satinder.

'Exactly. No — I think your call was right, Jilly. We have had a chance to see how this man behaves in his castle. We can form a judgement of him from his behaviour today.'

'So what *is* your psychological take?'

'I think he's a sociopath, all right. He displays the classic symptoms. It's a disorder characterised by a disregard for the feelings of others, a lack of remorse or shame, manipulative behaviour, unchecked egocentricity, and the ability to lie to achieve one's goals.'

'I noticed the way he greeted us warmly and then switched it off when he realised we were police.'

'Precisely. Typical manipulative behaviour: gregarious, presents a friendly face to the world when he wants to, then in private he is introverted, secretive, guarded — and the egocentricity was pouring out of him. He couldn't stop himself telling us that he had an eidetic memory. But remember: a sociopath has an antisocial personality disorder. It doesn't make him a psychopath; it doesn't make him a murderer.'

'But he could be, couldn't he?' asked Satinder.

'Possibly, but remember that serial killers are often people who feel undervalued, misjudged. They may not have the best job in the company but feel they are better than their boss. So their killings are part of their distorted make-believe — to be dominant. It is only when they murder, abduct, that they fulfil this fancy. But Franz Fischer doesn't fit this. He is not some inadequate who can only be dominant when he is raping, torturing, debauching his victim — he is already the alpha male in real life. He *is* a dominant personality. He has the organisation skills to run a business. He is successful, of that there is little doubt. He is prosperous in life and business.'

'So you don't think it's him?' Jilly turned to look over her shoulder at Leo.

'I didn't say that. If he is our killer, he will have his own distorted vision that he is acting out, but what I mean is, his fancy is not to be the dominant person. What we have to do is find what that quixotic vision is.'

'Well, it's not to taunt the police, to show us how clever he is, or to wallow in his fame, that's for certain. He would have left his victims' bodies for us to find if that was what he wanted.'

'I agree,' said Leo. 'Socially, he's a loner; he protects his privacy, and that fits the profile of an abductor. His business is a one-man operation — he can't delegate to subordinates. That fits, too — he doesn't trust other people. But, on the other hand, it's at odds with his peacock appearance — peacocks want to be the centre of attention. And he must have people skills to attract customers — that doesn't fit either. He's a bunch of contradictions, that's for certain. I'd like to bet that when Pete Reader investigates his favourite restaurant, we find he has a string of lady friends.'

'If that is true,' said Jilly, 'he has no need to get off on killing women. He can get as many as he wants. But I still feel it in my water — that this is our man.' She looked over her shoulder again at Leo and saw a smug expression on his face. 'Why are you looking so pleased with yourself?'

'Remember I said that if Fischer were our killer, he would be acting out his own distorted make-believe and my job is to find out what that is? Well, I think I may have a handle on it.'

Jilly's eyes widened, gesturing him to explain.

'Well, when you were talking to him, I took the opportunity to look at his bookshelves to see what his reading material was.'

'And?'

'And, he has books on chess, on military tactics, but interestingly also on German mythology.'

'But why is that surprising — what was his degree in? Oh yes, Viking and Old Norse Studies.'

'On its own, perhaps it's not, but he also had books on Hitler, on Nazism, and books on the occult — many historians think there is a link between Nazism and Occultism. Many of the Nazi hierarchy were into it in a big way. He has other related books too, mostly on subjects I know nothing about, but I did recognise books on the Vril and the Lebensborn.'

'And are they?'

'Whacko ideas the Nazis latched onto. The Vril are a mythological subterranean master race, if memory serves. Lebensborn was an SS-sponsored organisation aiming to increase the Aryan-pure birth rate. They linked up young, single, Aryan girls with SS officers who got them pregnant, then the children were adopted by the right sort of "racially pure" people, to be brought up in the pure, Aryan way.'

'So what are you thinking — that Franz is a closet Nazi?'

'I'm thinking exactly that. He has changed the family name back to its German origins. I believe he admires the Nazi philosophy, no matter how horrific it is to us. I think Franz's vision may be a Superman fantasy — an Aryan version.'

'You mean like a superiority complex?' asked Satinder.

'The term "superiority complex" in everyday usage refers to an overly high opinion of oneself. In psychology, it refers not to a belief, but a pattern of behaviours expressing the belief that one *is* superior. I don't think Franz is compensating for inner feelings of inferiority, if that's what you mean.'

'So why does he dress so stylishly, drive flash cars — isn't that trying to impress people?' Jilly needed more convincing.

'Good point. That bothered me, too, but when you think it through, it still fits. Yes, you could argue he is dressing to impress, which might signify compensating for inferiority. But I suspect he dresses that way not out of a need to impress — ultimately, I don't think he cares what other people think. To him, other people are lesser beings. No, he dresses to express himself, not out of a need to impress others.'

'But that will make him conspicuous, won't it? People don't like arrogance.'

'If he is our killer, then he doesn't want that. But he is also manipulative, remember. He doesn't care what others think about him, but he is savvy enough to hide his displays of egocentricity.'

Back at the station, as they left the pool car, Leo took Jilly's arm before she walked back into the building. She gestured to DS Kaur to go on without her.

'You're not convinced about my profile of Mr. Fischer, are you?'

'I may be coming round to it.'

'Would you like to discuss it over dinner?'

The words caught her unawares. She was momentarily tongue-tied. Another police car coming into the car park beeped, and they got out of the way, giving her a chance to formulate her words. 'Okay,' she said, 'that might be useful.'

'Do you like Indian food?'

'Yes, very much.'

They started walking back to the building, but then she stopped and looked up at him.

'Is this a professional dinner, or is it a…' Jilly paused, unable to find a way of expressing herself. 'Are you asking me to dinner … as a date?'

'Would you like it to be a date? It can be whatever you want it to be — it's your decision.'

She nodded, and they walked on. She was still unsure what she had agreed to.

CHAPTER 25

Day 19

Mac sat, as usual, on the corner table, listening to DI French's report of the interview with Franz Fischer. She had her notes, and her written summary was detailed and frank. Likewise, Dr. Adams had, overnight, written up his psychological profile of their suspect. While he passed copies around, he gave his report verbally. Mac's leg stopped swinging briefly as he listened.

'So, in Franz Fischer's case, we need to expand on what we have identified as a peacock syndrome,' Leo concluded. 'What we have is a man with a full-blown narcissistic personality disorder. It's all there — grandiose behaviour, expects obedience from others, takes advantage of people around him, has exaggerated feelings of self-importance, a disregard for others' feelings; he schemes endlessly to achieve his success. He wants power.'

Mac looked up. 'So you think Fischer may believe himself to be a man of destiny — that's his vision?'

Leo paused. 'I wouldn't have chosen those words, but, yes… That's a reasonable assessment.'

'Would that lead him into serial-killing?'

'The best answer I can give at the moment is — maybe. He's capable of killing, certainly — he has no empathy for others. Probably sees them as lesser beings, but I need more information before I could say *yes*.'

'Like what?' Jilly interrupted. They had discussed it at their dinner the previous evening, but she wanted the team to understand Leo's thought processes.

'Nazism and the occult give us a *handle* on the type of guy he is, but I have to establish what he is trying to achieve, what bit of it is his particular fancy.'

'So what's next?' she asked.

'Anything you can find for me, anything to beef up the profile.'

Jilly looked to her team, gesturing for their input.

DS Jackson came in first. 'Basic police work, guv. Take the suspect's home apart. Look in the attic, the loft, under the floorboards.' He addressed Leo. 'Serial killers take souvenirs of their victims, right?'

'Sometimes,' said Leo.

'Absolutely,' Jilly agreed, 'but we would need a search warrant, and that may be a bit iffy, convincing a magistrate.' She turned to Mac — he moved his head from side to side, suggesting it was difficult but may be possible.

'Why not?' asked Leo. 'Don't you have eyewitnesses at the car hire companies who can identify Fischer?'

'Yes, we do, but all that does is link him to rented cars seen following Karrie's vehicle. That's too loose to connect him to Karrie and doesn't put him at a crime scene. We have no bloody crime scene. Unless... Pete, how's the CCTV for the Travellers Rest in the days before the abduction, going? Does it show our man casing the joint?'

'I think I have him, eight days before the abduction, guv. I'm sure it's him.' DI French drew a breath, all eyes turned to Pete. 'He's checking where the CCTV cameras are. He got out of an Audi S6, and he's wearing a hoody. It's him alright; hoody wearers don't drive Audi S6s. I've had the picture going backwards and forwards, freeze-framed, enlarged, blown up, but I can't get a good image of him — that bloody hoody.'

'And the car registration?'

'I've got a partial, boss, enough to establish it's not registered to Fischer. There aren't many registered in this area, and the info we have from Swansea on the partial suggests it may belong to another hire company. If that's the case, there's probably little mileage in taking it further. They'll remember him, he's distinctive, but it doesn't connect him to Karrie or the others.'

'Bummer!' Jilly blurted. She paused, chewed the inside of her mouth. But then she stood up straight. 'Look, we're not going to hold back now; we need to keep the momentum going. I know a magistrate who I think I can sweet talk into giving me a search warrant. We present it to Mr. Fischer first thing tomorrow morning — I'll arrest him and bring him back here for questioning while you lot search the premises.' She saw the satisfaction on her team's faces — she had energised them. 'Oh yes, one last thing.' She turned to Pete Reader. 'What did the manager of his favourite restaurant say about his eating arrangements?'

'He wouldn't tell me anything, boss. He said his customers had a right to privacy. Fischer's too good a customer to piss off, I suppose.'

'You let it go at that?'

'Did I hell, boss. I've been down there and talked to the waitresses. They were more forthcoming. He's their local heartthrob, it seems. They call him Fish the Dish. He always has a looker on his arm, apparently, classy women, and he tips well, too.'

DI French turned to Leo. His expression said it all — *told you so.*

CHAPTER 26

Day 20

The team were at Fischer's house by 8.00 a.m. DI French rapped the door knocker boldly. It was wet from the driving rain. When Fischer drew back the bolts and opened the door, she brandished her warrant card. She was anxious everything should be done by the book; that there could be no grounds for the man's sharp mind to find a defect he could exploit.

'Good morning, Mr. Fischer. I have a warrant to search these premises.'

He opened the door fully, stepped forward and faced her, his legs spread as if to bar her entrance. He took the document and read its contents thoroughly, ignoring the flurry that wet his manicured hair and stylish clothes. His expression did not change.

'Very well,' he said calmly as he stood aside, 'but wipe your size tens before you come in.' Jilly turned to her team, gesturing for them to enter. They rushed past her, eager to get on with the search, disregarding Fischer's demand. 'I will be claiming compensation for any damage you do,' he added.

'Noted, sir,' DI French said. She was not going to be intimidated by this man. 'And I would also like you to accompany me to the station to answer some questions.'

'Is that a request? If it is, I won't come voluntarily. Am I under arrest?'

'In that case — yes, you are, sir.' Jilly handed him a copy of the arrest warrant. 'I am arresting you on suspicion of involvement in the disappearance of Karrie Talbot. You do not have to say anything, but it may harm your defence if you do not mention when questioned something which you later rely on in court. Anything you do say may be given in evidence.' *Everything by the book*, she thought.

Jilly and Satinder entered the interview room and sat at the table, placing their files before them. Jilly switched on the tape recorder and spoke: 'Interview commencing eleven-o-five a.m. on the thirtieth of September 2019. Present: Mr. Franz Fischer, DI Jill French, and DS Satinder Kaur. This interview is done under caution. For the purposes of the tape, Mr. Fischer, can you confirm you have been given written notice of your rights, they have been explained to you and that you have declined your right to legal representation? You have also rejected your right to be advised by the duty solicitor.'

Fischer nodded.

'For the purposes of the tape, can you answer, Mr. Fischer, please?'

'That is correct.' His words were unemotional, business-like, but with a hint of disdain.

DI French turned to DS Kaur to ask the first questions.

'Can you tell me where you were on Tuesday the tenth of September, Mr. Fischer?'

He turned slowly to take in her brown eyes. He gave her an arrogant look, as if she was beneath him, she thought.

'I was at home all day, working,' he said calmly.

'Have you ever met Karrie Talbot?'

'No.'

'Have you ever met Emily Jackson or Caitlin Morgan?'

'No.'

'Have you ever visited the Travellers Rest pub on Mapperley Top?'

'No.'

'What would you say if I told you we have CCTV footage of you in the pub eight days before Karrie Talbot was abducted?'

'I would say that you were lying.' He looked straight into her eyes, his own face a mask, yet she thought she saw something hawkish in his expression. He was calling her bluff.

In the next room, looking at Fischer through a video link, sat Dr. Leo Adams. His eyes were fixed on the suspect, assessing his every word, every gesture. He jotted notes down on his pad:

Egoism or egotism?
Places himself at the centre of his world.
Disregard for others.
Grandiose sense of his own importance.
Doesn't recognise others' abilities.

'Have you ever hired a BMW X5?' DS Kaur continued.

Fischer never took his eyes off her, as if goading her to do her worst. Then, suddenly, he seemed to lose interest and turned back to Jilly. She saw him look her up and down. His eyes paused briefly at her blonde hair, swept back into a ponytail. Then they dropped to her navy blue business suit and alighted on her bosom. She felt as if she was being judged, both as a sexual object as well as for her intellect, to see if she was good enough to even engage with him.

Leo jotted more notes:

There's a sexual nuance if I'm not mistaken.
He's looking at Jilly in a carnal way.
Is he aroused?
Does his egoism assume that he can have her?

Is his attraction distorted by his fantasy?
Does he want to do depraved things to her?

Fischer looked back up, took in her eyes, and gave her a dismissive look. The brief moment of lust had passed. 'I've told you … I was at home on the day you mentioned, and I do not know these women.' He spoke to DI French, dismissing DS Kaur deliberately. 'I will now invoke my right to silence.'

No, you don't, Satinder thought. 'Have you ever hired a Range Rover Sport SVR?'

He turned back to her. 'No comment.'

'What about an Audi S6?'

'No comment.'

'You know the courts will take your silence into account when deciding whether you are guilty or innocent?' Her words were intended to coerce him, but they failed.

'As this will never come to court, that threat is an empty one.'

Jilly watched him for some moments. There was something primeval about the man. She considered the top of her pen as she formulated her tactics. 'That tattoo on your hand is very distinctive, Mr. Fischer.' She gave him a withering look as she spoke.

He looked down at his hand, then back at her, but didn't speak. He chewed the inside of his mouth, she noticed, the first time that mask had slipped.

It was a small victory. He returned to his "no comment" tactic for the rest of the interview.

In the adjoining room, Leo gathered up his notes. He was anxious to join the search team. He wanted a good look at Fischer's home to get more of a handle on the guy.

Jilly looked out of her office window into the darkness of the rainswept night. She saw her own reflection and those of Leo, Satinder and Jimmy Jackson, blurred only by droplets running down the pane. She looked at her watch — 7.55 p.m. It had been a long day. She slumped back, letting out a long sigh. 'Honestly, Jimmy, you found nothing?'

DS Jackson saw the disillusionment in her eyes and felt as frustrated as she did. He shrugged his shoulders, scratching his white goatee as he did so. 'Sod-all, boss — sorry, absolutely zilch.'

'You must have found something?'

'I've been doing searches for years, and I know what I'm doing. We've been in the loft, under the floorboards, everywhere. No souvenirs of the victims. And the fingerprint guys tell me the place hasn't been wiped clean, either. So he hasn't erased anything expecting us to search — there's nothing to suggest any of the victims were ever in his house. Only three sets of prints were found, and we expect to match them to Fischer, his cleaner, and his cook.'

'No paperwork suggesting Karrie was a client?'

'Nothing, boss — but we have his laptop. Our techie guys might find something.'

'That isolated house is perfect for a serial abductor; it *must* be the crime scene?' Jilly's eyes drifted out into the rainy night.

'The SOCO guys disagree, boss,' said Satinder. 'They say it's not the crime scene.'

'Then he has somewhere else — he must have.' Satinder and Jimmy Jackson nodded. Jilly turned to the psychologist. 'Leo, what do you think?'

'In my existing profile, I said Fischer displays all the symptoms of being a sociopath, but, remember, I said that didn't make him a psychopath, a serial murderer. We may have to swallow that particular pill.'

'Is your professional assessment that we have the wrong man?'

'My profile of the *abductor* is fragile because he has left us so little evidence, so little information. My profile of *Fischer* is more detailed, and I am beefing it up all the time. His wardrobe is full of expensively tailored clothes. He has an extensive porcelain collection. His library has books on fine art, fine wines, fine dining — the man likes the finer things in life. He has the capacity, therefore, to embrace higher human values. But he also displays counter-traits: his personal value system is hedonistic and appears to be centred on what is important to him — that lack of empathy for others, for instance. He may also have baser animal instincts that drive him. I would ask you this question: has your basic police work been sound, has it been robust, has it been perceptive?'

Jilly looked at the ceiling. 'Goddammit!' she grumbled through gritted teeth. 'This case has been like swimming through treacle: no crime scene, no witnesses, fuck all to go on. Given that, this is a bloody good team who have done a fantastic job. Despite the difficulties, I believe we have the right man.'

'Well, if you think your coppering has been spot on, then I'll add my two penneth. If Fischer is not the abductor, you have got the wrong man for the right reasons.'

'What does that chuffing mean?' asked DS Jackson.

'It means I believe he is hiding something — something major.'

'Because of his excessive protection of his privacy, you mean?' Jilly's eyes widened.

'Exactly, but I think it goes way past privacy. He has constructed a secluded world where nobody can enter. He has no employees, other than two domestics. He trusts nobody with his business activities. He is self-reliant to the point of obsession — but he is not a recluse, and he's not a miser. He likes women, he likes beautiful possessions — his porcelain collection, for instance.'

'So all that has a purpose — and you think that purpose is to hide something from the world?' DS Jackson leaned forward in his chair. 'You agree, then? He is our serial killer?'

Leo uncrossed his long legs. 'Don't rush too far ahead, Jimmy. Yes, I agree he his hiding something, but with serial killers, something happens to them that releases base animal instincts; a perverted logic is unleashed, allowing them to do unspeakable things. I don't think, for Fischer, it is about basic animal instincts. I believe it's about something intellectual, doctrinal, to be more precise — and my deduction would be it is his obsession with Nazism.'

'So you think Nazism is the key?' Jilly was trying to pin Leo down.

'I do. Nearly half his library is about Nazism — I think he sees himself as a product of the master race. What form that takes is what we have to establish.'

'We can only hold him for twenty-four hours without charging him,' she said. 'I'll have to let him go at eight a.m. tomorrow.'

'No chance of the superintendent authorising another twelve hours?' asked Satinder.

'No chance, we've got nothing to take to him.'

'So where do we go from here?' Satinder followed up.

Jilly sat back. 'We'll have another go at Mr. Fischer now — do you want to sit in, Satinder?' She nodded. 'In the morning, we'll get Tim to start searching Nazi-style organisations to see if he's a member of any.' Jilly got to her feet.

Leo cast her a sceptical look. 'You know he'll hide behind his "no comment" tactic, don't you?'

'I expect so,' she said, 'but it's a time thing.'

'Do you fancy a late-night curry afterward?'

'Yeah, and a couple of lagers would be good.' She had accepted before she had time to think it through.

CHAPTER 27

Day 21

The pool car arrived outside a well-maintained bungalow with an extension to the side — the home of Oliver and Elizabeth Fisher, Franz's parents. The journey had been subdued. Franz Fischer had been released at 8.00 a.m., and the sight of his smug, condescending face was burnt into their memories.

Satinder looked at the first of the autumn leaves, spotting the lush, green lawn. 'They look to be comfortably off in their retirement,' she said to Jilly. 'How do we play this, boss?'

'Delicately — we are only fact-finding, so, a light touch. We want them to be open with us about their son, but their natural instinct will be to protect him. So let's not be too heavy-handed. We'll not tell them we suspect him of being a serial murderer. You agree, Leo?' she said over her shoulder.

'Absolutely, this can't be an interrogation.'

Mrs. Fisher answered the door. Leo assessed the woman: tall, slim — he knew from the team's research she was sixty-four, but she looked much younger, he thought. It was her eyes that took his attention — they had the same piercing intensity as her son's, the irises the palest flint-blue. He looked at her hair; it was blonde, but it was probably dyed over ageing grey.

Jilly presented her warrant card. 'Mrs. Fisher? We spoke on the phone earlier this morning. I am DI French, and this is DS Kaur and Dr. Leo Adams. May we come in and talk to you about your son?'

'I think we'll go through to the conservatory,' she said. 'There's still some life in the garden to enjoy.'

It was an odd thing to say, Jilly thought, but it gave her an opening to engage with her. In the conservatory she stood by the window, looking at the flowerbeds and the manicured lawns. 'Oh, I'd love a garden like this, Mrs. Fisher, but I haven't the time to devote to it. Mine is all chippings and imitation grass.'

'Neither had I when I was working, but retirement has given me all the time I need.'

Jilly noticed her husband coming out of a shed with some long-handled shears, and when he saw them, Mrs. Fisher waved him to come into the house.

Leo looked at the pictures on the back wall while Mrs. Fisher went to bring tea for them. One was a graduation photograph of their son. Mr. Fisher joined them, gesturing for them to sit, and they waited in uncomfortable silence for some minutes. Jilly saw a resemblance to Franz: a broad forehead, a square-jawed face, but shorn, spiky-grey hair. There were also dark shadows under his eyes, which detracted from his handsomeness. She wondered if she should start without Mrs. Fisher, but Leo made the decision for her.

'Graduation is always a very proud day for parents, Mr. Fisher,' he said pointing at the photograph.

Leo saw a sparkle of pride, but it was fleeting and quickly replaced by something else — perhaps sadness. 'Yes, Frank was a brilliant student; graduated with a first. But then, he has an eidetic memory. Learning and exams always came easily.'

'Oh, I envy him that, Mr. Fisher — if only I had perfect recall. The hours it would save me, going over and over my notes.'

'Too true, Dr. … Adams, was it? But it can be a curse as well.'

'In what way?'

Mr. Fisher opened his mouth to speak, then seemed to think better of it. 'What is your particular field, Dr. Adams?'

'I am a psychologist, attached to the Nottinghamshire police as an advisor.'

'As an offender profiler, you mean?'

Leo saw Jilly's expression darken. It had been going so well, he thought, diverting the conversation skilfully, but this was a danger point. He chose his words with care. 'Amongst other things — yes,' he said, his tone as businesslike as he could make it.

Mrs. Fisher entered with a tray of tea and biscuits, catching the last of Leo's words. 'What have you been telling our guests, Oliver?' There was admonishment in her voice.

'We were talking about Frank's eidetic memory, dear.'

Mrs. Fisher poured the tea with all the delicacy of a cultured lady, but it became apparent she had some steel about her. 'Do you suspect Frank of some crime, DI French?' she asked.

'Most crime investigation is about eliminating suspects, Mrs. Fisher, but Franz is hard to remove because he is so secretive. We were wondering if you can tell us something about him — let us form an opinion, so to speak.'

'Still calling himself Franz, is he?' Mr. Fisher cut across.

'He changed his name by deed poll to Franz Fischer — the German spelling, some years ago,' Jilly advised.

'Oh. I didn't know that.'

'You didn't, Mr. Fisher? He didn't tell you?' Leo was still trying to manoeuvre the conversation.

'I think you should know … we haven't seen our son for over ten years.' There was sadness in his voice.

'Oliver!' Again there was admonishment in Mrs. Fisher's tone, Jilly thought. She saw Mr. Fisher's eyes dart to his wife.

They'd made a pact beforehand, Leo thought, as to what they would volunteer — but Oliver had broken this agreement. He had to manipulate that, not let Mrs. Fisher rein him back.

'Why is that, Mr. Fisher? I can see the pride in your eyes at your son's academic achievements.'

'Of course I was proud of him, what father wouldn't be? A first at UCL, a brilliant rugby player — several professional teams were after him — a talented racing driver too, and a martial arts expert. He could have achieved anything he turned his hand to.'

'But he is a very successful businessman, is he not?'

'Is he? I don't really know.' His expression saddened, as if his son's success had been taken from him.

'He married a lovely girl — didn't he, Oliver? Emma? Met her at university.'

'Absolutely! They looked so good together. She's lecturing herself at UCL now. We couldn't have been happier.'

'So what went wrong?' Leo pressed.

The world around Mr. Fisher seemed to drift away; his eyes fixed on some faraway point.

His wife answered. 'They broke up — it didn't work out.' Her words were curt, as if she wanted to say no more on the subject.

Leo turned back to her husband. 'Did he confide in you, say what the problem was?'

'Oh, yes.'

'Oliver!' his wife said again, but Leo saw that the man desperately wanted to unload his pain.

'What was it, Mr. Fisher?' he pressed gently.

Mr. Fisher gave a humourless laugh. 'You wouldn't believe me if I told you.'

'Why not, Mr. Fisher?'

'Because … my son broke up with his lovely wife because she possibly had a great-grandmother who was mixed-race. Her great-grandfather was a ship's captain, and married a woman in Venezuela in the 1880s. So somewhere in her history there was white and Black parentage. The family were wealthy, apparently, but were treated with some hostility by the Spanish colonials at the time.'

'But why would he break up with her over that?' Leo was teasing the information out of him.

Mrs. Fisher got to her feet and gave her husband one last penetrating look, but he was going to tell the whole story. She left the room.

'I was so pleased when he decided to study Viking and Old Norse at university, a link to his German roots, so to speak, but it has turned out to be a curse.' Leo nodded, gesturing for him to continue. 'He studied ancient mysticism, sacred Northern gods — but he became obsessed. We are an academic family, Dr. Adams — I lecture in German, my wife in classics. We know about objectivity in our research, the need to be impartial, to take a dispassionate view, but with all Frank's advantages, his eidetic memory, it was something, it seems, he couldn't master. He got sucked into an imaginary world.'

'The way the Nazi leadership did, you mean?'

'You have read about that?'

'A little.'

'Yes, many of the Nazi leaders belonged to secret societies, and the rituals involved even included pagan worship. Societies such as the Thule, the Vril, the Black Sun. Frank studied these societies with a passion, but it was not a detached, academic passion; it started to consume him.'

'So it came between him and his wife — this obsession?' Jilly interrupted.

'Oh, it was more fundamental. It was a throwaway line in an argument — Emma, trying to show that "racial purity" was nonsense, told Frank she had a mixed-race great-grandmother. She thought it would bring it home to him that it was gibberish, bring him down to earth. But it had the opposite effect — it drove a wedge between them that finally broke them up.'

'Really?' said Jilly. 'He took it *that* seriously?'

'It was to do with the Vril — he was getting drawn into it at the time. According to the mythology, the Vril-ya were a subterranean master race who had an energy force called Vril. To harness this power, the subject has to be *spiritually elevated* to receive it. That requires him to have a robust hereditary constitution.'

'A robust hereditary constitution — what does that mean?' Jilly's expression showed her confusion.

'I think what Mr. Fisher means,' Leo interjected, 'is that it requires the subject to be "racially pure" — no Jewish or non-white blood.'

'Dr. Adams is right,' said Oliver Fisher. 'My son split with his lovely wife because their children would not be "racially pure". Can you believe anybody would think such a thing in the twenty-first century? His grandfather would turn in his grave — he was forced to join the Nazi youth in the nineteen-thirties and saw at first-hand all that nonsense. That obsession with the "purification" of the race, requiring people to declare their lineage when applying for a job; the measuring of the skulls and temples; they even called it a racial science. It has as much to do with science as palmistry. It is one of the reasons his grandfather came to this country — his revulsion at what his country had done.'

'So there were rows over his … interpretations?' Leo was not going to let this line go.

'It was an academic debate to start with. Scholarly examination of the facts. It should have been easy for me to shred these arguments; they were based on myth and pseudo-science, but you don't know my son. That eidetic memory of his — he can find a source to justify any whacko argument. It's like trying to debate with an encyclopaedia on speed. And he picks and chooses what will support his arguments, demolishing anything that would challenge his ideas.'

'He's in search of external self-justification to counter his dissonance,' said Leo.

Jilly and Satinder both looked at him as if he were speaking a foreign language.

'It happens to us all, at some times in our lives. A state of tension when we hold two opposing views. We frequently justify it to ourselves by external means, but it becomes a problem when we can't find those external justifications. Then people change their behaviour to explain their views. Frank's total recall must have helped him justify his acceptance of these societies — would you not think so, Mr. Fisher?'

'I hadn't thought of it that way, Dr. Adams, but I suppose you are right. Whatever, my relationship with my son began to break down — I couldn't get him to see sense. We started to have the most blazing rows. He only had that stupid tattoo done to spite me.'

Leo stiffened. 'The All-Seeing Eye, you mean?'

'What?' Oliver Fisher shot him a confused look.

'The tattoo on his hand. The All-Seeing Eye — the Eye of Providence.'

'Is that what you think it is?'

'Is it not?'

'No, it's the Black Sun.'

Jilly looked at Satinder. Was there something wrong with Leo's profile?

Leo ran his hand through his hair. 'Can you explain the significance of this ... Black Sun?'

'The mythology behind the Black Sun Society is connected to the legends of the Vril. The fabled Vril energy force was supposed to be derived from the Schwarze Sonne — the Black Sun. I guess his tattoo does look like an eye, but it represents this black sun. His version is a black sphere with plumes on its surface, with a yellow centre — yes, like a pupil, I suppose.'

'So what is it intended to symbolise?' Leo pressed.

'An opposing force, I think. The Nazis had their own version, with a swastika symbol in the design, but it's claimed the philosophy goes back thousands of years. There are modern versions of it created after the Second World War as well. Many occult societies use the symbol to the present day.'

Leo paused as he took in this new information. 'So what was Frank's ultimate aim? What was he trying to achieve?'

'The beliefs of some of the Nazi leadership obsessed him — that there was a hidden power they could harness. The Nazis swept across Europe in the early part of the war, remember. The idea was that they had tapped into a hidden force.'

'So Frank's ultimate aim was also to draw on this energy — this Vril?'

'Yes, daft as it seems, he believed his "racial purity" gave him the ability to do so.'

Leo caught Jilly's eye. She understood — he had a handle on what motivated this man, what his fantasy was. His profile could now be completed.

'A lamb pasanda, a masala special mix bhuna, pilau rice, two Peshwari naans, and two pints of Kingfisher, please.' Leo gave his order to the waiter.

The lagers arrived almost immediately, and Jilly took a long drink.

'Steady, tiger.' Leo's words were teasing. 'You feeling better about the investigation, then?'

'I was pissed off this morning when we had to release Herr Franz, but, after meeting his parents, I am more convinced than ever he is our man. I'll have to get Tim Book to repeat his searches for organisations using this Black Sun symbol.'

'Franz already feels superior to us mortals, and is in search of power to elevate that further. So, with him, it's about ritual, about a perverted ceremony. It's not about arousal. He's not *getting off* on these murders. But…'

'But what? You still have doubts?'

'No, I think we're right — but it's still not the full story.'

Jilly paused as the food arrived. She tore a piece of naan bread, scooped up some of her sauce and chewed. 'Go on,' she said.

'Well, I think Franz has this nonsense fancy that he can tap into some mysterious force. What I am not sure of is how murdering successful, Aryan-looking women will help achieve that.'

'I would have thought that was obvious. Isn't it like cannibalism? Didn't early tribes eat their enemy, thinking they would take on their powers? I know our Mr. Fischer is academic, but it doesn't stop him having a variation of the same idea.'

'Yes, maybe you're right — I may be overthinking this. If he is obsessed with — what was the phrase — oh yes, his own *robust hereditary constitution* — then perhaps he feels he can absorb the "racial purity" of these women.'

Jilly stopped eating. She cradled her beer glass and sat forward. 'It's down to police work now. My team has to find the evidence to get this guy.'

PART 3: THE GIRL WHO DID NOT DIE

CHAPTER 28

The new academic year could be a bit chaotic. The family holiday had done wonders for us, especially Carol and me. We even talked about the chronicle and what had happened to Margaret — it brought us back together in some strange way. Carol, with her legal background, had been the one who was the most cynical about Margaret's extraordinary story, but she became as enthused as me. She wanted me to get on with the translation. I started it again on my second week back in September, and emailed another passage to James, Grace and Carol:

You may be interested in this — a further translation of Brother Roger's chronicle. This bit is about what happened to Margaret of Wellow.

I arrived back at Rufford Abbey with Margaret in a cart that I had borrowed from Guy FitzHugh the under-sheriff. There was little sign of life in her frail, diminutive body, and I had her taken to the infirmary at once.

Brother Emanuel, who runs the hospital, confirmed, however, that he too could feel the merest pulse. He put her to bed with ample blankets to raise her body temperature and then put a few drops of broth, infused with nourishing herbs, into her mouth. He continued this throughout the night, and by morning the pulse was more distinct. He said that if he could get her to take sustenance, he believed she might recover.

There seemed little evidence of this in the next twenty-four hours, and she lay almost lifeless and unresponsive. By day three, however, it was as though a spark of life had come hither, and the spirit of God's good grace had entered her. I prefer to think about it as the spirit of God, but I suspect that the zealous village priest would advocate it was the spirit of Satan taking back his vassal.

Whatever, she was sitting up in her bed, taking the mixture of broth and herbs from Brother Emanuel. He had a look of satisfaction on his face.

Abbot Stephen thought carefully about the law, both clerical and secular, and came to the judgement that her sentence had been justly arrived at and that her punishment had been legally served. She had in fact been hanged according to the sentence prescribed. In these circumstances, she had nothing further to answer.

His problem was what to do with her. He feared that if he sent her back to the village and her family, she would be in danger. The village priest would certainly whip up fear amongst the villagers, and that would put her at risk. He therefore had her sent to the nuns at the Priory of St. Mary's and asked the prioress to assess her state of mind. She went there on the 12th December.

Grace replied to all of us with some news:

Have you seen the evening paper? Police are investigating the possible abduction of a Nottingham architect — Katarina Talbot, blonde hair, blue eyes. Last seen wearing a white suit, late yesterday morning after visiting a client in Rainworth. Remind you of anybody? How did Margaret describe the victim? 'The lady angel, though beautiful as a princess, was dressed as a man in white breeches, and she walked on the toes of her beautiful white slippers. Her hair was white and curled, hanging long down her back, her fingernails long and red.' She could be describing this Katarina Talbot — platinum-blonde would be white in her vocabulary.

Whoa! Let's not get carried away, I wrote in response. *That's one hell of a leap.*

Maybe, wrote Grace. *But remember what else Margaret said — 'It was in September that I first saw the devil's work.' It's September now.*

That evening, over dinner, I asked Carol if she'd had time to read my translation of Brother Roger's chronicle.

'Mmm,' she said while serving the kids' food.

'What's this?' asked Emma. I had shared the translation with Carol, so I thought I'd also share it with the kids. I told her the full story. It gave her some idea of what I did for a living. Surprisingly, she was taken with it. Even Tom looked up from his smartphone to show interest.

'I'm so pleased she didn't die on the gallows,' Carol said, and Emma agreed.

'You have to go to the police, Dad,' she said.

I laughed. 'I don't think they would take me seriously, sweetheart.'

'Why not?'

'Because the police won't see it as you — as we do. What is an academic historical conundrum to us, is of no importance to them. It's not evidence.'

'But this Margaret of Wellow witnessed the whole thing, didn't she? That's what this Brother Roger wrote in his … journal.'

'Well, she witnessed something. But time travel is something for novels and the movies. She can't have seen the abduction of Katarina Talbot. That sort of thing doesn't happen in real life.'

'Grace seems to think so, though, doesn't she?'

I looked at Carol. 'Your mum's a lawyer. She can explain it better than I can.'

Carol gave me a sideways look. 'Grace is being playful, Emma — she's teasing your dad. She doesn't really believe

Margaret of Wellow in 1151 witnessed an abduction in 2019. And even if it were true, in contemporary courts it would be regarded as hearsay, and hearsay is not admissible.'

'Hearsay — what's hearsay?' she asked, her forehead furrowing.

Carol sighed. 'Hearsay is when you say what somebody else has told you. To be allowed in court, Margaret would have to give that evidence herself and be subject to cross-examination — subject to questioning.'

That seemed to satisfy Emma for the time being, and she returned to her meal.

After dinner, Carol and I returned to the subject.

'Is that right — about hearsay, I mean?' I asked.

'Probably. It takes us into difficult areas — and I'm not a criminal lawyer, remember.'

'Accepted, but what do *you* think?'

'The judge has leeway — there are statutory exceptions to the hearsay rules.'

'What sort of exceptions? How does it work?'

'If the relevant person can't give the information to the court themselves, the judge may allow it because it is in the interest of justice.'

'When you say the relevant person can't give the information to the court themselves, do you mean they can't be found, or that they are dead?'

'Yeah, that sort of thing.'

'So — Margaret of Wellow has been dead for nearly 900 years. I would say it falls within that statutory exemption, wouldn't you? You can't get more dead than that.'

'It's not me you have to convince,' she said. 'It's the court.'

'But there's a possibility the chronicle would *not* be regarded as hearsay?'

'Yeah, okay — a chance.'

'And what was that Latin precedence you were on about the other week — *nemo moriturus* something?'

'*Nemo moriturus praesumitur mentire.* No-one on the point of death should be presumed to be lying. Dying declarations were admitted as evidence as far back as English law itself goes.' She gave me a knowing smile. 'I see where you are going — and yes, that will add weight to the argument. You're thinking about going to the police, aren't you?'

'No — no,' I lied.

'Don't give me that, I can see it in your face.' She was teasing me, but I wasn't upset.

'You think I'm nuts, don't you?'

'No, actually.'

I looked at her, surprised. 'But the other week you didn't believe a word of it.'

'That was the other week, but…' She didn't complete the sentence. I didn't think she could explain it, even to herself.

'So you *now* believe this chronicle could be admitted in evidence?'

'It's not that. I don't think that's the point. The point is whether the information in the chronicle will help the police find the abductor.'

'So you think I *should* go to the police?'

'I'm ambivalent. I think they will reject you out of hand — as you say, like a nutter. But it's the name Margaret thought she heard that's been nagging at me — "Catherine". It's not that far from Katarina, is it? Katarina is a northern European name, so she wouldn't have known it — she could easily have mistaken it for Catherine. And, on the other side of the coin, it may at least settle *your* conscience.'

'Yeah, I follow that. At least I will have done my best to help find this poor woman.'

I rang the helpline number the following morning.

'DC Reader,' a commanding voice said.

I was tongue-tied, not sure how to formulate my words. 'Erm … I'm ringing about the abduction of the architect. On the telly last night you appealed for anyone who had any information about her.'

'Yes, sir, that's right. Can I have your name, please?'

'My name … yes, my name is Toby Fielding.'

'And do you have a sighting to report, sir?'

'Well, not exactly…' I was still awkward.

'Do you have any information about her whereabouts?'

'No, not really, but…'

'Any information you can give us, sir, no matter how insignificant, may be useful.'

His words were encouraging, so I tried to recount the words I had been practising to myself before I picked up the phone. 'I think she was abducted from a clearing beside the A616 Nottingham Road.'

I could sense his interest intensifying. 'Did you witness the abduction, Mr. Fielding?'

'No, let me explain. I'm a historian, and I've been translating a twelfth-century chronicle from its original Latin.'

'I don't understand, sir,' he said. 'What's this got to do with the abduction?'

'Well, I know this sounds ridiculous, but there is a reference to a young girl who claims to have visited the year 2019 and witnessed an abduction. I regarded it as a fantasy of a naive young medieval woman, but then I saw your appeal last night

— and … well, her description of this Katarina Talbot seems to fit.'

He didn't speak, but I heard a disdainful *tsk* sound down the phone.

'Well, thank you very much for your information, sir. I'll make a note of it.'

The line went dead — he had cut me off. He must have thought I was tying up the line. I hadn't even had a chance to draw his attention to the similarity of the name Catherine to Katarina, but at that moment the link seemed weak. Perhaps DC Reader had been right to cut me off.

CHAPTER 29

I emailed the next part of the chronicle to James, Grace and Carol:

It was on Shrove Tuesday 1152, the day before Lent, that I accompanied Abbot Stephen to the Priory of St. Mary. It was a routine visit, but I knew he was anxious also to learn of the assessment the prioress had made of young Margaret. Her welfare had given the abbot some sleepless nights; he had been unable to sleep calmly and restfully since this whole matter had been delegated to him.

But Prioress Agatha confirmed my findings that Margaret was the most godly of young women. Dutiful in her work and her devotions, uncomplaining and obedient. She had settled into the priory life and had expressed a wish to be considered as a novice. This was good news indeed, I thought, but I saw Abbot Stephen's face wince at that notion.

He questioned the girl at length, and I was allowed to ask questions also. The girl has a generosity of spirit, most at odds with the view that she has been practising witchcraft. She is apparently devout, and in some ways, a monastic life would solve some of the abbot's fears, but herein lies his dilemma.

He confided in me afterward — to accept Margaret as a novice would cause him great spiritual unease, which would require much religious study. He has ruled that she was convicted, by the Church, of being a witch. That could not easily be cast aside. How, then, could she be admitted into the Order?

I have skim-read ahead, I wrote, *but there doesn't seem to be anything immediately relevant to Margaret. Perhaps Brother Roger returns to the subject later in the chronicle.*

Grace replied:

Did you hear the local news last night? The police are scaling down the enquiry into the abduction of Katarina Talbot. They can't do anything else until more information comes to light.

I think you should go and see them again. Stella McMillan, head of the archaeology department, is married to a senior detective. James has met him — perhaps he can have a word with her and get her to talk to her husband on your behalf.

PART 4: THE EYEWITNESS

CHAPTER 30

Day 65

'Dinner's ready,' called Stella, DCI Donald McMillan's wife. He went through to the dining room and sat down at the table. 'Pour me a glass, too, please darling,' Stella, added.

He poured the Chinon Blanc as she served two portions of pasta bake.

'How's that kidnapping inquiry going, Mac?' Stella asked, as though she was making light conversation.

They had made a pact when they had married. Being a copper had cost him his first marriage, and he did not want to make the same mistake again. If he spent many hours away from home, Stella would know why, and what he was pursuing. Promotion to DCI had standardised his hours; that helped their marriage, but the pact still stood.

'It's stalled badly, I'm afraid.' He gave her a rueful look.

'It upsets you, doesn't it?'

'You always try to harden yourself to the realities, the immorality of people, the vileness you meet as a policeman — but it's the sense we have let this poor woman down that gnaws at my insides.'

'Has your team not done a good job, then?'

'You can always question yourself, but…' Mac paused as he reflected on the question. 'No, they have done a first-rate job, taking into account what they have had to put up with.'

'How do you mean?'

'Well, in an investigation, we have various tools to use. Forensic science, scene of crime analysis, ballistic science.

"Identify the weapon, identify the killer" is an old adage. But we have nothing to give the forensic guys. We have no body, no crime scene, no sightings, nothing, and our timeline is broken very early after the abduction.'

'No body? You think she's dead?'

'Oh, yes. The stats tell us she was probably dead within seventy-two hours. We can't save her life, but I hoped we could bring her killer to justice.'

'So you have no suspect, no motive?'

'On the contrary, the team has done brilliantly. We believe we know who did it, and his perverted reasons, his warped fantasies — but we can't get any evidence to nail him. He's an odd cove — one of your lot, an academic — well, he was, with some whacko ideas about the occult and ancient Norse mythology.'

'You sure it's him?'

'Oh, yes. The criminal psychologist confirmed that the crimes fit the psychological profile of the guy.'

'So why can't you arrest him?'

'We desperately need the crime scene. These abductors always have their crime scene in some remote place, away from prying eyes, where they do their despicable things. It sounds ghoulish, but it's where nobody can hear the screams.'

'And you haven't found it?'

'We thought we had. He lives alone in an isolated country place. Just what you would expect, but despite taking the place apart, we've found nothing. So he must have somewhere else.'

'Who's the SIO?'

'DI French — Jill French.'

'Is she any good?'

Mac tutted. 'Fast-track graduate.'

'That's not what I asked, is it?'

He sighed. 'Yes, she is good, bloody good.'

'Hasn't she been able to crack him in interrogation?'

'This guy is the smartest criminal I've ever come across. Doesn't use a solicitor but knows police procedure backward. Answers all questions with "no comment", so we can't catch him out in any lies. And the bugger has an eidetic memory, total recall.'

'Like you, you mean?'

'What? Hardly.'

'I taught you, remember. You were the best archaeology student I ever had. You vacuumed up information.'

'Well, even if that is true, I would only be fourth division. This guy is Premier League.'

'Nevertheless, perhaps it's time to change tack.'

'What, take over the enquiry, you mean? It doesn't work that way — my job as DCI is to control and advise. And anyway, I have had to make the decision to downgrade the enquiry.'

'You've closed it down, Mac?'

'No, but I have to make the best use of the resources available to me. I've disbanded the Major Incident Team with effect from Monday of this week, and reassigned everyone. The enquiry is not an operational runner anymore.'

'What does that mean?'

'It means the enquiry is dormant until more information comes to light.'

'Another killing, you mean?' Stella saw his fist clench. He put his fork down, but struggled with a mouthful of pasta, as though unable to swallow. 'Sorry, Mac, I shouldn't make comments like that. *I* don't have to make life and death decisions as you do, so I shouldn't have…'

Mac took a gulp of wine and gave her a reassuring look. 'No, it's okay, Stella. You touched a nerve, that's all. I've struggled with the decision for so long — this guy will kill again, I'm sure of it. We have had him under surveillance for weeks, hoping he will lead us to his hideaway, the scene of crime, but nothing.' She reached across and caressed the back of his hand, and he patted hers to show they were still good. 'What about you? Have you had a good day at work?'

'I've had an odd one. James Postlethwaite, head of the history department, came to see me. You remember James — you've met him a few times at faculty dos.'

'Thick Lancashire accent?'

'Yeah, that's the guy. Well, one of his lecturers, Toby Fielding, has been translating a twelfth-century account written by a monk, Brother Roger of Hathern, who was chronicling the first abbot of Rufford Abbey, Abbot Stephen.'

Toby Fielding, Mac thought, wondering where he had heard that name before. 'What's that got to do with you in the archaeology department?'

Stella was hesitant. 'Nothing, actually. But he has let me read the translations — they are remarkable. I've never seen anything like them.'

'In what way?' Mac asked, but then the link snapped into place. 'Toby Fielding! He was the loon who contacted the team in the first few days — something about a girl from the twelfth century witnessing a murder in 2019.' He screwed up his napkin and threw it down. 'So that's what this is about. Postlethwaite came to see you because you're married to me, didn't he? Jesus! Stella, the loonies come out of the woodwork in every case like this. If I were to allocate resources to them all, I would burn my budget in quick order. We haven't got time for these people.'

Stella saw his anger, a pulse throbbing in his forehead, and was unsure how to proceed. 'Yes, perhaps you are right, Mac. I told James I would broach the subject — and I shouldn't have. I'm sorry.'

Mac took up his napkin and returned to his pasta bake. They were quiet for a time. 'I'm sorry. I overreacted, Stella.' The rancour had gone from his voice. 'It'll be a hoax — these things always are.'

'They thought that as well, so they were academically rigorous, and it all still seemed to stack up — passed the forensic tests. It's not only the police who use scientific tests, you know. It's just so strange to read a twelfth-century document suggesting time travel, and a girl who witnessed an abduction by a man with an eye tattooed on his hand.'

Mac's eyes darted to his wife. 'What? What did you say?'

'It's a twelfth-century Latin chronicle suggesting time travel.'

'No — the other bit. The tattoo.'

'Oh, the killer apparently had an eye tattooed on his hand. The medieval girl called it — the Eye of Lucifer.'

Mac's logical brain could not process the information. If this was a forgery, how did the forger know about the eye tattoo? The information had never been released.

'I need to read these chronicles,' he mumbled, more to himself than his wife.

CHAPTER 31

Day 70

'Come in, DI French. Take a seat,' said Mac over his shoulder. As Jilly stepped into his office, he turned, sat at his desk, and massaged his brow with his fingers. 'Have you read that email I forwarded to you?' He was almost ashamed to broach the subject.

'The one from the university?'

'Yeah, that one. Have you read the attachment — with the translation of the Latin chronicle?'

'Yeah, I've waded through it — that was a couple of hours I won't get back.'

'Oh … I found it interesting — but that's beside the point. No — what do *you* think of it as a lead, as evidence?'

'You're not serious, are you?' Jilly made no attempt to hide her disdain. 'This Toby Fielding guy may be a professor, but it doesn't stop him being a loony, does it? He's forged it — it's a hoax.'

'He's a lecturer, not a professor — but yes, that was also my initial reaction. I've been through it several times since, however, and it's not as ridiculous as I first thought.'

Jilly looked at him suspiciously. 'Go on, then — let's examine it, see how it stacks up,' she said.

'All right,' said Mac with a faint smile, 'you be the prosecution.'

She shuffled in her chair. 'Okay, Fielding is an academic. He is a man capable of forging this chronicle.'

'True, but I've spoken to his boss, James Postlethwaite. English Heritage found the chronicle — not Fielding. They approached Postlethwaite, who then allocated it to Fielding.'

'So, okay — Fielding is not the forger. It's someone else.'

'Why forge it?'

'Publicity, fame — somebody out to make money.'

'The paper and ink have been forensically tested. It's been verified as being from the twelfth century.'

Jilly sighed. 'Fielding is using our investigation to get publicity for his work, then. It will get him a book deal, or something.'

'So he's exploiting coincidences?'

'Exactly.'

'But what don't coppers like?'

'I know — coincidences, but even so…'

'What about the tattoo on the hand — the Eye of Lucifer?'

Jilly's mouth gaped — she had no immediate answer. 'Fielding added it to the text?' she said eventually.

'If he did, it was added before Karrie Talbot was abducted. Postlethwaite has an email string with Fielding and others which predates the kidnapping, and the emails mention the Eye.'

'So we have independent corroboration that the tattoo hasn't been invented to fit our case?' Jilly said, her voice uncertain.

'It seems that way — and even if we hadn't, we never released that information.'

Jilly took a moment to work out what to say. 'So we have to make a judgement call — crackpot or plausible.'

'That's about the size of it. It goes against all our police instincts, that's for sure.'

'We have no other outstanding leads,' she said.

'No,' said Mac. He could order her to investigate, but he wanted her on board.

'Okay, I'll arrange a search of the A616, near the village of … what was it? Oh, yes … Wellow.'

'Good,' said Mac, but there was no satisfaction in his tone. He was as ambivalent as she was. 'And I'll get in touch with the Crown Prosecution Service — see what they have to say about a twelfth-century deathbed confession being admitted in evidence. Get their take on the hearsay rules.'

Jilly headed for the door. 'Good luck with that,' she said over her shoulder.

CHAPTER 32

Day 73

'Franz Fischer agreed to come in voluntarily, then?' asked Leo, scratching his beard as if he were surprised.

'Yep,' Jilly said, 'and the arrogant sod is coming in *without* a brief.'

'And you feel confident enough to interrogate him on the basis of a twelfth-century chronicle?'

'No, I bloody don't, but we have nothing else, have we?' said Jilly.

Leo and Jilly had had this conversation before — in bed the previous night. Leo had returned to it — he thought she was taking a risk. 'Are you going to divulge the source of your information?'

'Not bloody likely,' she said. 'He'll make mincemeat of us if he thinks that's all we've got.'

'Wasn't that also the advice from the CPS — to leave this alone?' Leo knew he was being negative, but he wanted to protect her.

'Actually, they were not as definitive as that. I think they have had fun with this problem. Saw it as a conundrum, an enigmatic exercise, so to speak. They feel there is a case to be made — a contention that the deathbed confession should be admitted as evidence and not subject to the hearsay rules.'

'But their bottom line is they don't want to test that contention in court — isn't that right?' Leo leaned forward to emphasise the point.

Jilly's shoulders sank. 'Yes they did,' she admitted.

'So why go ahead with the interview?' Leo pressed. 'The fingertip search of the A616 near Wellow didn't find anything, did it?'

'No, we didn't find anything to suggest the abduction had taken place there — but even narrowing it down to the A616, it's still an extensive area. We looked at a two-mile stretch, but it could be five miles either side of our search. And the disappearance was over two months ago, remember?'

'So, you have none of her clothing, nothing to tie either of them to that place? So why show your hand?'

'Because I want to see Fischer's face when I tell him we have a witness — a witness that saw him abducting Karrie Talbot from a clearing beside the A616. *He* doesn't have to know our witness has been dead for 900 years.'

Jilly and Satinder entered the interview room, sat at the table, and placed their files before them. Jilly switched on the tape recorder and spoke: 'Interview commencing at ten-fifty-six a.m. on the twenty-first of November 2019. Present Mr. Franz Fischer, DI Jill French, and DS Satinder Kaur. This interview is done under caution. For the purposes of the tape, Mr. Fischer, can you confirm you have been given written notice of your rights, they have been explained to you and that you have declined your right to legal representation. You have also rejected your right to be advised by the duty solicitor.'

'Do we have to go through this rigmarole again? Can you get on with it, please?'

'For the purposes of the tape, can you answer, Mr. Fischer, please?'

'That is correct.' His words were a mixture of irritation and condescension.

Jilly took in the man before her: a large, athletically built man in an expensively cut suit, with a broad forehead and a handsome square-jawed face — but now that handsomeness was scarred by his snarling, twisted lips. Jilly smiled — he was irritated, that was good. A rare display of emotion.

'Can you tell me where you were on Tuesday the tenth of September, Mr. Fischer?' she asked routinely.

Fischer relaxed in his chair and gave a hollow smile. 'Let's save us all time, shall I? I will refer you to the answers I gave the last time you interviewed me. I was at home all day, working. I have never met Karrie Talbot. I have never met Emily Jackson, nor Caitlin Morgan.'

'You still say you have never met Karrie Talbot, Mr. Fischer?'

'No, I haven't.'

'Isn't it true you met her at the Travellers Rest pub on the tenth of September and she left with you in your car?'

'No comment.'

There was still that assurance about him, DI French could see. He believed he had covered his tracks. It was time to dispel that belief. She paused for a while and took in his eyes. They looked back at her, then dropped to her breasts as they had done the last time they had met. Then they shot to her hair, her dress. She knew she was being assessed by his dark mind. She leaned forward in her chair.

'Isn't it true you left the Travellers Rest, drove to the A616 and, in a clearing, you strangled Karrie Talbot and then bundled her into the boot of your car? I have an eyewitness who saw you do it.'

She studied his reaction intently. His cologne entered her consciousness for the first time — it was part of his immaculate image. His face remained a mask, but his eyes suggested he was on the brink of a reaction. At that moment, DI French knew that however ridiculous the source of the information, it was *right.* Their search had not found anything, but the scene of the crime *was* the A616.

'No comment.'

DI French had expected that. It was time to press home her advantage. 'What does the tattoo represent, Mr. Fischer?'

He looked first at the back of his hand, then impassively back to her. 'No comment.'

'It represents the Black Sun, doesn't it?'

The poker face remained, Jilly saw, but this time his response was delayed. It was enough to convince her he had not expected her to know about this.

'No comment.'

'You're fascinated with Norse mythology, aren't you, Mr. Fischer — the occult?'

'No comment,' he answered, but then he added, 'These are things you cannot comprehend.'

That's right, Franz, Jilly thought. *Let your ego lead, run free.* 'The Schwarze Sonne. It was a secret cult society, wasn't it? Along with the Vril and the Thule. You have studied them, haven't you?'

'Been on Wikipedia, have we?' He made no attempt to hide his disdain.

DI French didn't take the bait. 'You haven't been able to summon up the power of the Vril, have you, Mr. Fischer? Are you not "racially pure" enough?' She looked down, saw his hand curl into a fist. She hadn't expected it to be this easy.

'No comment,' he said, but now there was aggression in his tone.

She was suddenly in familiar territory. It was time to taunt him. 'So how does it work, Mr. Fischer? You abduct and murder Aryan women, then you absorb their "racial purity"? The power of the Vril is miraculously given to you? You become Superman, the Vril empowering you — is that how it works?'

'No comment,' he answered, but then spat out, 'Stupid woman!' He gave a humourless laugh and looked away, as if everything was beneath him.

In the adjoining room, Leo had noted Fischer's reaction — their assessment of his motives was accurate; he was now more convinced than ever. What he had not said was as important as what he had. He let out a sigh when Jilly wound up the interview. *Go and find the evidence now, Jilly*, he thought to himself.

CHAPTER 33

Day 193
Woodborough Village

Jilly French curled her legs under her on the sofa, reached down, picked up the bottle of wine and filled her glass. The fire was blasting out warmth to counteract the vicious March coldness outside. The retrieval of the wine bottle had disturbed Freud, Leo's Labrador. He circled to his feet and then went to stand by the door. Jilly's eyes flashed to the clock on the mantle. *Nearly ten o'clock*, she thought — the last thing she wanted was to venture out into the cold night.

But she realised her obligation. 'I suppose you've been on your own all day, haven't you, boy?' she said. Stirring herself, she laced up her boots, wrapped a thick scarf around her neck, and put her winter parka over the top. Slipping Freud's lead into his collar, she stepped out into the bitter night.

A flurry of icy rain immediately stung her face. 'I think we'll make this a quick walk, Freud,' she said, but he had other ideas as he tugged her forcefully along the road.

She turned onto Main Street, and they walked in front of St. Swithin's Church, then past The Four Bells Inn, all the while Freud leading the way as they headed towards Woodborough Hall, his usual evening route while staying with Jilly. At the edge of the main village, Jilly saw a man coming the other way, his collar up against the arctic wind, a woolly hat on his head, and his scarf obscuring the lower half of his face. As they passed, he stopped and patted Freud — it was usual in the village, and she thought nothing of it. He took a treat from his pocket, and Freud greedily snatched it and gulped it down. He produced another one, and Freud did the same again.

'Goodnight,' the man said, adding, 'It's a cold one tonight.' With that, he went on his way.

'Night,' Jilly said after him, politely.

They walked on for a hundred yards or so, before Jilly noticed Freud had stopped pulling and they were slowing down. 'Come on, boy,' she said. They reached the gates to the hall, at which point they normally turned around and walked back, but Freud's back legs slumped down.

'What's the matter, boy?' Jilly said, crouching. She rubbed the side of his head to encourage him. He tried to get up, but toppled over onto his side, his eyes distant. Then they closed. Her stomach knotted as she realised there was something badly wrong.

Her mind raced. She needed to get him home. She looked down the street, but it was deserted — no one to help. She considered leaving him, going back to get her car, but she couldn't abandon him, she thought. She took her mobile from her pocket, but Leo was away. Who could she ring? Perhaps Satinder.

Then she saw headlights coming down the road from the village. She considered flagging it down, but then noticed it was slowing down anyway. It came to a stop, a large four-by-four; the door opened and the man in the woolly hat and scarf got out.

'I need your help, sir,' Jilly said. 'My dog has collapsed.'

'I can see that, DI French.'

She was momentarily confused. He had used her name. She tried to see his eyes, but the light was poor. He was probably a villager who had seen her about and made it his business to know her occupation.

'Can you help me get the dog in your car and then give me a lift home?' Her words were businesslike.

'The dog will be okay in an hour or so, Jilly. He only needs to sleep it off.'

Alarm now washed over her — a villager would not know her Christian name, particularly not the familiar version. She got to her feet and stiffened. She had her mobile in her hand and she switched it on swiftly to call for assistance, but the man stepped forward and knocked it violently from her hand. She watched it bounce and disappear in a grassy clump. She stepped back.

'Who are you?' she asked, her voice even.

'Oh, I think you know, DI French.'

And she did. 'Franz Fischer,' she said in a fierce whisper.

'You are a smart woman, Detective Inspector. You taunted me with how astute you had been, didn't you? Your offender profile told you all about me, didn't it? You and Dr. Adams were so smug. You had established my motivation, my type. But you overlooked one thing.'

Jilly couldn't see his eyes clearly in the low light but, nevertheless, she felt them burning into her. He wanted her to engage, to re-establish his dominance over her, she saw that. She said nothing and looked behind to see how much room for manoeuvre she had if it came to a fight.

Fischer answered his own question. 'You have overlooked the fact that *you* fitted *my* profile, Jilly French. Blonde hair, green eyes. I've done my genealogical research — your parents are from a rural Durham village, and so are your grandparents and great grandparents. Your history is racially pure for generations. And you have a sharp mind, too — what more could I want?'

Jilly now went into survival mode. Her eyes darted left and right, up and down the road, but there was no one. She searched her pockets for anything that could be used as a weapon — but there was nothing. She would not be missed until the following morning, she thought; she had to survive the night — somehow. It was a cold March evening — there were few people about, she had walked to a secluded spot, and a pedestrian was unlikely. Perhaps there would be a passing car, somebody wending their way home from the pub. Fischer only had a short window to abduct her, to kill her, then — he must have known that, but he wanted to talk. *His ego is getting in the way of his intellect*, Jilly thought. The longer she could engage him, the more likely it was that a car would come down the road.

'I can't say I'm pleased to be of service,' she said, then bit her bottom lip.

She saw his mouth curl into a sneer. 'Ah, wit in the face of adversity. It gets better.'

Jilly had self-defence training, but this was a powerful man, an ex-rugby player, and he was a martial arts expert. If he killed her, he would be interrogated. She must at least make sure he had signs of a struggle on him — she would scratch his face. *Let him explain that.*

'So, in your crazy world, you will absorb my "racial purity", will you absorb my intelligence, my — chutzpah?'

He grunted. 'Chutzpah is a Yiddish word, my dear. You can do better than that — shall we say, I like your feistiness.'

She had not used a Yiddish word deliberately, but now she latched onto it, saw an opportunity to keep him engaged. 'Need to absorb a bit of chutzpah, do you? Are you running low on chutzpah, then? Will the Vril-ya allow you access to them if you can bring them more chutzpah?'

He gave a hollow laugh. 'Unfortunately, your Dr. Adams has made a mistake in his profile. The abductions are nothing to do with *absorption*, as you put it.'

Jilly started to say more, but over his shoulder, she saw headlights in the distance. Adrenalin kicked in, and she started to circle him, wanting to get to the side of the road. He allowed her to do so, making no attempt to cut her off. She got to the road edge, but the car was still some distance away, its headlights not illuminating her. But in her eagerness, she had made a mistake.

Fischer came up behind her, reached with his right arm over her right shoulder, and hooked the bend of his arm around her neck, the other hand clasped across her mouth. He now dragged her backwards, away from the roadside and into the driveway to the hall, up against the padlocked gates. She tried to reach behind, find his face with her nails — but she couldn't, nor could she shout out. Her eyes bulged in horror as she watched the car pass by. Not only had she missed her chance, but she had failed to defend herself.

Now he let go of her mouth with his left hand, his right hand grasping his own left bicep, and then he placed that left hand against the back of her head. She realised he had done this expertly. It was a choking hold. It would compress her carotid arteries without compressing the airway. It was a technique used in law enforcement; she had been taught it herself. Well applied, the chokehold would lead to unconsciousness in seconds. Her hands came up automatically to her throat, but she felt him apply pressure with his biceps and forearms to both sides of her neck, on her carotid arteries.

Her mind stopped calculating; her vision blurred. Her bulging eyes closed, and her grasping hands eased and fell away.

CHAPTER 34

Day 194
Nottinghamshire CID Central Division

The aroma of hot coffee and croissants accompanied by the buzz of gossip filled the briefing room. It was more pronounced than usual, since DI French was not there to dampen down the enthusiasm. The chatter stopped immediately, however, when DCI McMillan entered. He took up his usual place, perching on the edge of the desk with his leg swinging.

He looked around the briefing room. 'Where's DI French?' he asked.

DS Kaur spoke for the team. 'She's not in yet, Mac,' she said sheepishly, not wanting to get her boss into trouble. 'Might be traffic.'

'Has she rung in?' Mac asked.

'Not as yet,' replied Satinder.

'DS Jackson, will you take the meeting, please?' Mac ordered.

Forty minutes later, Mac looked up at the knock on his office door. It opened and DS Kaur peered round.

'Sir,' she said hesitantly, 'we can't contact DI French.'

Mac waved her in. 'You've tried her phone?'

'Yes, sir. No reply from her home phone and her mobile is going straight to voicemail.'

'Could be a dead battery. What about her partner?'

'I've spoken to Leo. He's away at a conference in Manchester and has been for two days. He said she didn't call him last night, but he assumed she was working late. He's worried now — I've put the wind up him, I think.'

'Okay, get in touch with the phone people. Find out where and when her mobile was last used.'

'Already done that, sir. I'm waiting for them to get back to me.'

Mac saw the concern in her eyes. He, too, had a sinking feeling. 'Keep me informed, will you? And send somebody round to her house.'

'Yes, sir,' she said as she stood. 'I think I'll do that myself.'

Satinder called Mac half an hour later. 'Sir, it's DS Kaur. I'm at Jilly's house.' He could hear her voice quavering over the phone.

'Is she not there?' he asked.

'No, sir, no sign of her.' She hesitated. 'But Leo's dog is sitting by the front door, with the lead still attached to his collar.'

Mac stiffened in his chair and a knot tightened in his stomach. 'I'll get a SOCO team down there right away. See if there is any sign of a break-in, and then you break in if you have to — I want to know if there is any indication of a struggle.'

At noon, Mac stood before the empty whiteboard in the major incident room, his jaw set hard. DI French was one of their own; any professional detachment was cast aside. 'From this moment,' he said, his voice soft yet compelling, 'we are treating this as a major incident.' He had the full attention of everyone. 'I am not bringing in another DI. I'm taking charge. I will be the SIO until DI French is found. DS Kaur, preliminary timeline? What do we have?'

'DI French left the office at six-thirty p.m. last night. Took her own car back to her home in Woodborough, about seven miles from here. We assume she arrived safely because sometime later she took Dr. Adams's Labrador for a walk. She didn't turn up for work this morning, and her car is still in the garage.'

Mac chewed the inside of his cheek. 'What about her mobile?'

'It was turned off at ten-forty-six p.m. — the last location we have for it is a country road near the M1.'

Mac looked up at his team. He knew what that probably meant — *smashed*, and he saw the same thought reflected in the faces of his team.

'Any sign of a break-in?'

'I went in with the SOCO team — they're still there, but I couldn't see anything. It looks as if she was taken last evening, sir, but not from her house.'

'I agree,' whispered Mac, then his professional mind kicked in. 'This is probably work-related. We need to examine the cases she's been working.' He looked around the room for input.

'Come on, Mac. This is Franz Fischer's work — he's got her. We have to get to him before he does for her,' said Pete Reader.

Mac cleared his throat. 'For once, DC Reader, I agree with you. DS Jackson, DCs Reader and Boone, you're with me. Let's get out to his place. DS Kaur, get me a search warrant. Get the magistrate out of his own courtroom if you have to. Ring me as soon as you have it.'

CHAPTER 35

Consciousness returned slowly to DI French. Her eyes opened sluggishly, but she failed to recognise anything around her. Awareness of her situation came gradually. Lying on her back, she looked up and around. She was in some type of chamber, rather than a room, she saw. The walls were decorated in terracotta relief of swords and axes, warriors and raiders, gods and creatures. It was a story of the Norsemen, the people of the north.

There was light, but it was subdued. The whole room had a hue of ochre; it was strange but then relaxing, oddly comforting. Jilly looked down at herself: she was reclining on a bed, but not wearing her own clothes. They had been replaced by a chemise, a loose-fitting dress, hanging from the shoulders and reaching to her ankles. She eased her hand below her waist, felt for her panties — but they had been removed. She had no underwear.

Her hand went to her head; her hair had been plaited into two braids, falling beside her cheeks.

It was disorienting — she sat up on the edge of the bed and forced herself to gather her thoughts. Her mind filled with Franz Fischer, with her abduction, with Freud the Labrador — with her strangulation.

She touched her neck; fear returned to stab her like a rapier. Her mind again went into survival mode. The chamber was sparse: one bed and a bedside cabinet. She bent and opened the drawer — but there was nothing she could defend herself with, only bedding and a replacement dress.

From somewhere she heard the sound of running water. She listened intently — there seemed to be muffled voices. She looked around the terracotta-decorated room; there was only one door. She padded towards it and turned the handle, expecting it to be locked, but it opened. She peered through the crack into a corridor and saw walls decorated with the same terracotta designs. She listened again — there was the sound of a baby crying.

Jilly tiptoed hesitantly into the ochre-hued corridor, following the sound of the baby. She held her breath, her sense of danger rising with each step as she tried to be as silent as she could. After about fifteen feet, the corridor opened into a large, circular chamber. The walls were decorated in a similar way to the chamber she had awoken in: lavishly carved terracotta relief depicted scenes from Norse mythology — ribbon-shaped serpents, entwined gods, mythical animals, swords and axes, warriors and maidens. But at the far end of the chamber, incongruously, was a modern kitchen, complete with an oven and hob, a dishwasher, a fridge, a washing machine, a kitchen table and several chairs. There were two babies in highchairs being fed by two women — their mothers, Jilly assumed. There were two other women present, attending to chores and chatting away. They wore the same dress as Jilly did.

She stared at this absurd scene of domesticity. Her mind and body were alert, in fight or flight mode, like a coiled spring ready for action, but then she'd stumbled on this… What exactly was this?

There was a tightness in her throat, but the words escaped easily. 'I take it one of you ladies is Karrie Talbot?' she said.

The platinum-blonde woman at the sink turned and looked over her shoulder. 'Oh, hello,' she said. 'Yes, I'm Karrie Talbot.'

'And who's Emily Jackson and Caitlin Morgan?' she added.

The two women with babies in highchairs confirmed that they were Emily and Caitlin.

Jilly turned to the fourth woman standing at the hob and eyed her questioningly.

'And I'm Nicole Petersen,' the woman said matter-of-factly. 'I've been here the longest.'

Jilly had not identified Nicole Petersen as a possible abductee.

'I'm a doctor, by the way,' Nicole added. 'I checked you over when Franz brought you in last night. I also undressed you — if you are wondering.'

'And was I…' Jilly struggled with the word.

'Assaulted, you mean? No, you weren't assaulted, but you should prepare yourself, my dear. Your purpose is to breed children for him, as he has from us. My son is three now — he's taking a nap in my room.'

Jilly turned to Karrie, looking down at her stomach.

'Yes, four months gone,' Karrie answered, stroking her tummy.

'Where are we?' Jilly asked, looking around the elaborate chamber.

Karrie answered for them all. 'No idea — all we know is we are underground. There are no windows, and if you cry out for help, no one will come. Either no one can hear us, or there *is* no one to hear us. And I have called out for help, I promise you.'

'You have running water and electricity?' Jilly looked around the kitchen. 'What about food?'

'Yep, water, electricity, even television. He delivers the food and groceries, comes to talk to us about his … beliefs. And then there are the … the initiation sessions.'

'When he rapes you, you mean?'

Karrie looked uncomfortable.

'How often does he come here?'

'Most days, sometimes more than once a day.'

'But he can't do,' said Jilly, confused. 'We've had him under surveillance for weeks.'

'I think you had better tell us who *you* are, my dear,' interrupted Nicole. She gestured for her to sit down.

She sat at the table. 'My name is DI Jilly French. I am a DI leading a major incident team for Nottinghamshire police. I am the senior investigating officer in charge of the abduction of — ' she paused and looked into Karrie's eyes — 'of you, Karrie.'

'So you have identified Franz as a suspect, then?' asked Karrie, her tone rising in astonishment. 'But how? I had never met him before he snatched me.'

'Oh, yes — he's our prime suspect. He fits our profile of the abductor. We identified him from your internet search history, comparing it to the search history of Emily and Caitlin. You'd all been looking at the webpage of a car broker called Valkyrie Classic Cars Ltd. And Valkyrie Classic Cars Ltd is our friend, Franz Fischer.'

'So why didn't you arrest him?' asked Emily.

'Because we haven't been able to find the evidence. Mr. Fischer is a super smart bugger, I promise you.'

'You don't have to tell us that. He says he designed and decorated this place,' Nicole said, looking at the walls with admiration.

'He designed the dress you are wearing, as well,' Caitlin cut across.

Jilly sighed. 'The key problem was that we weren't able to establish the scene of crime, the place where he killed his victims.' She paused, realised what she had said and shot a sheepish look at Karrie. 'Sorry, but, well, that's what we thought — history tells us that if we don't find the victim within seventy-two hours, they are probably dead.'

'But we're clearly not,' said Nicole.

'No — we got that wrong, alright. But we had him under observation, hoping he would lead us to his hideout, but he hardly ever left his house. He did all his business from there. Unless…' She paused. 'This place must be under his house, or one of the outbuildings — it's the only explanation. We took his place apart trying to find some trace of you lot, some forensic evidence — but nothing. We must have been standing directly above you.'

'Are you sure? We didn't hear anything,' said Nicole.

Jilly inclined her head. 'It's the only explanation. He has designed it this way, to be soundproof, and there must be a hidden entrance. Have you searched for a way out?'

'Oh, endlessly,' said Emily. 'You do when you first arrive, until you realise the futility of it. This place is the central chamber, with seven small corridors leading off it — five go to our bedrooms, the sixth is the Black Sun room, and the seventh leads to the entrance — and I assure you there is only one entrance.'

'Have you tried to escape?'

'How? There's a solid metal door with an electronic keypad lock. Only Franz knows the combination.'

'There are *four* of you,' said Jilly. 'Haven't you tried to overpower him?'

'In the past,' answered Nicole, her tone pragmatic, 'but he easily defeated us. He is some sort of martial arts expert, it seems. But that was before we realised…'

'Realised what?' Jilly interrupted.

'Realised what he was trying to achieve here.'

'We attempted to stab him once,' said Caitlin, 'but we weren't allowed sharp knives or scissors, only cutlery knives, and he then took *them* away from us for a couple of months. Preparing food with cutlery knives was bad enough, but without them, it was … well, you can imagine.'

'So you have settled down to accept this hell,' Jilly taunted them.

'Hey,' said Nicole, 'what makes you think this is hell? Franz brings us everything we ask for: food, wine, books, CDs, DVDs, toys for the children. He looks after our health — provides supplements for the children, vitamin pills for us.'

'But you're prisoners of this loony.'

'Yes, we are — but he doesn't treat us badly.'

'He rapes you, for God's sake!'

'It's not rape, it's initiation,' answered Nicole. Jilly could see that she recoiled at the word 'rape'.

'And he doesn't hurt us,' added Emily.

'What?' Jilly was unable to her hide her disbelief.

Emily's face relaxed into a dreamy smile. 'You haven't seen his eyes — when he fixes you with that stare, you feel unable to break away.'

DI French sat back in her chair and looked at each of them with incredulity. She wanted to say they were four intelligent women, that they should be aware of this man's evil, but there was some sort of Stockholm syndrome going on here.

'He's the most well-read man I have ever met,' interrupted Nicole. 'He knows so much about everything. He can discuss medicine with me, and I would swear he was a doctor. I promise you, when you meet him, you'll find him beguiling.'

There it was again, Jilly thought; Nicole was being protective of her captor. Her heart sank — she assumed Fischer had also studied brainwashing techniques, and she wondered how much help she would get from these women when she tried to escape. She had to break through this hold he had on them.

'I *have* met him. I have interviewed him three times,' she said. She sought out the eyes of each of her fellow captives, trying to gauge how much influence Fischer had on them. 'He's a condescending, delusional, alpha-male toerag with crackpot ideas about "racial purity" and the occult.' She spat out the words, then wondered if she had overdone it.

Each woman reacted differently. Karrie sat back in her chair, her eyebrows arching — she had been there the shortest time, Jilly considered, and was perhaps most likely to resist his indoctrination. Emily looked visibly deflated, as though the light in her world had been dimmed. Caitlin was harder to read; she seemed ambivalent, but Nicole's hand curled into a fist as she gave Jilly a hostile stare.

'Look, DI French,' she said, 'Mr. Fischer is the only person I have ever met that I can attach the word *genius* to. We are privileged to be part of his quest. What he is doing here is actually beautiful.'

'So you are privileged to be raped by him, are you?'

Nicole shuddered. Jilly could see desperation in her eyes. She was caught between one thing and another. She had been indoctrinated to the point where she was comfortable with her situation, even happy and fulfilled, but now she was forced to defend Fischer's rape of the women. Her emotional link to Fischer was still strong, but her rational mind could not find the words to justify what he did.

Eventually, Nicole's frustration turned into belligerence. She stood up, her chair falling behind her. 'You can't possibly understand this remarkable man!' she shrieked.

The babies were startled and began to cry. Emily and Caitlin leaned over to pacify them.

'I understand that this *brilliant* man has a set of nonsense ideas. He believes there is a hidden power that can be harnessed by the right sort of "racially pure" person. And he wants to be that man. In his mind, he has to validate his sociopathic behaviour, so he focuses on any piece of information that justifies this nonsense, and ignores anything that contradicts his delusional beliefs. For goodness' sake, woman, he is a pathological liar. Franz Fischer is not even his real name — it's plain Frank, Frank Fisher without the C.'

Emily and Caitlin took their babies from the highchairs to calm them — Jilly's words had bypassed them. Nicole and Karrie were the only ones still taking notice. Jilly looked at Karrie and noticed she was taken aback by her words, but when she looked at Nicole, she saw only animosity. Her hero had been challenged. She stormed away to her bedchamber.

CHAPTER 36

DCI McMillan, DS Jackson, DC Reader and DC Boone sat in the pool car on the gravel drive outside Fischer's house. They had been there for 25 minutes. Mac chewed the inside of his cheek, and the other three shuffled in their seats, irritated and anxious. There had been no indication that Fischer had noted their arrival, but Mac assumed they were on his surveillance cameras. Then his phone rang.

'DCI McMillan,' he answered, the words fired like bullets.

'Got it, sir — the search warrant,' said DS Kaur.

'Okay, bring it here ASAP.' The four police officers strode across the gravel, and the knocker of the solid wood door was rapped forcefully. Mac moved his weight from foot to foot as he waited; it felt endless, though it was only a matter of seconds. He heard the bolts shoot, and the door opened. Fischer stood there, as immaculate as usual.

Mac brandished his warrant card, identified himself and his colleagues, and fixed Fischer with a hard stare. 'I have a warrant to search these premises.'

'Can I see it, please?' Fischer said calmly.

'It's on its way,' Mac replied.

'Then when it arrives, I'll check it over.' Fischer's words showed the arrogance of a man in control.

He moved to close the door, but Mac pushed back at it with his shoulder, putting his body in the entrance. Fischer, visibly taken aback, let go of the door as Mac forced his way in. The other three followed him.

'My SOCO team will be here shortly, Mr. Fischer,' Mac added.

'You can expect another compensation claim,' Fischer called after him as Mac strode into his house.

McMillan ignored him, scanned the house from his position in the hall, and directed his team to various rooms. 'Be thorough; miss nothing,' he said. 'Jilly's life depends on you.' He'd called her Jilly — he never did that, and they all noticed the change.

'Yes, Mac,' they replied.

After an hour, they had still found nothing. The SOCO team were on site, dusting for fingerprints, taking photographs, looking for DNA traces. Fischer sat in his office, the smug expression on his face suggesting they would find nothing, Mac thought. He could have punched him, but there was work to do.

He called the station as his anxiety rose, requesting more officers, more resources. 'I want every floorboard taken up,' he said, 'and the loft examined in detail.' When this failed to reveal anything, he turned his attention to the outbuildings. He sent the SOCO team — there was a double garage, and one of the annexe buildings was also used as a garage.

'I want soil samples from the car wheels,' he shouted at the SOCO team leader, 'and get them back to your lab. I want a check against the soil at Woodborough.'

The SOCO man ground his teeth and thought about telling Mac that he was the scientist, better able to determine what tests to undertake, but he thought better of it. He could see the anxiety mounting on Mac's face.

However, he was back in a matter of minutes. 'Mac,' he said, rubbing his jaw, 'there are no soil samples to be taken from the tyres. All the cars have been thoroughly cleaned, right down to the tyres and wheel arches.'

'What cars are out there?' Mac asked.

'Three classics in the annexe, an Aston Martin Virage Volante, a Bentley Pininfarina Cresta and a Ferrari 246GT Dino. I think we can assume they haven't been out of the annexe all winter.'

'What about the others?' Mac pressed.

'In the garage, there's a Bentley Continental Flying Spur and a Mercedes GLS Coupé SUV,' answered the SOCO man.

Mac thought the Mercedes was the most likely to have been used, unless he had another car tucked away somewhere else. 'Get the Police Recovery Operatives to get that Mercedes into the police workshops. I want it forensically examined. I want any trace of DNA found.'

Mac feared there was nothing to be found here. Fischer had not brought DCI French back here at all. *The smug bastard*, he thought — *he's still hiding the scene of crime from us.* Horrible thoughts danced in his mind — bloodied clothes, a terrified face, eyes bulging in horror. He shook his head, trying to cast them away. He realised he had to be as cunning as Fischer. He must assume Jilly was not dead, he told himself — and if she was still alive, the longer he could hold Fischer, the more chance they would have of finding her alive. If he arrested him now, he would have 36 hours, and with a magistrate's approval, he could extend that, perhaps, to 96 hours. Fischer was coming back with him to the station.

CHAPTER 37

Jilly lay on her bed. She had tried to sleep, but her mind raced. Why were these women so in awe of Fischer? Why were his brainwashing techniques so successful? They were extremely intelligent, high achievers. They were not the sort to be brainwashed so easily. Then she realised. What was it Nicole had said? Oh yes, Fischer was bringing them *vitamins*. He was drugging them, bit by bit. What was that new Columbian drug? Jilly racked her brains — she had been told of it at a seminar. The Devil's Breath — she couldn't remember its chemical name, but it eliminated free will. It was made from the seeds of a South American tree, she recalled. *I bet it's that*, she thought, resolving not to take any of the vitamins — but now she had a more immediate problem.

Fischer would arrive soon to rape her. She had to formulate a plan to protect herself, but every scenario she considered ended in failure. She looked at her wrist, then realised her watch had been taken. Time deprivation was a brainwashing technique, she knew, but then she remembered there was a television in the main chamber — time awareness was available to them. That meant — what did that mean? She wasn't sure. Then she heard voices from the main chamber; she swivelled her legs off the bed, stood up and padded to the door. She opened it slightly and tried to listen, but she couldn't make out the words. The tone was clearly agitated.

She walked through and stood at the end of the corridor.

Karrie Talbot was the first to notice her. 'Hi,' she said, her face open and welcoming. The others were more circumspect, unsure of the woman before them.

Jilly took it as an invitation anyway and sat at the table. 'What time is it?' she asked.

'Seven-thirty,' said Nicole Petersen conversationally, but there was still hostility in her expression.

There was an uneasy silence, as though Jilly had interrupted their conversation. She took the opportunity to look at each of them in turn. Physically, they were like peas in a pod. All four were blonde-haired and blue-eyed, though their hair shades varied from Karrie's platinum blonde to Nicole's medium blonde — Caitlin's was an ash tone, and Emily's was flaxen. Their body language defined them more at that moment, though. Karrie was open and inviting and Caitlin was neutral, but Emily was wary of her, and Nicole was clearly defensive. But there was something more, something indefinable about them — they were a community, Jilly decided. They had bonded; they would defend each other. If she wanted their help, she would have to gain their collective acceptance, become part of the group.

Jilly decided to take the bull by the horns. 'What were you guys talking about?'

Nicole turned away to the kitchen sink, making a pretence of washing a pan. She wasn't going to engage without coaxing, it seemed. The other three looked at each other, but Karrie Talbot answered for them.

'Franz is late. He said he would be here at six — he's never late.'

'He always comes at six?'

'No — he keeps to his own schedule, but he told us to prepare for...' She didn't complete the sentence, and glances were exchanged with the others.

Jilly held Karrie's eyes firmly, leaned forward, and pushed one plait away from her face, looping it around her ear. 'To prepare for what?' she demanded.

It was Nicole who answered. 'To prepare for your initiation,' she said over her shoulder. Then she nodded towards the seventh room.

A knot tightened in Jilly's stomach. 'The Black Sun room,' she exclaimed. 'What exactly goes on in there?'

'Tonight is going to be your initiation,' said Nicole, gesturing towards a peg on the wall. 'That's your cape there, the white one. You'll need to wear it.'

'And the other capes?' Jilly nodded at the other black cloaks hung beside it.

'They are for us.'

'So you will take part in this initiation, will you? When he rapes me?' Jilly made no attempt to hide her anger, her revulsion. Then she realised her hostility wouldn't help with the bonding.

'It's part of our journey as Applicants — so that we will be admitted to the Vril-ya when the time comes.' Nicole's tone was positive; there was no hint of self-consciousness at the nonsense she was repeating.

'So, the Black Sun room is where all his crackpot rituals take place, is it?' Jilly bit her lip — again, she'd been unable to hold back her hostility.

'It's a truth that goes back thousands of years. When you have studied it, you'll come to appreciate it's not *crackpot* at all.'

'It's only natural you should be anxious about your initiation,' Karrie cut across Nicole. 'I was petrified. But the initiation was … uplifting. He made me feel like I was taking part in something special.'

Jilly tried to change tack and forced herself to be more agreeable. 'So, tell me all about it.'

Nicole answered for them. 'Well, we will be there, holding your hands as Franz goes through the rituals. We will chant in the Old Norse language he has taught us. Then he will cast the runestones and read them. He will worship the whiteness of your breasts with his hands, then the whiteness of your thighs, as a pure, Aryan woman, then all the other parts of your body. Then we will worship his phallus as the bringer of the pure, Aryan life to us all. At some time during the ritual, he will connect with the Vril, and at the moment of climax he will briefly transform into a Vril-ya.'

DI French was momentarily speechless. The meaning of this sexual ritual was not lost on her. As a police detective, she had studied such rituals, and discussed them at great length with Leo in this particular case. They were part of the psychopath's sexual need. The other women had fallen for Fischer's devious claims, but Jilly saw the ritual for what it was.

CHAPTER 38

DCI McMillan and DS Kaur entered the interview room, sat at the table, and placed their files before them. Mac switched on the tape recorder and spoke. 'Interview commencing at seven-thirty-six p.m. on the twenty-fourth of March 2020. Present, Mr. Franz Fischer, DCI Donald McMillan, and DS Satinder Kaur. This interview is done under caution. For the purposes of the tape, Mr. Fischer, can you confirm that you have been given written notice of your rights, they have been explained to you and that you have declined your right to legal representation? You have also rejected your right to be advised by the duty solicitor.'

'Blah-di-blah-di-blah,' answered Fischer, feigning a condescending yawn, as if he had heard it all before — which he had. 'Yes, that's correct.' He leaned forward, placing his elbows firmly on the table between them so that his face was only a couple of feet from Mac's.

Mac, holding his stare, also moved forward so that the distance between them closed further. He knew all about body language, how to negate it. 'Can you tell me where you were last night, Mr. Fischer, from six p.m. until eight a.m. this morning?'

Fischer relinquished his position, realising he no longer had dominance. He leaned back in his chair, adopting an air of indifference. 'At home, working,' he said, 'then I went to bed about twelve-thirty.'

'Are there any witnesses to confirm that, Mr. Fischer?'

'No — no witnesses, but then, I don't need them, do I?'

'When was the last time you saw DI Jill French?' Mac's voice was silky.

'Oh, I had the pleasure of meeting her in this delightfully decorated room,' Fischer sneered, looking around to emphasise his dislike, 'last November, I think it was?'

'You haven't seen her since?'

'No, I haven't had that pleasure.'

There was a knock on the door, and DS Jackson put his head round it. 'Sir?' he said.

'Interview suspended at … seven-forty-six ,' Mac said, moving to the door.

Outside, he confronted Jackson — his momentum had been interrupted. 'What is it, Detective Sergeant?'

'Dr. Adams, sir — he's back from Manchester. He wants to sit in on the interview.'

'Where is he?'

'I've put him in the next room, sir. He's observing through the video link. I wasn't sure what you would think about him sitting in — with him being romantically linked to Jilly.'

Mac rubbed his chin, contemplating the problem. The door opened, and Leo joined them. 'I need to be with you for this interview, Mac,' he said.

'I think you are too close to this, Leo. It's better if you observe. You can call me out if there is something you want me to challenge him on.'

'We're all too close, Mac. We're all emotionally connected to Jilly. Me romantically, you as a colleague. I will be as detached and professional as you are, I promise you.'

Mac could see the truth in his words. He tried to gauge his mental state, his emotional control. 'Very well,' he said, 'but as an observer. If you have anything to say, say it through me.'

Leo nodded. His intention was to be compliant, but his hands curled into fists.

'Interview recommenced at … seven-fifty-two,' Mac said. 'Dr. Leo Adams is also now present.'

Fischer sneered at Leo, looking him up and down.

Mac decided to change tack. He had read Jill's report of her interview with Fischer's parents when they had identified the tattoo as the Black Sun. Since then, he had been diligent with his research, reading about the mythical Vril. 'Edward Bulwer-Lytton,' he continued, leaning back in his chair. 'What do you know about him?' He saw the surprise on Fischer's face.

'What about him?'

Mac knew he had no evidence to place Fischer at the abduction scene. If Fischer followed his usual plan of action, to offer no information, to merely say *no comment*, then he would have nothing to challenge him on. He had to work on his ego, he thought — that was his Achilles heel. 'So you know about him?'

'English, nineteenth-century author,' Fischer said.

'Not German, then?' Mac prodded. He saw Fischer sneer, as if that were a cheap shot unworthy of his response. Mac re-evaluated — he had to be cleverer. 'Author of *The Coming Race*, published in 1871. It's about an adventurer who stumbles into a subterranean world occupied by beings that resemble angels. They call themselves the Vril-ya and they have telepathic abilities and extraordinary mental powers.'

'You *have* read it?'

'Yes,' said Mac, 'does that surprise you?'

'What — that policemen can read? Yes, it is surprising.'

Mac went on. 'The Vril-ya are descendants of an ancient civilisation who live in subterranean caverns linked by tunnels, but they were originally surface dwellers who fled underground to escape the great flood, where they developed their immense power to overcome the harsh conditions. They built an advanced utopian society based on an energy source that fuelled their powers — they called this the Vril.'

Fischer's eyebrow arched, then he nodded. 'A reasonable summary,' he said, but his words were still laced with condescension.

'But there was a problem for our adventurer, wasn't there? To control the Vril energy, you had to be... What did Bulwer-Lytton describe it as? Oh yes, *spiritually elevated.* Not for the common man, then?'

A humourless smile crossed Fischer's face. 'No, not for the ordinary amongst us,' he answered, giving Mac a withering look, which he then transferred to Leo.

'Why not, Franz?'

'It needs a strong hereditary constitution.' There was a perverse pride in his words.

Go on, thought Mac, *let your ego do the talking.* 'Hereditary constitution? What does that mean?'

Fischer leaned forward. 'It means racially pure.' The phrase was spat out, each syllable enunciated.

'It's a fine story, Mr. Fischer,' said Leo, 'but it's just that, isn't it? A story. Bulwer-Lytton wrote it as a novel, didn't he?'

'Or is the novel based on occult truth, an older truth, that the twenty-first century has forgotten? Bulwer-Lytton studied the occult and Nordic mythology extensively, just as I have. Did he put forward his ideas via the medium of the novel form? Yes, he did. That's why he published it anonymously. It was only later that his identity as the author was established.'

Mac paused for a moment and put his thoughts in order. 'The Vril women were larger and stronger than the men, weren't they?'

Fischer stiffened and hesitated, but then he sneered again. 'Yes, they were,' he answered.

'Is that why you feel a need to kill intelligent, capable Aryan women, Mr. Fischer — so that you can take on their power?'

'That would be a ludicrous course of action,' Fischer snapped.

'Why is that?'

'Because it is based on primitive beliefs.'

'Like the tribes that once engaged in cannibalism, you mean?' Mac said. 'Eating your enemy in the belief it will endow you with their powers?'

'Yes, that sort of thing.'

'So you don't believe in such primitive beliefs?'

'No, of course not.'

'But you defended Bulwer-Lytton. What was it you said? Oh, yes — the novel is based on an older truth, a truth that the twenty-first century has forgotten. How does that differ from *primitive* beliefs, Mr. Fischer?'

That thin, humourless smile returned — he was not going to be caught out that easily. 'I said an *old* truth, not a primeval one. Truths established by men of learning over thousands of years — there were such men before our time, I assure you. We now worship technological knowledge. We have forgotten an older wisdom.'

'Men of learning … like Himmler and Herman Wirth, you mean?' Mac's words were derisory.

For once, Fischer didn't have a response ready. 'No, not like them,' was all he could say.

'Tell me about Himmler and Herman Wirth, Mr. Fischer,' said Mac.

But Fischer just stared back, as if he could see the trap but was not sure how to avoid it.

Mac went on, 'They had the same whacky ideas as you, didn't they, Mr. Fischer? They believed in the superiority of the Aryan race, so what did they do, Mr. Fischer?'

Fischer continued to sit silently.

'What did they do, Mr. Fischer?' Again, no response. 'Wirth faked his archaeology in Sweden, didn't he, with the connivance of his master, Heinrich Himmler, to try to prove that the Aryan race was descended from the people of Atlantis. Is that the sort of old wisdom that you are talking about?'

Fischer leaned back in his chair, again feigning disinterest, but Mac knew he was shaken.

'First-year students of archaeology study those two bozos at university. The dangers of pseudo-archaeology are prescribed reading.' Mac paused, then went at him again. 'So, if it wasn't some wise old truth from men like Wirth, why *did* you kill these women?'

'Phaw!' Fischer blurted. He dropped his eyes and gazed at the table, as if the question was not worthy of him.

'Have you ever been a member of any secret societies, Mr. Fischer?' Mac smoothly changed tack again.

'Such as?' Fischer was clearly not going to volunteer information.

'The Vril Society?'

'Does it still exist?' Fischer snapped back, inclining his head.

'You tell me, Mr. Fischer. You have travelled extensively in Germany, Scandinavia. Did you attend any meetings while you were there?'

'No comment.'

'What about the Thule Society or the Black Sun Society?'

'No comment.'

'What about the Hermetic Order of the Golden Dawn?'

'Oh please!' grunted Fischer, as if such a thought was contemptible.

'But you have studied these secret societies?'

'I have studied German and Norse history.'

'You say history, not mythology?'

'The two words overlap.'

Leo made a note and slid it sideways across the table to Mac. He glanced down, read it, and decided to go with the prompt.

'"Racial purity", Mr. Fischer. Do you believe it is important?'

'No comment.'

'Your father says you believe in it.'

Fischer's expression darkened. It was as if some invisible barrier had been breached, a line crossed. 'No comment.' The words were now spat out.

For the first time, Mac saw that Fischer was riled. He knew he had to goad him further. 'Why is it important to you, Mr. Fischer? You split with your wife because of it, didn't you?'

'No comment.'

'Is it because you have to be "racially pure", to have a *strong hereditary constitution*? And you need that to connect with the Vril-ya, to have access to their Vril power source?'

'No comment.'

'Mr. Fischer, isn't it true that, despite your eidetic memory, your years of study, your "racial purity", all the rituals you have performed, you have been unable to connect to these mythical people?'

'They are not mythical,' Fischer blurted out.

He had finally lost it, Mac saw. He would press his advantage. 'You cannot face the fact that you have been wrong all this time, can you?' He turned to Leo. 'What's it called, Dr. Adams?'

'It's called cognitive dissonance, Mac.'

'I know what cognitive dissonance is,' said Fischer.

'Do you recognise it in yourself, then?' Mac pressed. 'You have that internal strife, don't you? You have accepted this mythology, this Vril-ya, but you haven't been able to connect to it, have you? So you have to get rid of this internal discord, but instead of accepting you have been wrong all this time, you have added a new explanation. You have convinced yourself that you haven't failed; you're just not *spiritually elevated* enough. Is that how it works, Mr. Fischer? You abduct and kill women to reduce your internal dilemma?' He turned to Leo. 'Isn't that how it goes, Dr. Adams?'

'Absolutely, DCI McMillan — a classic case of cognitive dissonance, leading to psychotic behaviour.'

The words hit Fischer as if, for the first time in his life, he had seen his own true reflection. He swallowed and looked at the ceiling.

'It doesn't hurt to take a good look at yourself from time to time,' Mac said, pressing home his point.

Leo passed him another note — it merely said *Superman*, but he knew what Leo meant.

'How does it feel, to know you will never be able to attain what you are striving for?'

'And what exactly is it you think I am *striving* for?' Fischer affected an amused look.

'Why, Mr. Fischer — you want to be Superman, don't you? Having a powerful intellect, an eidetic memory, "racial purity", a successful business, money — all of these are not good enough for you, are they? You want to be Superman, you want super-human powers. You want people to bend the knee before you, don't you?'

Fischer exchanged glances with Mac and Leo. He opened his mouth to speak, but no words came. He crossed his legs and sat back in his chair. Mac knew he would now revert to his "no comment" responses.

'Interview concluded at eight-forty-five p.m.,' he said, turning off the tape.

Outside, DS Kaur looked at her boss with admiring eyes. She thought she had witnessed a masterclass in incisive interrogation, and Mac hadn't even raised his voice. 'That was brilliant, sir.'

'Thank you, DS Kaur.' He didn't feel elated. 'But we still have nothing to pin on the condescending bugger, do we?'

'What exactly was your strategy in there?' Leo asked.

'At this point, just to get Franz to enter into a dialogue. If all we get from him is *no comment*, then we will have nothing to take to a magistrate, and he'll walk in thirty-six hours.'

'You'll try the magistrate, though, Mac?'

'Oh, yes,' he said, but his tone was unconvincing.

'So what now, Mac?'

'We start again in an hour, go over it all again, bruise his ego — shred it, if we can. We work through the night if necessary.'

CHAPTER 39

Day 195

Jilly lay on her bed. She had slept little and thought it might be about 5.30 a.m. Her mind had raced throughout the night, and she had decided her best option was to try and find a way out. She turned off her bedside light, not wanting it to spill out into the corridor, and she walked to her door, opening it slightly. She needn't have bothered — the hallway was permanently lit. She listened — it was quiet. She padded down the corridor to the main chamber and peered in, but it was empty. The others had not stirred yet — that was good, as she wanted to explore before they rose, unsure of the help she would get.

Jilly tried to get her bearings. Seven corridors, she had been told, five leading to bedrooms — these were easy to identify, the corridors were no more than fifteen feet or so, the same layout as her own bedchamber. That left two, the Black Sun room and the hallway leading to the entrance. She took the corridor closest to her room. She explored it hesitantly; there was a gentle S-curve, so she couldn't see the end from the chamber but, about thirty-five feet in, the corridor ended with a door. And emblazoned on it was an image of a black sun.

She approached, looking behind her to confirm she was not being observed. Then she saw her own footprints. She realised, in her anxiety, she was perspiring profusely, and the sweat was causing the prints. She took a deep breath, pressed her ear against the door and turned the handle, expecting it to be locked, but it opened.

She eased herself through the crack, closed the door behind her and leaned her back against it. She realised she had been holding her breath and exhaled deeply. But when she took in the room before her, she inhaled again at the sight. The chamber was circular, about twenty feet in diameter, and domed. The dome was a representation of the Black Sun, the terracotta having been painted that colour. In the centre, about five feet in diameter, was a smaller circle painted yellow, to represent… What did it represent? An iris, perhaps. Around its circumference were painted red plumes, and they reached down the circular walls.

Jilly was no expert in architectural styles, but it seemed to her to be a fusion of Celtic revival with its interlaced images, and Nordic visual metaphors. The motifs, to her eye, were Scandinavian, lavishly carved decorations in terracotta relief — more elaborate than those in her bedchamber. In front of the walls stood four alabaster statues, spaced equidistantly as though at the four points of a compass. They looked like beautiful Nordic angels, standing almost ten feet tall. *They probably represent the Vril-ya*, Jilly thought — *and I bet that bugger sculpted them himself.* At the far end, there appeared to be an altar: an oblong piece of marble, six feet by three, maybe, standing three feet above the ground, but there was no indication that this room was in any way Christian; it looked more pagan.

A realisation made her shudder. It wasn't an altar of prayer to a pagan god. It was the ritual place of impregnation. This was where Fischer would rape her. She tried to dispel this horrible image. 'Not if I can help it, Herr Fischer,' she said out loud.

She left the Black Sun room, returning to the main chamber, and took the last passage. It too had an S-curve, then it straightened out, and after forty feet she was confronted with a solid metal door, as Emily had said. It looked like the door to a security vault controlled by an electronic keypad lock. There was a raised step, and Jilly surmised there were stairs on the other side leading up to ground level, coming out … where? Probably to a hidden entrance in Fischer's house somewhere.

Then she noticed a small, sliding door to the side of the main door, about two feet square. She slid it back to reveal a shaft. She put her head inside and looked upwards, but there was not enough light to see the top. She knew at once it was a dumb waiter; a food lift to get provisions down from the surface. They hadn't told her about this. She tried to get inside, to measure herself against the width of the shaft, but no matter how hard she tried, she couldn't get her legs in — she wasn't supple enough. Who was the smallest? Emily? Could she persuade her to get in after they had emptied the waiter of its provisions? She put that thought on the back-burner, as she thought Emily wouldn't do this willingly.

She stepped back, took in the scene, and tried to formulate a plan. She saw no way of opening this heavy door, but … but perhaps she could ambush Fischer as he came in. He was a martial arts expert, though. She would not be able to overpower him; she needed a weapon — but what? *Come on, Jilly*, she said to herself — she had investigated so many crimes. *What weapons do people use in the heat of the moment?* Cutlery had been tried and had failed. A sharp edge would be good, but Fischer had stripped his hidden world of any such thing. She needed a heavy object to use as a club. She would search this cavern for anything that would be weighty enough.

CHAPTER 40

Day 195

'What's our strategy this time, Mac?' Leo was looking for reassurance. They were all tired, running on adrenalin, but they knew Fischer would be in the same boat.

'It'll be the third interview in the last twelve hours. We go over everything again, and then again and again if necessary.'

'There were signs Fischer's grip is beginning to loosen, did you notice, Mac?'

'Oh, yeah, I noticed. Fischer is the brightest bugger I've ever interviewed, but he's also the most arrogant. That's his Achilles heel. He didn't think we had the ability to trip him up intellectually, but now he knows we can. His self-esteem will have lessened — he'll have been dwelling on that all night. We press that home — do you agree, Dr. Adams?'

'Absolutely, Mac. Fischer is a complicated character, a sociopath, but he's struggling with his internal cognitive dissonance. And paradoxically, I think he also has a narcissistic personality disorder. It's all there — exaggerated feelings of self-importance, taking advantage of people around him, the pursuit of power, the importance of the way he looks.'

'Does he recognise that in himself?'

'People with the disorder frequently do not consider themselves to have a problem, and Fischer is no different. But I think we have punctured some of his arrogance — I agree we have to twist that dagger.'

'In what way?'

'It's the other edge of the sword, Mac. People with NPD also exhibit an inability to tolerate criticism, and a tendency to belittle others in an attempt to validate their own superiority.'

'You mean their ego is fragile?'

'I mean exactly that.'

'Then we are agreed — we go for the throat?'

Leo nodded.

Mac smiled; this was his territory. But then reality sliced through and a knot tightened in his stomach. There was still no crime scene, no forensics, no fingerprints, no DNA.

'What's the matter, Mac?' Leo asked. 'We're making progress, aren't we?'

'Yes, progress — of a sort,' he said, but his tone was less than convincing. 'But disparaging this guy is not enough. We need evidence, Leo — he has been in custody for twelve hours. Unless we get something, anything, he walks tomorrow.'

Leo grunted in acknowledgement and clenched his fists.

Mac turned to DS Kaur. 'Okay, Satinder, let's get the bugger in again.'

Unusually, there was no chatter when Mac entered the incident room. Everyone was quiet in their anxiety. Mac went straight to the whiteboard and tapped his knuckles on the picture of Franz Fischer.

He briefed the team about the three interrogations so far. He could see the satisfaction on their faces that Fischer had been brought down a peg or two. But that was not what he wanted.

'We know what this fucker is, guys. He's a super smart bugger with horrific crackpot ideas. Dr. Adams says he has a narcissistic personality disorder. We've managed to puncture that arrogance, but that's not enough. So he still walks tomorrow, and I don't have to remind you what that means —

he'll do for DI French if he hasn't already. I need you to revisit your research, look for anything we may have missed, something we can charge him with, or can take to a magistrate to ask for an extension so that we can keep him longer.

'DC Book,' he said, turning to the computer whizz kid with the backward baseball cap. Book sat up and turned the cap the right way round. 'See if you can connect Fischer to any organisation using the symbol of the Black Sun.

'DS Kaur, go back to his bank accounts, especially his expenditure. Anything that might suggest he owns another property — or anything that simply looks unusual.'

Mac looked up at his team. They were good, but he needed more from them. He clapped his hands. 'Come on, guys,' he said, 'we need to find something.'

PART 5: THE GIRL FROM THE PAST

CHAPTER 41

Thursday, 26th March 2020

I'd gone into work after picking up a strange email from DCI McMillan. I had been musing over it for about an hour or so when James Postlethwaite came bursting into my office. I knew why he was here — he had been copied into the email. He'd guessed I would come into the university. He pulled a seat up next to mine and saw, over my shoulder, the email open on my computer screen.

'What do you think?' he asked, enthusiasm emanating from every pore. 'This will be good for your book,' he added without waiting for an answer.

'I think we should concentrate on helping the police first,' I snapped. 'They want my help in getting something to pin on their suspect — some guy called Franz Fischer.'

'Yes, yes, you're right, Toby,' he said. 'There's a life at stake here, isn't there?'

'They haven't released news of this abduction to the public yet,' I added, 'but to ask for my help suggests they are desperate. The DCI is looking for anything he can take to the magistrate to keep Fischer in custody.'

'And have you anything for him?'

'I'm desperate to help, but I've been racking my brains, James. I can't think of anything.'

'What about your translation of the chronicle — anything more about Margaret?'

'Yes, but it doesn't help. You remember Abbot Stephen was reluctant to accept Margaret as a novice because she had been convicted, by the Church, of being a witch? He didn't know how that could be cast aside.'

'Yeah, it was an ecclesiastical dilemma for him.'

'Right, well, he must have resolved it. After a year, he allowed her to enter the Order as a novice. She became a nun some years later. She disappears from the chronicle then, so I assume she lived out her life as an ordinary nun devoted to the Order.'

'Hardly your regular nun,' James said, 'but I see what you mean.' I nodded my agreement, but my mind was elsewhere. James must have noticed that. 'What are you up to?' he asked.

'You remember Margaret's story after she had been to the Easter Sunday service?'

'You mean when she went back to the copse, where she met a man who said he was from the year 2020 and knew her name?'

'Yeah — that's right. She thought he was an angel from God, and he said he had come to speak to her. He asked her to show him where the lady angel had been taken.'

'Yeah, go on.'

'I've been checking the date of Easter Sunday in 1152 — it was the twenty-ninth of March.' I paused, unsure what I was suggesting. 'Well, this Sunday is the twenty-ninth of March — what if she will appear then? What if *I* am the man she met from 2020?'

James whistled. 'That's an accumulation of — "ifs" — Toby,' he said, rubbing his chin, 'and I'll give you some more. *If* time travel is actually possible. *If* you jump to the same day in different years. *If* you can find her when she appears. *If* you can understand what she says and vice-versa.'

'I know, I know, James,' I said. 'I've been sitting here for the last hour telling myself the same thing. Damn it! I'm supposed to be a detached professional historian.'

'On the other hand, what have you got to lose?' There was mischief in his tone. 'And if you *do* find her, who is more likely to understand her than you — you're a medievalist, aren't you?'

'True, but even that won't be easy.'

'But you *have* studied Middle English, haven't you?'

'Yeah, but it was developing all the time, you know that. We now use the term *Middle English* to refer to the varieties of the English language spoken after the Norman conquest of 1066 until the late fifteenth century.'

'So when is Middle English dated from?'

'It's a bit nebulous, but the scholarly view is that it developed from 1150 through to about 1500.'

'And Margaret says her vision was in…'

'Easter 1152,' I answered.

'So right at the beginning of Middle English,' James said, nodding. 'I see your point.'

'It's even more complicated than that. Middle English was the consequence of the adoption into English of Norman French. It's a sort of Anglo-Norman, but it was hardly ever written down. There's virtually no standard Middle English to study. And as it developed, it was mainly used by the ruling classes — for politics, the law, that sort of thing.'

'And Margaret is a peasant Anglo-Saxon, not a Norman.'

'Exactly. Her everyday English may still have been profoundly Old English, Germanic in origin with perhaps Old Norse influences. And there were many regional dialects, different inflections, and different pronunciations.'

'Not easy, I see that — but you also have knowledge of Old English, don't you?'

'Yeah, I do,' I said.

'So, as I say, you're just the man, Toby.' James patted me on the back.

I gave him a hesitant smile. I *was* the best equipped man to meet Margaret, I could see that, but all these obstacles were swirling around in my mind. And then there was the absurdity of the whole conversation — it was based on the assumption that time travel was possible, and I still didn't quite believe that.

CHAPTER 42

Sunday, 29th March 2020

That saying came to my mind: *March comes in like a lion and goes out like a lamb.* It had been bitterly cold for a week, but the old adage seemed to be coming true. The wind swirled, but there was no icy sting to it. The trees and bushes were still bare, but the buds promised new life. Snowdrops and crocuses caught my eye.

I looked down at my feet; my boots were covered in mud, and it had splashed up my trousers. Fatigue was beginning to take me. I had walked around the village of Wellow, up to the A616 Nottingham Road, six times. And each time I walked up and down the road searching for a sight of — well, what was I searching for? A young girl dressed in medieval garb. I was starting to feel ridiculous.

I had varied my route along the rustic trails and paths around to the village, but there was no guarantee that they were the same as those that had existed in 1152. I looked at my watch — 5.30 p.m. I was hungry. I was thirsty; I had finished, hours ago, the coffee in the vacuum flask. Sunset was scheduled for 6.28 p.m. I shivered; I had not been bitterly cold, but now I'd been out in the open for eight hours. Every inch of me wanted to give up and go home — but I was determined to stay until the light failed.

Monday dawned overcast and drizzly. I had crawled out of bed, breakfasted and made a flask of coffee and sandwiches. I was more prepared for nine hours outdoors than yesterday. I left my car in Wellow and was walking in the open countryside by nine. I followed the same routine as the previous day, walking along pathways around the village to take me towards the A616, but I found nothing all morning. That feeling of ridiculousness was back. I stopped for lunch, sitting on a stone mound.

I took a bite from my sandwich and a sip of hot coffee, but I stopped chewing abruptly. I had heard something; I listened intently. It was the sound of singing; a young girl's voice floated on the breeze. I stood, looking around tentatively, crouching near the bushes — then I saw her.

I felt my skin goose-pimple, my face suffuse. I tried to keep myself hidden so as not to frighten her. She was diminutive, barely five feet tall, looking no more than twelve years old, but I knew from the chronicle she was fifteen. She wore a sleeveless surcoat of homespun, undyed wool, a voluminous garment open at the sides, covering her from neck to mid-calf. Beneath the surcoat, I could see a long tunic, belted at the waist, which looked like it was made of the same material. It was basic, without any embroidery — I remembered her father was a weaver and he had probably made the peasant outfit. She also wore winingas, strips of cloth wound around the lower leg to keep her warm in winter. Her hair was not visible, her head being covered by a headrail.

I watched her for a time. She was engrossed, as if looking for something. Then I moved slowly towards her, into her eyeline. When she saw me, she turned as if to run.

I shouted after her, 'Are you Margaret?'

She stopped and looked back — there was fear in her eyes, but then it seemed to evaporate. I remembered the chronicle — she thought I was an angel, sent from God to explain what he wanted of her. She demurred, dropped her eyes submissively, then fell to her knees. Her face was alabaster pale, without blemish, her sky-blue eyes a picture of innocence — how could anybody have believed she was the devil's disciple?

I had practised what I would say to her over and over in my mind, but now the words caught in my throat. Then I simply said, 'I am Toby, I am a historian.'

A few simple words said without much forethought, but it was as if my whole body had been stunned. What did the chronicle say that the angel had said? *He was the man To Be, and his name was Ristorian.*

Oh, my God, I thought. *I am Toby. Toby — To Be. I am the man To Be. I told Margaret that I am a historian, but she heard, 'My name is Ristorian.' Oh, my God, I am the man from 2020 mentioned in the chronicle.*

Glances were exchanged, and I knew what I had to do. Suddenly, it was mapped out in front of me.

I asked her about the killing of the angel. I saw her eyebrows furrow in confusion — she didn't understand. I tried again, changing the inflexions, the pronunciation. She still didn't comprehend, playing with a loose thread on her sleeve. I persisted, and we talked for a couple of hours until, finally, we were on the edge of understanding. We shared, to her wonder, the hot coffee, even though it was clear she found it bitter. Eventually, a tentative joint recognition began to emerge. I then asked her about the man in black, but she inclined her head, still looking at me, puzzled. I called him the black angel, but she was still confused. Then I pointed to the back of my hand.

Her face lit up, her expression a mix of understanding and fear. She blurted out some words, nodding vigorously. At first, they didn't register, but then they began to make sense to me.

'Yes, the Eye of Lucifer,' I said. 'Can you take me to where he killed the white angel?'

She took me to the main road. We walked for several miles until we came to a clearing, and she gestured that the killing had taken place there. I searched the ground, looked in the undergrowth, got on my hands and knees, frantically looking for any evidence that might be useful to the police. Margaret was plainly mystified as to what I was looking for, but I was not even certain myself, and I was unsure how to explain it.

After another hour, I sat on the damp ground; my body language must have indicated I was giving up. Margaret sat beside me and put her hand in mine. To her, I was an angel. She trusted me, as I was from God. She spoke, and I realised that she was saying the white angel had lost a slipper. I nodded eagerly and asked her to show me.

She stood, still holding my hand, and I had the sense to leave my vacuum flask so that I would be able to locate the exact clearing again. She led me back along the A616 and down a path to a copse. She gestured that I should climb down into a ditch beside some brambles. I did so, scratching myself as I descended. It was dark when I was inside; I could not make anything out clearly. Margaret climbed down after me, took my hand in the darkness, led me along a few paces, and took out a small bundle hidden in the undergrowth, beneath scrub. I unfolded the coarse material — it was dark, but the object was a shoe, I could make that out.

We both clambered out again and I saw that the shoe was white and high-heeled, but inside was something else. I forced my fingers down inside, but I couldn't dislodge the hidden items. I hit the back of the shoe against the heel of my hand, and the items dislodged and rolled into view — three false fingernails, painted red. The chronicle — what did it say? I asked Margaret, 'Did the white angel scratch the devil in black?'

She nodded. I knew what this meant: the false fingernails would have traces of Fischer's DNA.

I asked if I could take the shoe and the nails. Margaret agreed readily — she thought I was an angel from God; she was never going to deny me.

We talked for another couple of hours; I was reluctant to let her go. I took several photographs of her on my mobile phone and showed them to her. There was wonder on her face, although I am unsure if she recognised herself. I felt privileged above all my fellow historians, all the historians of the past. I was doing the impossible — I was meeting a time traveller, even if Margaret did not know that was what she was. To her, *I* was the vision.

After a time, I noticed the first signs of the fading light. I shot my cuff to reveal my watch — a quarter after five. I looked back and saw another look of incredulity on Margaret's face. It was the last thing I remembered of her.

She climbed back down into the hole, and I heard her scrambling along its length, but then the noise stopped. She was gone. For hours I had been engrossed in an alternative world Margaret had shown me. If I wrote my book, would anybody believe me — would my fellow historians ridicule me?

CHAPTER 43

I drove straight from Wellow back to Nottingham, and to the police headquarters. It was after 6.30 p.m. when I arrived. I asked if DCI McMillan were still in the building. After a phone call, I was shown into his office; he was staring out of his window, looking dishevelled. He turned, leaning backwards against the window frame. 'What can I do for you, Mr. Fielding?' he asked.

'I've found your scene of crime,' I said bluntly.

His body stiffened, his gaze burning into me. 'Where?'

'A clearing off the A616,' I answered. 'Will you be able to hold Fischer now?'

His face creased into a scowl. 'We had to release Fischer half an hour ago. We got the magistrate to give us a thirty-six-hour extension on little more evidence than that a police officer's life was at stake, but despite our best efforts we still had no physical evidence to link him to the abductions.'

I dwelt on what he had said. I realised I had been self-indulgent, wanting my meeting with Margaret to go on forever. If I had come back half an hour earlier…

DCI McMillan grabbed his phone, interrupting my reverie. 'DS Kaur,' he said, 'will you come to my office now? If DS Jackson is still here, bring him, too.'

He slammed the phone down and looked at me. 'Would you be able to find it again, in the dark?'

'I think so,' I said. 'I left my vacuum flask as a marker.'

The door opened and two officers entered. I was introduced to DS Jimmy Jackson and DS Satinder Kaur.

'Mr. Fielding here believes he has found the scene of Karrie Talbot's abduction,' McMillan said. He turned back to me. 'How do you know it's the scene of crime?'

'Because Margaret took me there,' I said confidently.

I saw immediately the change on the faces of Jackson and Kaur. I knew what they were thinking — *it's that bloody loon again, wasting our time.*

McMillan's face was more open. 'What exactly are you asking us to believe, Mr. Fielding?'

I reminded him what the chronicle had said about a meeting on Easter Sunday, and explained I had gone out into the countryside near Wellow with the express intention of meeting the girl from the twelfth century. 'I'm asking you to believe that I have met Margaret of Wellow,' I confirmed.

I saw Jackson adjusting his weight from foot to foot. He was anxious to leave, I could see. 'I knew you would find my story difficult to accept.' I picked out Jackson's gnarled face as I spoke. 'Margaret told me that after the abduction, the white angel lost her slipper, and her fingernails, which she retrieved and then hid.' I reached into the pocket of my parka and took out the parcel of rough material. 'Perhaps this will convince you.'

I placed it on the DCI's desk and pared back the material to reveal a white, high-heeled shoe. McMillan sat up. Jackson and Kaur came forward to get a closer look. I shook the false fingernails into view.

'Your forensics people should be able to find traces of Katarina's DNA on the shoe, and traces of Fischer's DNA under the false fingernails. Will that be enough to link him to her abduction?'

'DS Jackson, get the SOCO team out to the A616 now. It's dark, they will need floodlights.'

'Mac, there's only one SOCO officer on call from ten p.m. to seven a.m. It's a big ask for him, in the dark.'

Mac chewed the inside of his cheek, nodding. 'Tell him to get his colleagues out of bed. If there's any reluctance, refer them to me. DI French's life hangs in the balance. Mr. Fielding, you will have to show them the exact location.' He turned to DS Kaur. 'Get the shoe and the fingernails to forensics; put them back to work if they've gone home. I want the results by eight in the morning.'

'What about Fischer?' DS Kaur asked. 'Do we re-arrest him?'

McMillan sat back in his chair pensively. 'Until we get the SOCO report and forensics, we don't have corroboration. We don't have that link between Fischer and Karrie Talbot.'

'But he'll do for Jilly tonight, if we don't arrest him, Mac.' DS Kaur's large brown eyes were pleading.

He turned to me. 'Mr. Fielding,' he said, his voice low and imploring, 'one of my officer's life is at stake. If this is a fucking ruse, tell me now. If I arrest this man and forensics show nothing, it will compromise our future case against him. Have you fabricated this shoe and the false nails?'

'DCI McMillan,' I said, 'I am a professional historian. I was as dubious as you and your fellow officers are about the story in the chronicle of Brother Roger of Hathern. I have only come to believe it reluctantly. But I promise you this is not a ruse of my making — I don't fully understand it, but I am not deceiving you. If your forensics people find nothing, it will not be because I have falsified anything, I promise you.'

McMillan returned my stare. Then his eyes darted to Jackson and Kaur. 'Get out to Fischer's place and re-arrest him. And bring the team back in. It's going to be a long night.'

DS Kaur left the room hurriedly. Jackson followed, but turned at the door. 'Nobody's gone home, Mac. Everybody's here, still trying to find something to pin on Fischer.'

McMillan gave him a knowing look. It seemed that he expected no less.

PART 6: THE CEREMONY

CHAPTER 44

Monday, 30th March 2020

Mac's phone rang, and he grabbed it from its cradle. 'McMillan.'

'Sir, it's DS Kaur.' Satinder's voice was shrill. 'Sir,' she repeated, her tone hesitant, 'it's Fischer's place. It's all in darkness. We have been hammering on the door, but there's no response.'

'But I sent a surveillance team to track him when we released him not three hours ago — we can't have lost him. What do *they* say?'

'He entered his house shortly after seven, Mac, and we've had the front and back under observation ever since. They are adamant he hasn't left. Should we break in, Mac?'

Mac hesitated. Fischer had to be there. 'Yes — go!' he shouted. 'Break the fucking door down if you have to — and keep me informed.'

Mac stood, his back against his window, looking at the floor between his feet. He shot his cuff, looked at his watch — 8.46 p.m. Then the phone rang, and he dived to his desk and grabbed it. 'McMillan,' he blurted.

'It's DS Kaur again, sir. We've broken in, but we can't find hide nor hair of Fischer.' Her voice fell away as she completed the sentence.

'But he must be there, Satinder.'

'But he's not, sir.'

They were both silent, knowing what that meant. They had been outwitted, but it was much more than that. They had messed up their last chance to save Jill.

'What shall we do, sir?'

'Stay there, DS Kaur,' he said, 'and keep looking. Go over every inch of that place again.'

DCI McMillan went through to the incident room and briefed the rest of the team. Everyone was subdued as he spoke — there was a collective sense of foreboding. Glances were exchanged, none willing to say out loud what they were thinking.

Then DC Book raised his hand hesitantly. Mac gestured for him to speak. Anything was better than silent despair.

'Sir,' he said tentatively, 'you know you asked us to go over everything again.' He waited while Mac nodded. 'Well, you remember you previously asked the Financial Investigation Unit to get details of Fischer's bank and credit card details?' Mac nodded again. 'I've been looking at them again, specifically at his outgoings.'

'But we did all that before, didn't we?'

'We did, sir, and there was no unusual expenditure that opened up a line of enquiry.'

'Do you think you have now found something new, DC Book?'

'Well, not new, exactly, sir, but it's his groceries, his food.'

Mac looked puzzled. 'Groceries? Everybody has groceries — what's unusual about that?'

'It's not that he is buying groceries, sir, it's the cost of them. He has his food delivered from the supermarket, sir, but there's too much. Even accepting he is ordering top quality produce, the cost suggests significant volume.'

Mac tuned into Book's line of thought but still wanted him to articulate it. 'Go on.'

'He lives alone, sir, and has a cook to prepare his meals, but the amount of food suggests he's … well, he *must* be feeding far more people than himself.' DC Book looked down at his desk, as if arranging his thoughts. 'We have assumed Fischer was abducting women to kill them — a psychopathic killer. What if his perversion is to abduct them as — as sex slaves, or something like that?'

Heads turned to Book, then one by one they started nodding. Mac turned to the desolate-looking Dr. Adams and saw a spark appear in his eye — Jill might be alive.

DC Reader was first to comment. 'I see that, Tim … but we've had Fischer under surveillance,' he said. 'If these women are alive, he must have them stashed away somewhere. So his hiding place is not the scene of the murders, but a prison for his abductees — either way, we've never found it. And anyway, we'd have noticed him transporting produce to wherever this hideaway is, wouldn't we?'

'Yeah, that bothered me as well,' said Tim, 'so I got on to the Land Registry. They got back to me at about six-thirty this evening, but Fischer had been released by then.' He looked from Peter Reader to the others, and then back to Mac. 'Sir,' he said, 'when do you think that house of his was built?'

Mac chewed the inside of his cheek. 'A period, stone-built, character dwelling, with outbuildings and a paddock. I don't know, the 1890s, perhaps — a bit later, maybe Edwardian, say the 1910s.'

'No, sir, it was built in 2009. There *was* a period building on the site before, but he had it pulled down.'

Mac jumped in. 'So we ask ourselves — why not renovate the existing building, retain its original character, rather than building a reproduction of it?'

'Exactly, sir.'

'Go on, DC Book, you've done the hard work. Fill in the blanks for us.'

'I've been reading up on the Josef Fritzl case, sir — from 2008. Fritzl had kept his daughter captive for twenty-four years behind eight locked doors in a concealed corridor, part of the basement area of the large family home. He serially raped her and had seven children by her, some of whom were raised by Fritzl and his wife.'

'So you speculate that Fischer is doing something similar?'

'I suspect we may have to multiply what Fritzl did by ten, sir. I think he had the house knocked down in order to build an underground complex, complete with a concealed entrance ready for when he started to put his plan into action.'

Mac turned to Dr. Adams. 'Could this fit in with your profile, Leo?'

Dr. Adams sat forward in his chair as if suddenly energised. 'I've said all along that the kidnapper didn't fit the standard profile of a sexual abductor. As far as Fischer is concerned, he's a sociopath, with a full-blown narcissistic personality disorder. He schemes endlessly to achieve his aims; he wants *power*. The fact he is abducting, not killing, does not change my profile of him. But it's now clear that he hopes to establish his own Aryan society, to pool his and these women's "racial purity" as his means of accessing the Vril. Oh my God!' he exclaimed. 'Lebensborn — I should have realised.'

'Lebensborn? What's that?' DC Reader spoke for them all.

'Lebensborn was an SS organisation who wanted to increase the Aryan-pure population. SS officers were paired with Aryan girls and then the children were adopted to be brought up in the "racially pure" way.' He looked around and saw that he had to explain further. 'When we first visited Fischer's home, I looked at his bookshelves to get a handle on what he was reading, to see if it would give us an insight into his mindset — he had a book on the Lebensborn. Oh my God! He's going to father children and bring them up to be believers in his cult.'

Fritzl's name came thundering back to Mac. *There will be children down there*, he thought. 'Right — I want a team at Fischer's place as soon as possible, ground-penetrating radar, that sort of thing. If there is a complex down there, I want to find it. In the meantime, we go there now — we need to discover that concealed entrance.'

CHAPTER 45

DI French's eyes flashed open — she listened intently; something was happening in the main chamber. She had not been asleep, but she *was* on her bed, formulating her strategy for Fischer's return. She swivelled her legs sideways onto the floor, crept to the door, and opened it. Faintly, she heard a man's voice. He was here, and she was not sure she was ready. She closed the door.

She realised what this meant — Mac had been forced to release him. She worked out the timeline in her mind; they must have arrested him at about six p.m. on Friday, and that was why he hadn't turned up for the initiation. Today was Monday, she knew from the television, so they'd had him for 72 hours — they must have got another 36-hour extension from a magistrate. Mac was the best interrogator she'd ever worked with, but she also knew they must have failed to get an admission out of Fischer. Without that, they had no evidence to link him to her abduction.

She heard footsteps coming down the corridor and sat back on her bed. There was a knock and Karrie Talbot popped her head around the door. 'Can I come in?' she asked, her expression warm and friendly. Jilly nodded. 'Franz is back,' Karrie went on matter-of-factly and then leaned back against the door.

'Oh yes,' Jilly replied sourly.

'You're making it harder for yourself, you know.'

'Oh, really? I thought I was making it more difficult for Herr Von Nutcase.'

'He's not that, honestly.'

'Look, Karrie, I've interviewed him, listened to him for hours — I've had an in-depth assessment of his mental state from a criminal psychologist. I think I have a better handle on this guy than you have from this underground dungeon. For God's sake, Karrie, he's got you all in quarantine.'

Jilly looked at Karrie's expression. There was a flicker — something had been breached. She knew she needed to press this home — work on her resolve. She adopted an appeasing tone.

'He keeps you isolated for a reason, Karrie. He's using it to warp your mind — it's a well-established brainwashing technique. He has you underground to deprive you of daylight, because that messes with your brain. Come on, Karrie — you have to wake up to that.'

Karrie stared at her. Jilly could see she had planted a seed of doubt.

'Karrie,' she pleaded, her voice soft and encouraging, 'I will need your help.'

'I can't, Jilly. You don't know what he's like.' She pushed the braid of platinum-blonde hair behind her ear. 'When I am with him … well, it's like you *have* to comply with his wishes.'

'Of course — that's because he's drugging you all.'

'No — I'd know if he was, Jilly.'

'Would you? They're not vitamins, Karrie. He's feeding you small amounts of drugs to make you compliant. They're accumulating in your system, making you do what he demands. Karrie, you're an intelligent woman — come on, think for yourself. I need your help, Karrie — the others won't help, will they?'

Karrie looked down at the floor and shook her head. She had no words.

'That's because he's brainwashed and drugged them into obedience. Do you want to be one of them, Karrie — to obey his every command? You tried to escape when you first came — remember?' Karrie's eyes remained fixed on the floor. 'Karrie, this is your last chance — if you don't help, you'll stay here forever. You'll never see your husband or your family again.'

Karrie sobbed. 'I've been sent to tell you your initiation will be at midnight.' She was still unable to look at Jilly. 'You should prepare yourself.'

'Karrie!'

Karrie looked up. Tears were streaming down her face. 'I can't, I just can't,' she blurted. She turned and groped for the door handle, finding it clumsily. She pulled the door open and fled down the corridor, still weeping.

Jilly closed the door and leaned back against it. She inhaled deeply, the air trembling as it entered her lungs. She would have to do everything herself, she knew.

At 10.50 p.m., DCI McMillan burst into Fischer's house, followed by DCs Reader and Boone, Dr. Adams and the rest of the team. 'DS Kaur, everybody, here — now!' he shouted. 'I've redeployed the SOCO team. They were on their way to the A616, but are coming here instead. I want all the hands we can muster. DS Kaur, what about the ground-penetrating radar?'

'Promised by first light, sir.'

'See if you can get it here earlier. We'll use the SOCO's floodlights.'

'Will do, sir.'

Mac continued, 'Now, look, all of you. DC Book has a theory that there is an underground complex below this house, and I agree. We have to find it. Right, we go room by room, three to a room — and that includes the outbuildings. We are looking for a concealed entrance. We don't do this delicately. The priority is to find it, and find it fast, have you got me? I don't care if he sues the arse off the department — let me worry about that. I'll take the blame. Do you all understand?'

'Yes, Mac,' everyone chorused.

'Right, all the floors come up — you are looking for steps to a basement complex of some kind. Take a hammer to every wall — you are looking for a false one with a concealed entrance behind. Get the books off the bookcase shelves and see what's behind them — move them, if you have to. I know we have already searched the attic, but we do it again just in case there is access from up there. I don't care if this place is falling down by the time we've finished. Have we all got that?'

'Yes, Mac,' the team chorused again.

'Right, go!' Mac clapped his hands, and DS Kaur began allocating the teams.

CHAPTER 46

Emily and Caitlin knocked and entered Jilly's bedchamber without waiting for an answer. They were dressed in long, black, hooded capes with billowing sleeves. Caitlin carried a white cloak over her arm.

'We've come to prepare you for your ceremony,' said Emily, as if it were an honour.

'What are you going to do?' DI French's words were defensive.

'We'll braid your hair, and then dress you — you want to look attractive for Franz, don't you?' There was no irony in her words; she was being sincere.

The two sat either side of Jilly, took out the existing side plaits and brushed her hair through. Then they expertly took most of her hair and braided a long plait down her back, with two smaller side plaits to give the impression of an Aryan Norse maiden.

Caitlin stood and picked up the white cape, holding it by the shoulders. 'Come on, Jilly,' she said. 'Slip off the Viking tunic.'

They heard a noise, and eyes darted to the ceiling. Jilly knew instantly what it was. *Oh, thank you, Mac, thank you, guys*, she thought.

'Do you hear that?' she said to her fellow abductees. 'That's the police. They're coming to get us out.'

She saw Emily and Caitlin look at each other, but strangely she saw no concern on their faces. 'Franz will keep us safe,' Emily said.

Jilly needed time. She feigned embarrassment, put her hand to her throat, and blushed. 'I don't want you to see me naked,' she said, dropping her eyes.

'But that's what you will be in the ceremony,' Emily said.

Caitlin put her hand on Emily's arm and nodded at her. 'Okay, Jilly,' she said, 'but be quick, the ceremony is about to start. We'll be outside.'

DI French watched them leave, then pulled the tunic over her head. Around her left arm was a length of unbleached fabric. She had torn it from the hem of the replacement dress she'd found in the bedside cabinet. She had unpicked the stitching with her teeth and then vigorously bit at the side so that she was able to tear it along its width. She now had a length of sturdy cloth about three feet long by two inches wide that she could use as a ligature, if necessary. She wound it around her upper left arm, checked the end was not loose, tucked it in tightly, then put the white cloak around her shoulders, her arms in the sleeves, making sure the cloth thong was not visible.

'Are you ready, Jilly?' Caitlin shouted from outside.

'Coming,' she said as she stood, shaking the sleeves so they fell down to their full length. She heard the banging again from above and looked at the ceiling. It gave her reassurance. She swallowed hard and opened the door.

Emily and Caitlin took Jilly along the terracotta-hued corridor to the Black Sun room. They walked behind her as if in some ancient procession. As the door opened, she looked up at the circular domed ceiling, the representation of the Black Sun, the centre a depiction of a yellow iris. She saw the painted red plumes reaching down the circular walls, but now they looked more intimidating; the interlaced terracotta images and Nordic visual metaphors more menacing. The four alabaster statues seemed to be standing in judgement.

Jilly was taken to stand in front of the altar; she was the tallest and in the middle. Emily and Nicole were either side of her, Karrie and Caitlin on the outside, going down in size. Her apprehension rose as she waited for Franz Fischer to make a dramatic entrance.

The door opened, and music started playing. DI French looked around but could not see the source. Then he entered, black-cloaked with yellow and red piping, to represent the colours of the Black Sun, she assumed.

Suddenly, it was as if an invisible hand was guiding her. Her fear should have mounted at the intimidating sight — that was obviously his intention — but instead it subsided, and she saw only a proud peacock before her. He was no more than a fool with a narcissistic personality disorder — a need to behave grandiosely, to exaggerate his own self-importance in an immature pursuit of power. She saw him for what he was, and scorn took the corner of her mouth.

Fischer entered slowly, in time with the tempo of the regal music. He came and stood before them. He spoke to the women in Old Norse, Jilly thought. She looked around at her fellow abductees as they replied in the same language, and she wondered if they understood the meaning. They parted, and he approached the altar — there was a cloth and a compass, displayed for ceremonial purposes. He unfolded the fabric and used the compass to carefully position it along an axis. She looked over his shoulder; it was east to west — why that mattered, she didn't know. Then he took a pouch from his cloak pocket and took out tablets with symbols on them, which she assumed were runes. He looked at the dome above, the image of the Black Sun, then cast the tablets carefully along the east-west axis. Some fell, right side up, with the runic symbol showing; others fell with the symbol down. He continued his chant as if he had the power and knowledge to decipher the way they had fallen.

Jilly looked at the symbols, then at the images on the walls — they were reflected there. In Fischer's world, everything had importance, was interconnected. But it was only Fischer that could interpret the meaning, the other women, intelligent and prosperous as they were, were merely his followers.

Then the altar was cleared. The women joined hands and, alarmingly, formed a circle around DI French.

'Who is the candidate?' Fischer intoned, his words echoing in the chamber. He had reverted to English.

'This is the candidate,' the women said in unison.

'Bring her forth.'

Jilly was manoeuvred to the altar, pressure placed on her shoulders so that she sat on the edge of it. Then her feet were raised up and she was turned so that she lay on her back along the length of the altar. Every inch of her wanted to fight them, but she resisted the impulse. She had her strategy in place, and that was her best chance. Fischer pulled down the hood from his cloak. That open and inviting expression was there; the one he used to manipulate people.

She heard a noise again from above her and saw Fischer's eyes shoot to the ceiling. There was a hint of anxiety in those sharp, flint-blue eyes — his expression darkened. She felt reassured. If his lair were about to be discovered, she thought, her initiation would be his last chance to connect to the Vril-ya.

'Show to the Vril-ya that this candidate is racially pure,' his words rang out, but now there was a hint of panic.

Nicole slowly pulled the left side of Jilly's cloak away. She paused, then followed with the right side. Her complete nakedness was now exposed as if she were a piece of meat on a butcher's slab. They all chanted while gesturing with their upturned palms to her pale calves. Fischer, without touching her, ringed his hand over them in small circles, then faced each of the four Vril-ya angel statues in turn. He held out his hand and spoke some Old Norse words, which Jilly assumed was an entreaty for them to acknowledge her white skin as evidence of her Aryan purity.

They repeated the ritual with her thighs, her stomach, the blondness of her flaxen pubic hair, her chest, her breasts, her throat. The ritual was mounting, the tone of the chanting rising; a crescendo, in harmony with the music.

Fischer came and stood before her, in the middle of the altar. Jilly raised her head to see what was coming next. He put his arms out sideways. Nicole and Emily came to either side of him, undid the cloak, pulled it back off his shoulders and let it fall to the ground. Jilly took in the sight before her. The handsome, square-jawed face stood atop a muscular torso and powerful arms. She noticed he was already fully erect.

He turned his back on her, faced his initiates and the Vril-ya statues, then looked at the symbol of the Black Sun on the dome. The women began to worship his phallus, encircling him as they chanted, their upturned palms gesturing to his manhood as they passed by in turn. They seemed to be goading him to take Jilly, impregnate her. The crescendo mounted further, and then he thrust both his hands into the air. The chanting stopped.

The women looked at Fischer, the common expression one of submission, obedience, adulation. But DI French was no such disciple; she knew this man's self-worth was delusional, a figment of his warped imagination. With his hands raised to the Black Sun image, he rang out words in Old Norse, and his disciples raised their eyes and repeated them.

Jilly saw her chance. She furtively reached across with her right hand, down the sleeve of her left arm. She loosened the edge of the cloth ligature and unwound it until it was free. Her movements were slow and deliberate; the last thing she wanted was to draw attention to herself. She wound one end around her left hand until it was firmly gripped and repeated the action with the other hand. She moved her arms down flat against her body, keeping her eyes fixed on the women initiates, then pulled her hands apart until the cord went rigid — she was ready.

She listened. Fischer was still chanting, but then he stopped. Jilly held her breath, she wanted to catch him off guard, gain the advantage that surprise would give her. But his arrogance came to her rescue; his Old Norse chant started up again. He had his back to her; this was her best chance. She took a deep breath, gently sat up and put her knees under herself. She saw Karrie's eyes dash to her, and for a moment she froze. She shook her head slightly, a gesture Karrie must have understood — she didn't betray her.

Jilly acted quickly. She rose up on her knees, crossed her arms, looped the ligature over Fischer's head and pulled her hands apart, tightening the thong as much as she could. His hands went instinctively to his throat, trying to pull it away. She could feel his considerable strength trying to get a grip, to squeeze his fingers under the thong. She pushed her right knee into the back of his neck just below the ligature, using it as a lever. She fell backward onto the altar as she increased the pressure, lying on her back and making the rope even tighter.

He fell back with her — she felt his strength lessen; he was off his feet and had much less purchase, much less power.

He abandoned the ligature and tried to reach behind to get at Jilly's face. An image shot into her mind. She had tried to do the same when *he* had her in a chokehold. She hadn't been able to do so, and because he had compressed her carotid artery she'd been unconscious in less than twenty seconds. The ligature would not do this; she would have to strangle him — that might take a couple of minutes, maybe longer. She pulled her head out of reach of his groping hands, shaking the braids so that they fell away from his grasping fingers, and luckily that also increased her force. She pressed her knee harder.

'Face it, Fischer,' she said through gritted teeth as she strained, 'you can forget about connecting with the Vril today, transformation into a Vril-ya at the moment of climax — it's not going to happen, pal.'

But her euphoria was short-lived. Nicole, Emily, and Caitlin came and grabbed at her hands.

Nicole prised the fingers of Jilly's right hand, pulling them back one by one. As she moved from one finger to another, however, Jilly snapped the first back into place and kept up the pressure. Caitlin was doing the same to her left hand, but using her teeth to try to loosen Jilly's grip. Emily went around her back and put her arm around her throat in a headlock. Collectively, they all pulled at Jilly's rigid, strained body.

Jilly was counting the seconds. She had to keep pulling, straining, keep strangling. As the women heaved at her, she heaved back. She could hear Fischer gagging, gasping for air, but his strength was still there, she could sense it. Bit by bit, the collective strength of four against one began to tell. Nicole was learning how to counteract Jilly's grip. She pulled her middle finger away from the ligature and concentrated on it.

She pulled it back and back, against the joint until it was almost touching the back of Jilly's hand. Jilly felt pain — the rush of adrenalin was no longer counteracting it. Her counting reached ninety agonising seconds, but she knew it was not enough. She had to gamble, move to the next part of her strategy.

She released her grip abruptly. Fischer slid to the floor, coughing, spluttering, gasping for breath, his hands pulling at the ligature. The three women also released their grip on DI French, rushing to Fischer to help him. The gamble paid off. Jilly jumped to the floor and ran to the statue furthest from the altar. She groped around its base, the side out of view of the ritual. She recovered what she had hidden there in the early hours of the previous day.

It was a two-litre orange juice bottle. She had refilled it to the top with water. A litre weighed one kilogram, she knew. Two kilos — that would be roughly four and a half pounds, she had calculated. Gripping the bottle neck with her right hand, she slammed it into the palm of her left hand, feeling the considerable thump it gave. She looked back at Fischer — he was ashen-faced, holding his throat, those piercing, flint-blue eyes looking up at her with an evil stare. Not only had she hurt him, she had diminished him in the eyes of his followers. He would regain his strength soon. She had to act, and quickly.

She bound across the chamber, raising the bottle high in the air, and brought it down in an arc like a cudgel, striking him across the forehead. She then brought it upwards, hitting him under the chin as he was sinking down from the force of the first blow. Two strikes with the same movement, she remembered from her self-defence training. Fischer slid sideways to the ground, dazed, his eyes rolling and his brain addled. Jilly raised the bottle again, ready to strike, but Karrie grabbed her wrist at its summit.

Jilly looked at her imploringly. 'No, Karrie,' she growled, 'you mustn't. I need your help.'

She saw a whirlpool of conflicting emotions on Karrie's face. She wanted to help Jilly, but she didn't want to see Fischer battered. She addressed the women kneeling on the floor. 'Get him out of here,' she said, her grip tightening on Jilly's wrist.

They obeyed, dragging Fischer out through the door.

'Sorry,' Karrie whispered, and she followed them out.

DI French stood as if paralysed, like one of the Vril-ya sculptures — her strategy had worked. Momentarily she felt exhilarated, but it began to subside almost immediately. The sense of danger re-emerged — ascending as her elation drained away. She had played the scene in her head over and over in her chamber and she had executed it perfectly, but she had not thought it through to its end game. How did she stop them coming back?

Adrenalin came to her aid again. Her eyes darted all about her, assessing her options. She didn't like the odds for any of them. Once more, she heard noises above her — Mac was close, she reasoned. That meant she didn't have to hold them off indefinitely, only until she could be rescued.

As if a starting gun had sounded, she rushed to the alabaster figure closest to the door and pushed at it, but it stood rigid. She was too low to get enough leverage. She took in the chamber but could see nothing to stand on — except, maybe, the altar. Crossing to it, she crouched down, pressed her shoulder against it and engaged her body weight — it moved; it was not fixed to the floor. It had slid by a foot. She repeated her efforts and the altar moved gradually, foot by sluggish foot, sometimes inch by agonising inch until she had manoeuvred it next to the statue.

Mounting it, she paused and took a deep breath, allowing the oxygen to reinvigorate her muscles. She put her shoulder behind it, spread her legs so that she got maximum purchase, and heaved. There was movement, but then it rocked back into its original position. She heaved again, grunting, sweat pouring from her forehead, stinging beads rolling down into her eyes. It moved again, but as it rolled back, she reapplied her force, using its momentum to help her. It had started to rock, and with each movement, she pushed, and the arc increased each time. She gulped another mouthful of air, but now it was getting easier — she was approaching the tipping point. Then she felt its weight ease against her shoulder and looked up, seeing it slowly toppling. Frantically she tried to manoeuvre the angle of its fall, the enormous mass now rendered weightless. She guided it towards the closed door.

Slamming into the floor, it broke into three substantial pieces. Jumping down, she found she could move the headpiece easily, and the upper body part with difficulty. She placed them closest to the door, wedging them in front of the larger lower body part of the Norse angel. She tried the door, and it opened an inch or so before slamming into the debris. It wouldn't keep Fischer and his candidates at bay forever, but it would give her time — give Mac and *her* team time.

Jilly collapsed onto the wreckage, gasping for air. Suddenly aware of the pounding of her heart against her ribcage, she wiped her forehead with the back of her hand. She started to tremble, a chill running down her spine as the sweat on her body cooled. Looking down, astonished, she realised for the first time she was still totally naked. She looked around for the cloak to warm herself and saw it on the floor beside where the altar had been. She was too exhausted to get it.

CHAPTER 47

'Sir, sir!' DC Reader rushed into the hall, where DCI McMillan was coordinating the search. He was holding a hammer in his right hand, waving it to emphasise his words. 'I think we've found something.'

'Where?' snapped Mac.

'There's a boiler cum utility room at the back of the house. I think there's a false wall.'

'Show me.'

There was a large American-style fridge-freezer standing against the back wall. Reader gestured with the hammer at the wall to the side of it. He tapped the wall and then the adjacent wall to show the difference in tone. The hollowness was evident.

'Hit it!' Mac's words were emphatic. Reader hesitated. 'Go on,' he repeated. 'Hit it! Hard!' Reader swung the hammer — a significant dent appeared. 'Harder!' Mac yelled.

He swung the hammer again, this time without restraint. The hammerhead went straight through. He repeated the strike a dozen times or so until a jagged hole appeared, about a foot across — he peered into it. Mac brought his torch and shone the beam into the cavity.

'Aw, fuck!' said Reader. 'It's only a stud wall; there's a chuffin' toilet on the other side.'

The banging continued throughout the house — though now there was less restraint. Mac's instructions to Reader had released their inhibitions. Mac returned to the hall, where he was coordinating everything, and heard the hammering above him. But after a time the din began to subside, and he knew what that meant.

He walked through into Fischer's plush office. The surveillance team had been allocated it. He sat behind the large vintage oak desk and surveyed the carnage; that sense of the country house library was gone — it was a wreck and looked as if it had been hit by a hurricane. One by one, his team returned from their allocated rooms with negative reports and dejected looks on their faces, hammers held limply by their sides.

'It's got to be here somewhere!' Mac said, grinding his teeth, the muscles in his cheek twitching. 'Where do you hide a concealed entrance — anybody?'

Glances were exchanged; they didn't have anything more to contribute other than the obvious. DC Reader stood rigidly, desperately trying to help. 'You're right, Mac, a false wall is the most obvious, but we've drawn a blank.'

'What about the bookcases?' He looked at DC Terry Redman.

The young surveillance man shuffled to his feet. 'We've pulled each bookcase back away from the wall, sir. There's no hidden entrance behind any of them,' he said, rubbing his chin.

'What about behind a fireplace?' Peter Reader's words were said without much expectation.

'There's only one fireplace,' said DS Jackson. 'It's in the living room. I've checked it — didn't find anything.'

'Did you take a hammer to it?'

Jackson shook his head.

'Go and do that now, Jimmy,' Mac ordered, 'and take DC Reader.'

They waited, the sound of hammer on stone reverberating back. When they returned, Mac looked at them with little expectation. They shook their heads. Mac chewed the inside of his cheek and played with his wedding ring, a sigh escaping. He had reached an impasse — they all had.

'Mac?' said Terry Redman, his tone rueful. 'I don't know if this is relevant, but…'

'Go on, son — anything at this stage.'

'Look in the top right-hand draw, sir.' Mac pulled it open. Redman went on, 'There are two remote controls. Press the left one.' Mac did so, and an oak cabinet slid open to reveal Fischer's printer. He pushed another button and a cover glided open. A computer rose from its hidden place below the desk. 'Now push the right one.' Mac did so — and nothing. 'It doesn't seem to operate anything in this room,' Redman added.

Mac sat up. It wasn't much, but it was something. He stood and went into the hall, Redman, Leo, Satinder, Reader, and Jackson following. He aimed the remote at each surface. A light went on each time he pressed it, but nothing operated. He went from room to room — the kitchen, the living room, the dining room. Again, nothing. 'Upstairs,' Mac said, and the train of police officers followed. He came to the foot of the stairs, but something made him stop. It was an impulse, nothing more.

He looked up the stairs. There was a landing halfway up, then it turned right and continued to the upper floor. He pointed the remote control at the stairs themselves, not entirely sure why he did so.

He heard the hum of an engine. He saw the first step of the staircase move. Then the whole stairway ascended like a drawbridge, hinged at the first landing, revealing the hidden room. There was a cheer behind him, and Mac's heart raced. At the far end, he could see a massive steel door with an electronic keypad and at the side, a steel hatch with a deadbolt lock.

Mac led them through and examined the steel door. They exchanged glances.

'This will take time to open, time we don't have,' Reader said, knowing they were thinking the same. They turned and looked at Mac for guidance, but he had no answers this time; his brief moment of elation had departed. DI French's life was at stake, and he knew it would take several hours to open this door.

'We need a specialist locksmith. I suspect he will have to drill out the electronic keypad. Get onto it, will you, DS Jackson — and in the meantime, get some cutting equipment down here as well. We need heavy-duty bolt cutters or a grinding tool. At least we can get rid of that deadlock on the steel hatch.'

Mac rushed outside, Dr. Leo Adams at his shoulder — the diverted SOCO team had arrived. 'I want the floodlights set up around the perimeter of the house,' Mac shouted.

He called over the lead technician, Mark King, and told him about the hidden room they had found, with the massive steel door with an electronic keypad. He agreed it would take many hours to open.

'Ground-penetrating radar and electromagnetic location is probably going to be quicker. We've used GPR and EML before — it's good,' King said. 'It was developed commercially, to confirm natural subterranean features or manmade ones, pipelines, that sort of thing. It's used before development and excavation — but it adapts well for use forensically.'

'Can we hope to have a unit here by the morning?' Mac said.

'I might be able to do better than that,' King said. 'The university archaeology department are using a unit at an old

Anglo-Saxon dig — I wonder if we can divert it. Let me make some calls — get some other people out of bed.'

'The burial site at Southwell, you mean?' Mac said.

'Yeah, I think it is — how do you…'

Mac cut across him. 'My wife is head of that department,' he said. 'We have discussed the dig at home.'

'As I say, let me make some calls.'

'No, leave that to me. My wife will know who to call. You get your guys over to the utility room and that metal door. See what you can suggest.'

King started to walk to the house then stopped and looked back. 'Mac,' he called, 'if GPR does show something down there, a digger might be the quickest way in.'

'Go in through Fischer's subterranean ceiling, you mean?'

'Exactly.'

One of the SOCO team put his head and shoulders through the front entrance, surprise evident on his face. 'Mac, your wife's here,' he said.

Mac looked at his watch. It was less than an hour and a half since he had called her and got her out of bed.

He rushed outside into the night. Stella was wrapped up in her thick winter coat. She turned to the young man beside her. 'This is Stuart,' she mumbled through her snood. 'He'd just got back home when I rang him; he'd been out drinking with his mates. He's not fit to drive, so I picked him up.'

Mac looked at the dishevelled young man beside her. His shoulders sank at the sight — a thin, unshaven face, black shadows beneath his eyes, red rims around them. 'I take it you had a good night, Stuart,' he said. Stuart nodded with a roguish smile. Mac looked back at his wife.

'I know,' she said, 'but you wanted somebody here tonight. This is the best I can do.'

Mac looked at the equipment on the floor. 'Are you capable of operating this … radar thing?'

'Sure, guv. Can do it in my sleep.' He was swaying as he spoke.

'Right, get to it, then. I want you to cover the perimeter of this house. I want to know what's under it.' Mac watched as Stuart unpacked and assembled his equipment — it looked like an oversized lawnmower when he had finished. 'How does it work?'

'It sends a tiny pulse of energy via an antenna,' Stuart said, pointing at the relevant component. He seemed much less drunk, now that he was concentrating. 'There's an integrated computer that records the strength and time required for the return of the signal.' He pointed again. 'Sub-surface variations will create differences that are picked up by the system, which identifies any change in geological structure.'

Mac interrupted. 'Like manmade objects, you mean?'

'If that's what you want to find — yeah.'

'That's *exactly* what we want to find.'

'Okay, then,' Stuart said, accessing the controls. 'We need to calibrate it for a low frequency. That will identify large objects at low depths. Will you get your guys to turn off their mobile phones, please? Otherwise, they'll affect the readings.' Mac gave the order.

Stuart set the controls accordingly and then manoeuvred the unit out into the floodlit grounds. He started to map the surroundings, wheeling backward and forward, setting down a grid — Mac walked beside him.

'How long will it take for the results to be ready?' Mac asked.

'All detected items are revealed on my computer screen in real-time,' Stuart said, pointing proudly at the display. 'Look, there,' he added, pointing at the waist-high LCD display on the front of the unit.

Mac stared at the screen — to him, it was only a collection of squiggly lines. 'Is this it?' he asked, perplexed.

'That's it — yeah. So now you need someone like me with field experience to interpret the data images.'

'I'll leave you to it, then, Stuart,' Mac said, walking away.

'Okay. I'll give you a call when I've completed the survey.' He paused. 'Chief Inspector,' he called after him, 'I can tell you one thing now, though. I've got the edge of something concrete — there looks to be a substantial structure down there.'

Dan'll Boone, his eyes bulging, strained at the handles of the heavy-duty bolt cutters. 'Aargh! Come on, you bastard,' he grunted. He stopped briefly to redouble his efforts, tensed and engaged. 'Aargh!' There was a shearing noise as the blades cut through the deadbolt lock.

He pulled it clear and opened the hatch. DC Reader shone a light into it. 'Well?' asked DCI McMillan.

Boone put his head inside. 'Looks like a food shaft,' he said, his words echoing in the chute, 'to get provisions down from the surface. There's a pulley system here…' He pulled at the rope, and a small cabin started to descend. He reversed it, and it came back up to the starting position, then he raised it as high as it would go — they both looked down.

'A dumb waiter — can we get someone inside it?' Leo's words were anxious.

'It's about two feet square,' Boone replied, assessing it as he spoke. 'I doubt any of us would fit.'

Mac turned to DS Jackson. 'Where are we with the specialist locksmith for the steel door, the electronic keypad?'

'Got somebody back at the station making calls, sir — they haven't got back to me as yet.'

'Get an update, will you, Jimmy?'

'Sir.'

'The radar man wants to see you, sir.' It was DS Kaur at the entrance to the false wall.

'DS Kaur, DS Jackson — with me, please,' he said as he strode through the opening. They pursued him without hesitation. Leo followed, frustration all over his face — he desperately wanted to help, but there seemed to be nothing he could do.

Outside, the young archaeologist was staring at his computer screen through his red-rimmed eyes. They gathered around it, gazing at the incomprehensible squiggles.

'Talk me through this, will you, Stuart?' Mac said.

'Never seen anything like this before, guv,' he said, scratching his unshaved chin. Then he pointed at the images. 'There's a complex down there as extensive as the house above it.'

'What about fresh air?' asked Mac. 'Where does that come from?'

'Yeah, an underground bunker like this, close to the surface, will have a vent by the entrance and will need a couple more to deliver enough fresh air for survival and cooling.'

'Could we find a way in via them?'

'Unlikely. It would only need standard air vents; they wouldn't be big enough to get a man down. And you'll have to find them — your guy will most probably have concealed them to prevent his secret being discovered. If he designed the whole thing not to be found, they could be anywhere — hidden behind rocks, shrubs or flowers, maybe.'

'I can't visualise the complex,' Mac said.

'The computer program enables me to show you a three-dimensional representation,' Stuart mumbled as he moved the cursor around. The screen image changed, showing a revolving 3D illustration. 'Look,' he said, pointing. 'Some of it is missing, as it's hidden under the house. But if we link this to this —' his finger swept across the screen — 'then it's like a wheel. Here's a central chamber at the hub, and then spokes leading off it. They are probably corridors, seven of them — five go to small rooms, one to a large one, and the last one disappears under the house — that's probably where the entrance is.'

They all grouped closer, eager to get a view of the screen. Stuart stood back slightly to make room for them.

'If this were an archaeological analysis, I would say it was…' He paused. 'I don't know what I would say — a secret place of ritual, perhaps.'

'That's exactly what it is, Stuart,' Mac interrupted him. 'It represents a symbol of a secret cult, the Black Sun Society. They've used various images over the years to represent the Black Sun, one of which was the Sonnenrad — in English, the Sun Wheel. This complex has been designed by Fischer to represent the Sun Wheel, to follow the old rituals.'

Things had temporarily stalled. Mac shuffled his weight from foot to foot, then snapped at DS Jackson, 'Have the station found a specialist locksmith yet?'

'They can't find an out-of-hours number, Mac. Can't raise anybody. Specialist locksmiths seem to be nine 'til fivers.'

'There's no point in you hanging around here, Stella,' Mac said to his wife.

'No, I'd like to stay, if you don't mind —' she started to say, but she was interrupted by the SOCO man, Mark King.

'Mac!' he shouted as he approached.

'What you got, Mark?' Mac said.

'Been onto the Highways Department, Mac.' He saw the DCI's brow furrow, so he explained further. 'I wanted to know if they had any overnight roadworks going on in the vicinity.'

'And?'

'And yes — construction work *is* going on — building a bridge over the M1. They gave me the site engineer's mobile number.'

'I've seen that,' Satinder interrupted enthusiastically, 'and we're only about five miles from the M1 here, aren't we?'

'Yep,' said King, 'and the new bridge is another seven miles further down on the southbound carriageway. They've got a Caterpillar excavator there.'

'Will it be able to dig down deep enough?'

'According to the engineer, it has a maximum digging depth of four metres.'

'Stuart, the GPR man, says that if we dig down, we should crash through into the ceilings of the compound at about two and a half metres.' Mac paused, his mind now teeming with questions, but his spirits were rising. 'And a transporter?'

'Yep, they have a lorry to bring it here, as well.'

'When?'

'The shift finishes at six a.m., but I told the engineer it was a matter of life and death. They're on their way — it's a big unit to get loaded, but they think they can have it here by four-thirty.'

Mac's face reflected his satisfaction, the creases of apprehension fading briefly. 'Right,' he said, 'we start 'em digging down as soon as they've unloaded.'

CHAPTER 48

DI Jilly French sat on the broken pieces of the alabaster statue, her back against the door. It had been several hours since Fischer had been dragged away — how many hours, she didn't know. There was no clock in the chamber. It was uncomfortable, but with her head against the door, she could listen for him coming back. She was shaking uncontrollably, although she was now wearing the white cloak of initiation. It was a symbol of her projected violation — she hated the thought of it, but she had to keep warm.

It wasn't working, though; she continued to tremble. She pulled the cape tightly around her and drew her legs up against her body. Her heart had started to race again, and she had a pain in her chest. She could smell faeces and urine — it was her own. It was coming from the corner where she had gone to relieve herself. She knew what was happening — her body had gone into shock. Her skin was clammy and pale, hypotension had irritated her large intestine, and her breathing was fast. She knew light-headedness came with shock, and she fought to keep her mind active. What was it you did for people in shock? Oh yes — it was the ABC. *A is for airways*, she thought. You had to keep them clear — yes, she could do that. *B is for breathing — what the fuck, isn't that the same as airways? Come on, Jilly.* She couldn't remember what C was for.

She was still in danger; she still had to be vigilant. Her eyes shot up to the ceiling; she knew Mac and her team were up there, but she hadn't heard anything for an hour.

'Yes, I'm down here, guys!' she yelled up. 'Don't go away now.'

The bottle, the one I used as a cudgel. The thought sprang into her mind. It was beside her as a ready weapon, but she needed fluid as well. She grabbed it, unscrewed the top and gulped down the diluted orange juice. Then she stopped abruptly and put her ear against the door. They were coming back. 'Oh, come on, Mac,' she grunted through her teeth.

'Mac!' Mark King yelled. 'It's here, the digger.' He waved his arms at the driver, directing him where to park.

DCI McMillan rushed over, followed by the rest of the team, relief showing on their faces. 'DC Reader!' Mac shouted, then his voice fell away as he realised he was with him. 'Get Stuart, the GPR man.'

Reader knew Stuart was keeping warm in the hallway of the house, slowly sobering up. He came back with the tousled young man.

'Where's the best place to start digging?' Mac asked.

Stuart wheeled his machine to them, booted up the computer display, opened the image he had of the underground complex, and pointed. 'This chamber, the largest one, is closest to the surface,' he said, 'which means it must be the tallest, as well as the largest.' He saw the confusion on the faces around him. 'You are unlikely to build a large chamber with a low ceiling, are you?' he said. 'It possibly has a vaulted ceiling, or maybe a dome.'

'Right!' Mac exclaimed. 'This chamber it is, then. Stuart, you're with me. I need you to show the operator where to start digging.'

The door slammed violently into the broken alabaster statue — it moved no more than an inch and didn't dislodge the debris Jilly had piled there. She had her back against it, however, and was jerked forward. She then slid down the broken pieces, grazing her thigh as she fell. She grabbed at the displaced head to steady herself.

'DI French.' The words escaped through the crack in the door, the timbre of Fischer's voice as smooth as melted chocolate.

Jilly wasn't fooled, however. This was what Fischer did: he manipulated people; he could be charming and sociable when it suited. 'Yeah, what do you want, Fischer?' Her words were caustic.

'Will you open the door, please?'

'Why would I fucking do that? You're not coming in, sunshine.'

'Okay, I won't come in, but will you let your sister candidates in?'

'Why? They're not my chuffin' sisters, mate.'

'They'll take you to the entrance chamber. You can go free.'

Thoughts swirled in Jilly's mind — was he giving up? Was it all over? Could she believe him? No, she decided.

'The police are here, aren't they?'

There was a pause. She assumed Fischer was gathering his thoughts. 'Yes — the police are here.' His voice was quiet and sincere.

She exhaled a long sigh of relief, pulled her head back and looked at the ceiling, to where she assumed Mac was. Then she closed her eyes — she knew they were there, but it was such a relief to hear him say it.

'Did you hear that, Karrie?' she shouted. 'You're going home to your family.'

She listened, but Karrie didn't answer.

'The police won't find you down here, Jilly. They'll go away again soon.' Fischer's tone was now as thick as treacle.

'So why are you letting me go?'

'It's clear you will not fit in with our community.'

He must have known, she reasoned, that if he released her, she would come straight back with the cavalry. She was no helpless victim of abuse, brainwashed into subservience. At that very moment, she heard a dull rumbling sound above her. It was muffled, but it throbbed through the concrete structure.

'I think I'll wait here and take my chances, thank you very much.'

'Jilly,' he smarmed, 'there's no need for this unpleasantness.'

'Let's face it, Franz, you've failed, haven't you? The years of planning, all this building work, the hours you must have spent sculpting your terracotta images, your alabaster statues, all your efforts to join the Vril-ya. You know what, Franky boy? It's been for nothing.'

'OPEN THIS FUCKING DOOR, YOU CLEVER BITCH!' His words exploded. 'OPEN THIS FUCKING DOOR!' He pounded on it — opening and closing it with all his force. She heard him kicking it, then shoving his body weight behind it. The debris moved back another inch — it wasn't much, but then, Jilly realised, he wouldn't need much of a gap to squeeze through.

She heard female voices trying to calm him down, and for a moment they succeeded. Leo's words suddenly came back to her. What was it he had said? People with narcissistic personality disorder often exhibit an inability to tolerate criticism and a tendency to belittle others to validate their own superiority. He was right, she thought; his ego *was* fragile.

Fingers squeezed around the door. A voice followed; the face must have been pressing against the fissure. 'Jilly,' it said pleadingly — it was Caitlin. 'The ceremony must be completed; you must see that. Open the door, please?'

A humourless smile took DI French's face. *Unbelievable*, she laughed inwardly. *Let's see how fragile that ego of yours is, Franz.* 'No comment,' she said.

'We are so close to connection, Jilly.'

'No comment.'

'Jilly, the Vril-ya are waiting for us.' This time it was Nicole's voice.

'No comment.'

'Jilly,' Nicole went on, 'the connection is imminent — we just have to engage it. You will be exalted by the Vril-ya when that happens. You have an unusually robust hereditary constitution — that's obvious. This is your destiny, you must see that.'

Robust hereditary constitution, Jilly thought, sniggering. 'No comment!' she shouted back.

The door rattled as Fischer pounded on it. 'OPEN THE DOOR, YOU FUCKING BITCH!'

Ochre-coloured dust fell from the ceiling, coating one of the alabaster statues. A small amount settled in Jilly's hair. The muffled engine noise was getting louder. Jilly's eyes shot to the ceiling and back to the door. *That's right, Franz*, she thought. *Lose it big time — you'll bring the roof down before that machine up there does.*

The excavator operator mounted his cab as a smattering of rain pricked his face — the engine roared to life as he turned the key, a cough of smoke escaping the exhaust. He disengaged the safety lock, then used the left and right controls to operate the tracks on either side to manoeuvre his vehicle into the position the radarman had indicated. He used the two joysticks to run the boom, the bucket, and the swivel. The rain began to run down his windscreen, blurring his vision slightly, but he was used to such conditions. He lowered the bucket into the earth, pushed his control forward — the blade went down, biting into the ground. He made his first pass, took off the turf and the topsoil to start a trench. Leo watched, his chin trembling, but his apprehension eased slightly when he saw the blade cut like a knife through butter.

With the bucket full of dirt, the arm rotated, and the contents were deposited on the ground beside it. The SOCO team and the police team stopped what they were doing, came to watch the excavation man at his task. As they watched, what started as a flurry of rain, built into a torrent, but none of them relinquished their viewing point. Leo looked up into the heavens, but the floodlights obscured his view; nothing was visible beyond the edge of their illumination. The only thing he saw were the sheets of rain picked out by the powerful lights. The trench became deeper with every scoop, and the mound grew higher. Deeper and deeper, the hole descended, the knoll rising like a monstrous molehill, rain beginning to cascade down it in rivulets of mud.

The endeavour was persistent, relentless, the focused eyes of the operator purposeful, fixed on the growing chasm. Yet there was a tension, and it mounted with every bucket of dirt as if it were a race in slow motion, the winning post agonisingly just out of sight.

Then there was a scraping sound as the bucket hit something solid. The driver stopped, and the spectators came forward to look into the hole.

The operator stood, took off his ear defenders, and leaned his head sideways out of his cab. The rain lashed his face, but his eyes automatically picked out a figure hunched against the driving rain — he recognised DCI McMillan as the man in charge. 'We're down to what you were looking for,' he said. 'What now?'

Mac waved his arms. 'Keep going!' he bellowed.

The digger man's eyes narrowed. 'If that structure is hollow,' he shouted back, 'then some of the debris will fall inwards. If there is anybody inside — they could be buried.'

All eyes turned to Mac. He dropped his eyes and studied the soggy ground between his feet. He had a judgement call to make — probably the biggest of his career. Whatever decision he made, it seemed he was putting his DI's life in danger. He looked at the faces around him, and saw nothing to encourage his decision either way. They were glad they didn't have to make the call.

He looked back at the driver. Stopping now was not an option, he decided. He puffed out his chest. 'Punch a hole in that fucker,' he said.

'YOU FUCKING BITCH!' Fischer ranted, and the door shuddered, rattling on its hinges. Jilly realised he was using his heel, using his martial arts training. Again, there was a thud, carefully placed — then again, and again. She heard him urge his disciples to put their weight against the bottom of the door, to keep it rigid — then his foot impacted higher up, sledgehammer-like. The door creaked, the effect of the strike more potent. He repeated the stroke three of four times, then Jilly heard a sound that made her freeze — something had splintered. Fischer stopped; he had heard it too. He examined the wood, determined where the crack was — then aimed his foot again. The splintering sound intensified.

Jilly glared at the door. She could see the crack, then another thud and a large shard broke away and flew past her. She followed it with her eyes, but when she looked back, she could see him looking at her through the hole, a single, piercing, manic, flint-blue eye, now aflame with unrelenting fury. At that moment she knew she was not only in danger of violation, but he would also kill her.

Another thud and another piece of door flew off, the hole enlarged. He started to hit the surrounding area with the heel of his right hand, and more and more wood split away. He shoved his shoulder against the weakened door, thrust his full weight on it — a larger piece was dislodged, and a crack rose upwards, two feet or more. Bit by bit the door was disintegrating.

Fischer leaned back, raised his right leg, stabbed his heel against the long crack, putting his full weight behind it — the upper central panel came away almost in one piece.

Jilly backed further away, she could see he could now squeeze through. She retrieved the orange juice bottle — realised immediately its weight was reduced, it would be less efficient. She watched as his right leg came through the gap. He ducked his head, and then the rest of his body followed. Clumsily he scampered down the debris of the fallen statue, started towards her, but Nicole called after him.

'Franz,' she said, her tone guttural, assertive, 'don't forget your destiny.' She reached out with her hand, gesturing for him to help her.

He was undecided, his rage undiminished. He looked at Jilly's terrified face and then back to Nicole. His shoulders sank; he desperately wanted to hurt this woman who had thwarted his meticulous plan, but… Yes, his destiny was more important. A deep sigh escaped his lips. His revenge would wait for a few minutes. He helped her through the gap, and then the others.

Jilly was faced by Fischer and the four women, and she had only the orange juice bottle to defend herself with. She padded backward and looked behind her, but there was nowhere to hide. She went behind one of the statues, but knew it offered her only temporary respite — they could come at her from both sides. Her mind tried to calculate her options, but she found none. There was a scraping sound on the roof, and a cascade of ochre dust came down, but it was no longer a sprinkle, it was a deluge. It covered them all, and when it hit the ground, it rose back up in a misty cloud. Fischer coughed but then gestured for the women to take her, and they advanced, two coming from either side of the statue, emerging through the hazy veil, their blonde braids now covered in brown grime. Jilly raised the orange bottle, but Fischer had been cunning — the women were not her enemy, and this caused her to hesitate. That hesitation was enough; she had lost what advantage she had, and was taken by each arm as the bottle was wrestled from her grip.

Fischer came and stood before her, his thick, handsomely groomed hair now reddened by the cascade, the greying at the temple hidden. He looked like one of his own terracotta warriors he had sculpted on the wall, but those eyes pierced through the orange face — there was venom in his stare. He swung his arm, the back of his hand hitting her face. The force was unrestrained; it was about malice and hatred. DI French saw it coming and then — blackness.

She slumped, held up only by the women. Then, following a nod from Fischer, they let her fall to the floor. He barked out orders, and they moved the dense altar back to its place for the ritual.

Consciousness returned to Jilly slowly. At first, there was a hazy image above her of the Black Sun. The blur was partly the dusty cloud and partly her own senses fighting to assert themselves. And then — pain; her nose felt as if it had exploded. She tasted warm blood in her mouth, ran her tongue across her lips for confirmation. Then words registered, but not their meaning — until she realised it was Fischer spouting his Old Norse nonsense.

An elemental fear took her like an electric shock. She felt her face flush, then it swept across her whole body. It made her raise her head and look down — she was horrified to find that she was entirely naked again. She looked upwards and saw Karrie pinning her shoulders to the altar; downward, she saw Caitlin was pinning her feet. Both were covered in brown dust. She looked about her — Fischer was standing at her side, naked, his arms raised to the ceiling, booming the ancient invocation.

Comprehension now emerged like an image coming into focus. Her initiation had been resumed. She would be violated so that Fischer could commune with his fantasy — the Vril-ya. But something was wrong; at first, she couldn't decide what it was. He had little time, he must know that, so why was he chanting again? And then she saw his penis — it was no longer erect. What was it Leo had told her? Serial killers are often *lust murderers*, they get off on degrading women. Perhaps Fischer was on the same spectrum. This whole Vril-ya thing, his quest to be Superman, must have been how he got off. This was his route to arousal, and she had messed it up — messed it up big time.

'Keeping the Vril-ya waiting, are we, Franz?' Her tone was mocking. 'Not rising to the occasion, big boy?'

He leaned forward and struck her again with the back of his hand. Her head juddered with the force of it, but this time the punch was pulled; it was about punishment. He hit her again, and again, and with each punch, his arousal grew. Through the pain, Jilly realised she had made a mistake — she had given him a route out of his dilemma.

His chest swelled as he walked to the foot of the altar and climbed on it, resting on his knees. He forced her legs apart, leaned forward and gripped her throat with his left hand. The other two women came and held her arms — she was completely pinned, and at his mercy.

Jilly braced herself for the inevitable. She averted her gaze from his snarling, reddened face, his belligerent eyes, and looked over his shoulder, up at the ceiling. Then her world seemed to go into slow motion. The roof imploded; that yellow centrepiece disintegrated; the fragmented pieces started to descend. The women looked up. Instinctively they let go of Jilly, bent down on their haunches, and covered their heads to protect themselves.

Fischer sat up on his knees and looked up at the disintegrating roof. Jilly saw those malicious eyes fill with fear. A hefty piece of concrete was descending; its trajectory would take it directly down onto the altar, like a meteorite. He seemed to be paralysed. All his planning, his unshakeable superiority, his absolute belief in the power of the Vril — and yet … now, his whole life was in a tailspin.

Jilly realised she had been holding her breath. Now, a massive burst of adrenalin surged through her veins. She swivelled and jumped down from the altar just as the yellow decorated concrete hit Fischer. He raised his arm to his face at the last moment, but it impacted on that hand and his face. The slab and his head hit the altar and the concrete fragmented. Smaller pieces cascaded down onto Jilly's crouched, naked body. Dust rose like a sandstorm in the desert, all clarity dispelled. Instinctively she crept away on her hands and knees, through the rising clouds, holding her breath, her back stinging as smaller pieces of concrete hit her, until she reached the outer walls of the chamber. Here it was out of the fall zone, but the dust rushed outwards, and she was still enveloped. She had no clothing to cover her mouth, protect her breathing, so she cupped her hands over her face, buried her head between her knees and waited.

Gravity slowly acted upon the clouds of dust, aided by the rain now streaming down, but Jilly didn't see them beginning to dissipate. She kept her head buried, holding her breath for as long as she could. When she had to breathe, the particles filled her lungs, and she erupted into paroxysms of coughing. Slowly, though, the air began to clear, and she peered at the scene through her fingers. She stood to rise above the last of the veil, all the time still coughing. Then a voice entered her consciousness — it was Mac's.

'Jilly, are you down there? Are you all right, Jilly?' he shouted in strangled tones.

She looked up and saw several rain-soaked figures staring down with anxious faces. She recognised Mac and Leo, then Pete Reader and Dan'll Boone, then Satinder and the white goatee of DS Jackson.

She forced herself to swallow — it was as if she had swallowed a mouthful of sawdust, but the coughing subsided. 'You lot have taken your time, haven't you?' she shouted. She then remembered her nakedness as the rain touched her dust-covered skin, and she put an arm across her breasts, a hand before her loins. 'And get me something to fucking wear!'

PART 7: THE PARADOX

CHAPTER 49

Tuesday, 31st March 2020

James Postlethwaite burst into my office while I was trying to write up my notes about the meeting with Margaret of Wellow. This was to be the defining moment of my career, I knew that, and I was trying to get it down while it was fresh in my mind. I would be open to ridicule when I published — if I published — I knew that, too. I had to get it down accurately, not give people grounds to mock me more than was necessary.

I gave a deep sigh of annoyance. 'Leave me be, James,' I blurted, not trying to hide my exasperation. 'I'll give you a full briefing when I've finished this report. It'll be well worth the wait, I promise you.'

'Have you got an email from DCI McMillan yet?'

His question took me by surprise. I broke off and shot a look at his smirking face, then back to my computer screen. No new emails. 'Why, have *you* got one?' I asked.

'No,' he said. 'He's probably still sleeping. He's done over forty-eight hours straight.'

'If he hasn't emailed you, why are you expecting him to email me?'

'Because you met Margaret of Wellow yesterday, didn't you, you lucky bugger?'

I gaped. 'How do you…?'

'How do I know?' he interrupted. 'Stella McMillan, from the archaeology department — she's been to see me. She's been up all night too, with her husband and the police. They've rescued

DI French and Katarina Talbot, and three other women.' He told me the full story of the rescue.

'Have they arrested that Franz Fischer guy, then?'

'Stella said he's in hospital, in a bad way. A fractured skull and possible brain damage. He's in an induced coma. And the rescue is down to you, Toby. You got the evidence from the girl from history, didn't you?' His enthusiasm was growing by the second.

I sat back, chewing the inside of my mouth. I didn't know why, but I didn't share the elation. 'How am I going to publish this, James?' I said. 'If you didn't know me — if you were a historian at, say, Cambridge or Harvard, you'd think I was a hoaxer, wouldn't you?'

When I showed him the photographs, now downloaded on my computer, his excitement was undiminished. 'You've come this far, Toby — why on earth would you stop now?' he asked.

'But the pictures will just be seen as part of the hoax, don't you think?'

'Maybe,' he answered thoughtfully, 'but those thoughts are for later — not now, Toby.'

I supposed he was right about that.

CHAPTER 50

Franz Fischer stood trial for the abduction of the five women. I gave evidence for the prosecution, having found Katarina's shoe and false fingernails. His counsel tried to deride me when I testified that I had learned of the abduction from a twelfth-century chronicle. I was uncomfortable in the witness box, and I knew I would also get the same treatment from my peers. As I squirmed, however, another thought took me. By delivering the shoe and fingernails to the police, I had provided the evidence to convict Fischer and had also saved five abductees. But what if I had not taken them from Margaret? I would have left her with the means to prove to Abbot Stephen that she was telling the truth, that she *had* had a vision of a future time.

I wondered how much else I had failed to see. As a historian, I knew the pitfalls of interpreting the past. To look back into history, you had to look back at a point in time when the people had an entirely different set of references. These people did not behave as I behaved, did not think as I thought, did not have the same values as I had. They had an entirely different set of sensibilities — they took their children to see the hangings on a bank holiday.

My failings were now plain to see. I had lost sight of these fundamental principles; I had been consumed with the fate of Katarina Talbot in the present, and the uniqueness of a chronicle that suggested time travel. No other historian had been afforded the honour of physically connecting with history. These thoughts were like a nagging toothache — I had failed to see Margaret's dilemma from her historical perspective.

All the time I was struggling with my shortcomings, my fame was growing. The newspapers were full of the trial — it was a sensation. But after the conviction, the notoriety didn't subside. I was offered an amazing publishing deal. I was to write an academic book, but also a mainstream book, concentrating on Margaret's experiences as I saw them.

I should have been elated, but the ironies mounted in my mind. Poor Margaret was hanged as a witch when she was no so such thing. Yet she'd witnessed an abduction by a man who was motivated by the occult — and despite his prison sentence, *he* would suffer no such fate.

I needed to unburden myself, and I confided in James. He thought I was nuts, making far too much of it. My reasoning, he said, was unsound — what happened to Margaret was history, and that could not be changed. He said I should accept the accolades coming my way — I deserved them. My unease remained undiminished, however.

I went to see Bill Owens, the head of the physics department. I was a little sheepish about it, assuming that he too would think I was either nuts or a hoaxer. On the contrary, I was invited into his office with open arms. The guy saw me as a pioneer not only in history but in physics as well. He had read about the court case and had listened to the university gossip. He insisted I tell him the whole story from start to finish.

'How can I be a pioneer in physics?' I asked. 'Isn't there something about the scientific method?'

'Oh, absolutely,' he said, 'to test hypotheses, you have to be able to control and replicate an experiment. We can't do that, so your story is hearsay, an unconfirmed report. But, if you are right, you will create a paradigm shift.'

'A what?'

'Well, a paradigm is the basic theory, a conceptual framework within which scientific theories are constructed, if you like. Every now and then, new findings or theories come along which challenge that, the way Einstein's theory of relativity challenge the accepted Newtonian theories. So the whole scientific community has to shift its thinking. You could be responsible for that.' He raised his eyebrows and grinned at me.

I sighed; this wasn't helping, but I took advantage of his pause to specifically ask him about my dilemma. 'If I hadn't taken the shoe and fingernails from Margaret,' I blurted, 'could she have avoided being hanged?'

He spoke quickly, excitedly, his voice rising. 'Ah!' he said. 'The time travel paradox. Physicists, science-fiction writers, and filmmakers have been struggling with this for years.'

'Go on,' I prompted.

'Well, it goes something like this: Einstein puts forward his theory of relativity, and there is nothing there to rule out time travel. But if time travel is theoretically possible, then it throws a spanner into the theory of causality.'

He looked at me. I nodded, although I was afraid I was falling off the horse before the first hurdle had been jumped.

He continued, 'If the laws of cause and effect no longer apply, it throws up a number of paradoxes that physicists struggle to explain. Have you heard of the grandfather paradox?'

I nodded again.

'The grandfather paradox says — what if you travelled back and killed your grandfather? You would *then* never have been born, and so would *never* have been able to travel back — a paradox, see. So let's consider some hypotheses — firstly, that when you go back and shoot your grandfather, the gun fails to fire. It will fire if you point it at anyone else, but not your grandpa. The universe won't allow you to change what is history.'

'Yeah, okay,' I said, encouraged. That would mean that if the shoe had gone back with Margaret, it wouldn't have changed what happened to her — right?

'Then there is the multiple universe hypotheses. You pull the trigger, and it does indeed fire; your grandfather is now dead. You return to the present, but you've never existed here. Everything about you has been erased. You have now created an alternative timeline — you have entered a parallel universe.'

Oh, bugger, I thought, *parallel universes* — but Bill Owens was not finished.

'Then there's the predestination paradox. That's where the actions of a person travelling back in time *cause* the event he is trying to prevent.'

'What?' I made no attempt to hide my incomprehension. 'You'll have to try me again with that one.'

He grinned. 'Our time traveller then becomes trapped inside a temporal causality loop, in which event *one* in the past influences event *two*, which is time travel into the past, which then causes event one to happen.'

Well, if this was an explanation, it passed me by. I was more confused than before. Bill must have seen that in my face.

He continued, 'There is then a circular loop of events, do you see?' I didn't, and he tried to explain in a different way. 'This circular loop of events stops history being changed by the time traveller. In other words, any attempt by the traveller to stop something happening in the past will just lead to the cause itself — it won't stop it.'

'So you are saying you can't change the past, and anyone trying to do so may find themselves trapped in a…'

'A repeating loop of time, yeah, you've got it.'

'Look,' I said, 'how will all this affect Margaret of Wellow?'

'Ah, the world's first known chrononaut — do you mind if I call her that? I've always wanted to use that word.'

'Knock yourself out, Bill,' I said.

He took it in good spirit. 'Okay, let's speculate about Margaret. If I believe your story, this girl may have proved to the world of physics that time travel is not just theoretically possible, it's a reality. She appears in 2020, but she has only been an observer, so we could argue she hasn't changed anything, hasn't created any paradoxes.' He stopped as something apparently occurred to him. 'Oh!' he said, holding his breath. I saw him start to grind his teeth as he wrestled with his difficulty. 'You spoke to her, didn't you?'

I nodded.

'Shit!' he exclaimed.

'How does that change anything — simply talking to her?' I asked, puzzled.

'The butterfly effect,' he said, his mind still struggling with this.

'I've heard of that. That's where a small change can result in substantial differences at a later time, isn't it?'

'Yes — chaos theory,' he said. 'You'd better let me struggle with that one.' He shook his head, looking up at me, then raced on with his thoughts. 'Now, if Margaret had taken the shoe back to 1152, that's clearly a different matter.'

'Why?'

'Because that shoe has no origin in the twelfth century, so it exists without ever being created. That's a paradox — it's called a bootlace paradox.'

'So?'

'Well, it could result in an infinite time loop.'

'Oh, bugger!' My heart sank. 'So let me go back to my original question, Bill,' I said. 'If I had allowed Margaret to take the shoe back, could she have avoided being hanged?'

'Dunno,' he said. 'It's a paradox.'

CHAPTER 51

I emailed my final translation to James, Grace and Carol:

I've finally got to the end of the translation of Brother Roger of Hathern's chronicle of Abbot Stephen. Thought you might be interested in the following — Abbot Stephen died in 1179. Brother Roger is now the sub-prior of the abbey.

AD 1179. 29th April. The 25th Year of the Reign of King Henry II. Fluffy white clouds were speeding across a blue spring sky as I walked around the cloister. There was warmth in the air for the first time in the year, and my old bones welcomed it. I had been yonder to see Brother Boniface at the abbey's vegetable garden, and as I walked, the newly budded trees swaying in the breeze were welcome after many months of bitterly cold winds.

Newborn lambs were frolicking, and there was new growth everywhere — crocuses, celandines, primroses. It was a season of new life, a season that always brought joy to my heart, but not today. My heart was heavy. Abbot Stephen lay on his deathbed.

I entered the abbey infirmary to find him attended by Brother Emanuel, the abbey infirmarian, and the goodly Mother Mary Lazarus, the prioress of St. Mary's. Brother Emanuel's once plump, blotched face was now wrinkled with old age and sorrow. 'How is he?' I quoth, and he said that the abbot had not spoken since Vespers yesterday, but he was sleeping peacefully.

He was not suffering from any ague; there was no physic that could cure him. He was just expiring from old age. I looked at his frail, sleeping body; he seemed so insignificant, a shadow of his former, robust self. His closed eyes were sunken, his cheeks hollow over his toothless mouth, the remaining hair around his tonsure sparse and white, his skin pale and creased. Yet despite his aged face, there was still something venerable about his appearance. I am so pleased that he hasn't lost that.

Stephen has been abbot here for 32 years, since AD 1147 when the abbey was founded. He has led us all with wisdom and piety over many years. Forsooth, he will be sorely missed.

After the last rites had been administered, I sent a message to Mother Mary Lazarus, and she had come hither from the priory at once. I am so gladdened she arrived in time.

I sat beside his bed, praying for him, and she sat on the other side, holding his hand and occasionally mopping his brow with cool water from the abbey well. She has always been such a diminutive figure and still looks as undernourished as she was when I first met her all those years ago. Her holy habit with her apron worn over it made her appear like a child that had dressed up in an adult's clothes. But I knew she was a formidable woman when she had to be.

The abbot stirred and opened his eyes, looking first at the ceiling. Mother Mary Lazarus stood, leaned over him and mopped his brow, and he turned and recognised her at once. From under her coif, her kindly eyes smiled back, and I saw him squeeze her hand thankfully. They had always had a connection since he had been called to pass judgment on her all those years ago.

He closed his eyes again, and an expression of contentment came over his features. I think he was consoled, in his final moments, that his judgment of Mother Mary Lazarus had been correct. Then his shallow breathing stuttered, then stopped — the good Lord had taken him unto His self.

I added a further note:

James, nuns do not usually keep their birth names, so I can't be certain, but this Prioress Mary Lazarus must be Margaret of Wellow, don't you think? She will be 42 in 1179. If she entered the Order in 1152, at the age of fifteen, it's entirely conceivable that she could have risen to the rank of prioress by that time. The name Mary Lazarus cannot be a coincidence; she was hanged but didn't die — it's surely a reference to Lazarus being raised from the dead by Jesus. The reference to Stephen judging her also fits, doesn't it?

Well, it's conjecture, James replied, *but, yeah, it looks to be a fair assumption to me. She also fits the description of the young Margaret. Can we forget all these time travel paradoxes now?*

Yes, perhaps I can, I wrote. *It's been tormenting me for months now — the thought that I had had a hand in her hanging. The Order must have given her some learning for her to have risen to prioress. So it seems she turned out okay, doesn't it? My mind has been put at ease, James, it really has.*

Carol replied next:

Yippee, she made a good life for herself. You know, if she thought of you as an angel from God, it may be that instead of contributing to her hanging, you actually made her feel that God had a purpose for her. Anyway, will this mean that you'll stop moping about the house now? The kids are beginning to notice.

Yow! Margaret girl, wrote Grace.

HISTORICAL NOTE

I have used the date for Easter Sunday in 1152 as being the 30th March. This will be correct according to the Gregorian calendar, but this was not used before 1582! People living before 1583 would have used the Julian calendar to celebrate Easter.

Abbot Stephen was indeed the first Abbot of Rufford Abbey. I was unable to establish a date of death for him, however. The date of 1179 is, therefore, a fiction.

Brother Roger of Hathern is a fiction. However, there is precedence in Brother Jocelyn de Brakelond, who chronicled Abbot Samson of Bury St Edmunds monastery.

The Priory of St. Mary's in Nottinghamshire is purely a fiction of my making.

Toby's translation from a twelfth-century chronicle wouldn't have used archaic words like sooth, hither, thither, and sext. He would have used the modern-day equivalents. By using these outdated words, however, I hope to enhance the flavour of the twelfth century to the reader.

The internal decoration of the underground complex is loosely based on the Watts Cemetery Chapel at Compton in Surrey. That has a Celtic Revival architectural style.

BIBLIOGRAPHY

Websites:

Auto Express (www.autoexpress.co.uk)

British History Online (www.british-history.ac.uk)

Citizens Advice (www.citizensadvice.org.uk)

College of Policing (www.college.police.uk)

Courts and Tribunal Judiciary (www.judiciary.uk)

History Learning Site (www.historylearningsite.co.uk), 'Positions of responsibility in a monastery' by C N Trueman, 2015

History on the Net (www.historyonthenet.com)

Mercian Archaeological Services CIC (www.mercian-as.co.uk)

Mental Floss (www.mentalfloss.com), 'A History of "Trial By Ordeal"' by Arallyn Primm, 2013

Sky History (www.history.co.uk)

Wikipedia entries on the following subjects: 1150s in England, Medieval Latin, Nottingham, Newark, Father figures as sexual partners, Die Walküre (The Valkyrie), Nazism and Occultism, Offender Profiling, Scene of Crime Officers (SOCO), The Black Sun Society, The Thule Society, The Vril Society, Viking Art, Viking Dress, Anglo-Saxon Dress, Stockholm Syndrome, Sexual Ritual, Ground Penetrating Radar, Electromagnetic Location, Runes, Herman Wirth, Brother Jocelyn de Brakelond, Bavarian Illuminati, Aryan Race, Racial Hygiene, Egotism, Cognitive Dissonance, Narcissistic Personality Disorder, Superiority Complex.

Articles:

Daily Telegraph, 'Should you use a car broker?' by James Foxall, 2014

OSV News, 'Understanding roles of brothers, deacons and monks', by Chris Meadows, 2012

Astronomy Trek, '5 Bizarre Paradoxes Of Time Travel Explained', by James Miller, 2014

Books:

Vril: The Power of the Coming Race, by Sir Edward Bulwer-Lytton

Reich of the Black Sun, by Dr. Joseph P. Farrell

The Occult Roots of Nazism, by Nicholas Goodrick-Clarke

The Black Sun, by Peter Moon

A NOTE TO THE READER

Dear Reader,

Thank you for getting this far. I hope you enjoyed *The Mystery of Rufford Abbey*.

Nowadays, reviews by knowledgeable readers are essential for a writer's success. If you found this book entertaining, I will be in your debt if you would consider leaving a review on **Amazon** and **Goodreads**. I love hearing from readers, and you can contact me through my website: **www.stephentaylorauthor.com**.

Thank you!

Stephen Taylor

SAPERE BOOKS

Sapere Books is an exciting new publisher of brilliant fiction and popular history.

To find out more about our latest releases and our monthly bargain books visit our website:
saperebooks.com

Printed in Great Britain
by Amazon

15757872R00163